inner brynner

by

RAPHAEL FOREST

ROOF MEDIA

A Roof Media Release

First US Edition

Spelling and grammar have been adjusted to
US English for ease of comprehension, but some
Australian/ New Zealand slang remains in place
to maintain authenticity. In most cases, context
should provide adequate clues as to meaning.
If not, please consult an online Australian/
New Zealand slang dictionary.

ISBN 978-0-473-40645-5

Available on Kindle and other devices

www.raphaelforest.weebly.com/

PART ONE

1

The real trouble started in London, on a filthy Friday evening in April.

I'd been invited to speak at the World Annual Revolutionary's Forum – *WARF* – because I'd been a troublemaker from way back and they wanted me to share a little of the verbal strife that came so naturally to me. A return ticket to Heathrow from my native New Zealand costs way too much, especially when you have no kind of regular income, so I'd paid dearly for the honor. But I was keen to get among fellow troublemakers and maybe meet a few kindred spirits.

Alnweth Castle was not really what I'd expected. The only part of it that even remotely resembled a castle was a small crumbling section of wall that snaked down one side of the venue's dome-like steel structure. A sign out front explained that the wall was all that remained of the twelve-hundred-year-old fortress. Seemed to me they should really call it Alnweth *Ex-*castle.

But in any case, the place was way bigger than I'd expected, and the WARF audience was huge – I heard somebody say twelve thousand – which, to be honest, gave me the willies. I don't remember my journey up onto the stage at all, or much of what I said. It's lucky there was a video.

'Ladies and gentlemen... All the way from New Zealand... Misterrr REAGAN JAMES!'

I stepped out onto center stage behind the microphone, and the audience went completely quiet. Watching the recording later, I could see why. They'd mistaken *scared-shitless* for *smoldering intensity*.

It's ridiculous, really. When I'm seriously freaking out, something weird happens to the set of my jaw, and my brow V's into a deep frown. My back straightens, and my head stands tall and erect. A prickly, warm feeling starts in my body, then moves up through my head and takes control of my tongue. My gaze is rock-steady and I appear calm and collected. You'd never guess I was deathly afraid.

People are either frightened by it, or impressed. I've come to accept it as a part of life, and I call it the *Brynner* – after the actor Yul Brynner, who did *intense* without even trying.

There on the stage at Alnweth Castle, I stood peering slowly around the auditorium. It took me a good five seconds to pull myself together, which only magnified the illusion of bulletproof confidence.

'Who are you?' I began at last. My voice is also fairly deep and resonant. '*Who... Are... You...?*' I repeated.

Silence. A bearded guy at the front's mouth fell open, but no sound came out.

'How do you define yourself?' I asked. '...Country of birth, perhaps? Culture? Traditions? Religion...? Job? Education?' I could see heads nodding thoughtfully.

'Well, that would be a serious mistake. All those things are *other people's* ideas. If you define who you are by even *one* of 'em... you're a moron who's incapable of thinking for yourself. *More* than one of 'em, and you're an absolute imbecile that should not be allowed out of your house to roam around and fuck things up.'

2

Assorted guffaws and growlings from the audience.

'Well, of course! A mind that runs on second-hand reasoning is very crude and is just not going to work properly. *Come on!* It's perfectly logical isn't it? If you adopt other people's ideas wholesale like that, your mind's nothing but a *prefabricated puff-pudding; a piss-poor, paint-by-numbers patchwork of plundered presumptions.* If that's enough *'p*'s for you.'

I got a few chuckles with that.

'The sad fact is, a lot of us are in this category. *Sheep.* Happy to hand over our most important choices to parents, politicians, police, principals, priests.'

I squared up to the mic, and asked, 'Are there any Christians here tonight?' I'd had my eye on the bearded guy at the front, and sure enough, he hesitantly raised his hand. 'You sir – you're a Christian?'

He muttered something.

'Pardon?'

'I'm a Christian. Yes.'

'Great. How about you? Did you look at all the other possibilities before you chose Christianity? Did you read the Koran and the Talmud and look deeply – I mean *deeply* – into all the other religions before you decided to become a Christian...?'

The beard took a breath and shook his head.

'... No? Just adopted Christianity wholesale, did you? The bible and the cross and church and the whole package...? Yeah. Because it was there, and your Mum and Dad believed it, yeah? Well your Mum and Dad know best, so it must be true. It's okay, mate. I don't mean to make you angry, I just want you to think about it a bit...'

Some mixed laughs, but this time, more than a few outraged protests.

'... Because this is why we fight wars, isn't it.' I tapped my head. *People don't think for themselves.* I know, I know,' I said, raising my hands. 'I'm so bloody confrontational. People tell me that a lot, believe me. You believe me? Good.'

I pulled the mic from its stand and paced the stage. 'We depend way too much on other people's ideas,' I continued. 'Sure. It's hard when our parents and our teachers and our friends and our workmates are mostly morons who make terrible examples. But it doesn't have to be like that.

'*Every single one of us* is unique, and that uniqueness is there at birth. —Yes! Many studies have found this to be true.' I thumped a closed fist against my chest. 'But we *know* it's true. We know it in our hearts.

'When we're born, we love the world. And we want to join in — we *need* to join in. But as things stand, how do we do that...? How do we join in? Okay, well, this is how:

'From when we're very little, we start ditching our unique, sovereign beauty, so we can get along. So we can play with the others. So we can eat. So we can live a mean, shitty... *safe* little life like the rest of the morons.

'And this makes us so empty and so sad, that we're ready to grab anything, *anything at all* that gives us a sense of identity. Even something completely second-hand. And to think... '

Nodding slowly, I put the mic back on its stand.

'... To think we'd each of us have a wonderful, truly original sense of identity, if we'd just nurtured and maintained the one we started out with...'

Like I say. Due to the *Brynner*, I finished up my speel without much memory of what I'd said, or of what troublesome seeds I might've sown that could come back to bite me on the ass later.

There was after-forum drinks at a cramped, smelly little pub near the venue, which should've been my cue to get sociable and meet with my fellow revolutionaries, but there I was, sitting alone and grumpy and disappointed on a high stool at the quiet end of the bar, elbows in puddles of spilled beer. Consoling myself with a bowl of pork scratchings.

It had started out all right. The event organizer – a wide, hairy bloke called Bill Sykes (yeah, I know!) greeted me warmly and told me the first drink was on the house, then he sat himself in a corner with an ancient Frenchman called Herbert Drus, who was a bit of a legend in revolutionary circles, and therefore one of the major attractions at the event.

Drus was a core member of an organization founded nearly two hundred years ago called SIR: *Société Internationale des Révolutionnaires.* The elite of the world's revolutionaries. Which is kind of an oxymoron isn't it, given that historically, revolutions have been fought against the elite.

Now to be fair, I was basing my opinion of them on a general lack of real knowledge about who or what they were. Unlike WARF, which sold tickets to anyone willing to come along and listen, SIR's annual forums were a closed-doors affair. Invitation only. Honestly? It seemed to me they were all flash and mystery. No one really knew whether their superior revolutionizing had any actual substance or worth.

But I was interested to know more. After I'd downed my free pint, I went over and introduced myself to Herbert Drus, then in my rusty French, I offered to buy the great man a drink. *Je peux t'offrir un verre?* I'd done a year's exchange in the rural northwest of France when I was eighteen, and could just about hold my own in a French conversation. Just about.

Herbert (pronounced *Air-bear*) Drus was a small, wiry little man, with a wrinkled, prune-like face, bright green eyes and an electricity about him. He also had a reputation for being a bit of a prickly pear, and my brief encounter with him that night did nothing to discount that.

'I'll take the drink on the condition that it doesn't obligate me to talk with you all night.' he answered. He was smiling when he said it, but I decided Air-bear was a rude old fucker and moved quickly away.

So, yeah. I was already in a bad mood when the bearded Christian from the front row at the forum appeared and stood next to me at the bar. A sour-looking cove with a shaved head and a roll-neck sweater took up position a few paces behind him.

'I was um... I was offended by the things you said tonight,' said the beard. I turned around on my stool and eyed him.

'Oh, okay... Why?'

He shuffled about a bit. 'It's a free country. It's my right to be a Christian and not get hassled for it.'

'Fair enough,' I nodded, scrabbling for memory of what I'd said. 'Uh, what was it I said that offended you?'

The beard looked pained, but remained silent. I was beginning to feel nervous, and no doubt the Brynner was starting to kick in.

Scowling over his bearded mate's shoulder, Roll-neck responded with a sneer. 'He don't have the fancy words like you do,' he said. 'He just wants an apology. So tell 'im yer sorry an' we can all get back to our drinks.'

'An apology? ... For what?'

'Like the man said. For hasslin' him about bein' a Christian.'

The Brynner kicked in some more, and some of the memories started coming back: *Bearded guy in audience... Informed choice to be a Christian... Don't mean to make you angry, mate...*

'I didn't hassle him about being Christian,' I said. 'I hassled him about letting other people make his choices for him. For living his life like a sheep.'

Roll-neck's eyes glinted dangerously. He took a step closer and spoke in a menacing growl. 'Orright. You're gonna apologize to my friend here... Or you an' me, we're gonna have a problem.'

I sighed dramatically. 'This is the Christian way to deal with stuff then, is it?'

I should mention here that I'm absolutely hopeless in a fight. No physical coordination to speak of, and none of the rage that gives a brawler the urge – and often the ability – to kick ass. Yes: up to this point in my life, the *fancy words* Roll-neck mentioned had helped me talk my way out of potential strife again and again. Plus, I would hazard a guess, the *Brynner* had helped a fair bit. But I'd always thought there might come a day when neither would have the desired effect, and I wondered now if this was the day.

The *head-butt* is well known as an effective fight-finisher. Apparently. It's said that the top of the forehead is solid bone, and a quick launch forward – *POW!* – can cause real damage: a mashed nose; split brow or cheek. The recipient is usually too stunned and messed-up to respond, and they lose the fight. Excellent weapon for a person of any ability and I wish I'd thought of it. But it was actually Roll-neck who launched the head-butt. His thick neck was obviously solid muscle, because there was devastating momentum in his thrust.

But. For some inexplicable reason – luck or premonition – I chose that very moment to look down at my shoes. With an almighty *CRACK*, the solid bone in his upper forehead connected with the solid bone in *my* upper forehead, and I sprawled against the edge of the bar, seeing multiple stars and flashing lights. My vision cleared just in time to see Roll-neck stagger towards me and grab my collar, only slightly more recovered than me from the impact. He shouted something at me and raised his bunched fist.

Then a shape whizzed from out of my peripheral vision and brought Roll-neck down with a solid rugby tackle. The shape had blond hair and was wearing a green jacket. It punched Roll-neck repeatedly for all of ten seconds until the bouncers came and scooped us all up. Before I had time to think, I was out on the street, peering at the cold, damp pavement close-up. My head was pounding.

I heard the Beard's whiny voice somewhere close. 'No, Terry, Terry... leave it. Terry! I don't want you to...' Terry grumbled in reply and I recognized his voice as Roll-neck's. I thought it might be prudent to get up and protect myself, but when I tried to, a wave of nausea washed over me and I puked.

When I finally managed to sit up, I saw my rescuer – the blond guy in the green jacket – silently standing between me and the diminished threat that Terry now posed. Terry was swaying on his feet, glaring down at me with glassy-eyed animosity while the Beard fussed about, trying to calm him.

The Beard started wringing his hands. 'I'm sorry... I didn't mean this to happen... Lord forgive me.'

'Yeah, yeah. You've proven what an idiot you are, mate.' It was my blond protector speaking. He spoke with a relaxed, even tone. 'Just fuck off, now. Go on. And take your gorilla with you.' The Beard finally managed to coax his unsteady mate away, and they turned a corner and were gone.

'Oh my God. Stupid people.' Another voice came from behind me – it was a woman's voice, breathy and heavily accented. She clopped over on shiny black high-heeled boots to join my protector, and the pair looked down at me, half concerned, half smiling.

The woman had exaggerated Asian features – strongly slanted eyes, small nose and full, sexy lips – slightly down-turned at the edges like she was permanently pouting. Her hair was cropped short and died bright blue, and she wore a cream puff jacket with a black miniskirt. She stood straight-backed; proud and confident.

The guy was lean and muscular. He had an open face. Early thirties, but prematurely aged, I guessed, by sun and wind – an outdoors life. Unshaven. Not quite handsome, but a long way from ugly. The eyes were big and bright and intelligent. 'You right there, mate?' he asked, offering a hand. 'Pair of fuckin' dickheads, eh?'

A half-hour later, the three of us were sitting around a table in a St. Pancras café. My headache was a little better because the Asian girl had given me some panadols from her purse.

He was Karl Donovan, proudly from Sydney Australia, near-neighbor to my hometown in New Zealand. "Just across the ditch".

She was Akemi, *not* proudly from Japan. She was living illegally in Britain, having outstayed her three-month visa by nearly three years. She told us in her strong accent that she was never, *ever*, going back to Japan. I didn't hear what else she said because she'd put one foot up on the chair beside her, exposing a white-pantied crotch. I had to work very hard not to look.

'So. Whaddya think of WARF?' Donovan asked.

I blinked. I didn't remember half of it. But also, having spent a lot of money and a lot of energy to get to London and speak at the forum, I was probably reluctant to admit it was anything less than wonderful.

'Hmmm. Not much in the way of new material,' I managed.

Donovan waved a dismissive hand. 'It was a diabolical pile of *shit*.'

We all laughed.

'Same old piss about the powerful versus the powerless,' Donovan continued. 'A bunch of sad, unoriginal presumptions that we're all powerless numbos, and we gotta make a stand and *fight* the powerful. To take the power *back*.' He threw up his arms. 'Oh, give a me fuckin' break!'

I laughed and nodded. 'Morons.'

'Yeah, mate. The so-called powerful are *not* powerful if ya don't *give* them power by the way ya *think*, and the way ya *live*.'

He leaned back in his chair and crossed his legs. There was no room under our tiny table, so his legs blocked the passage between our table and the next, and the waitress chose that very moment to arrive with our coffees. Donovan didn't seem to notice the detour she had to make before placing our drinks on the table.

'How 'bout my spot, then?' Donovan asked, taking a pull from his cup.

'Your *spot*?'

'You know, my *spot*. My speel.'

'Oh... You spoke at the forum today?'

Donovan looked at me oddly. 'Ah... *yeah...?* Two slots before yours. You were there. I saw ya. Coupla rows from the front. '

I explained my nervousness and its amnesiac effects. He seemed a bit put out, like maybe he'd gone in to bat for someone who didn't even know he existed. Akemi leaned towards me.

'Your speaking was very *plovocative*.' She gave a double thumbs up. 'Nice talking.'

'Thanks. I wish I could remember it.' I was yet to see the video.

Donovan shook his head. 'Seriously?'

'Seriously.'

'Okay. Well, you're not nervous now, right?'

'Um... Not really, no.... Actually, yes.' I pointed at Akemi's raised leg. 'That's very distracting.'

Akemi gave an amused pout and lowered the leg.

Donovan grinned. 'So we're on the record now?'

'We're on the record.'

'Good.' He leaned forward, arms on the table. 'See, I think you an' me oughta get together and brew some trouble.'

2

'Whaddya do for a living...' said Donovan in a loud, deliberately-stupid voice. 'People always ask that, don't they? The *fuckers*. I mean, it's gotta be the most irritating question *ever.'*

We were at an apartment in the upmarket London suburb of St. Pancras, where I'd been invited to stay for a bit. Nice place: cream walls, tasteful furniture. All the latest appliances in matching silver finish. I was sitting drinking coffee on a leather couch.

'They wanna know a bit more about you,' I suggested. 'Polite conversation.'

'Trust you to find some generous shit to say about it,' Donovan answered from out on the balcony, where he was standing smoking a cigarette. 'It's an appalling assumption to make. Like it's a given that you work most of your waking hours to put food on the table. Your chief purpose in life is survival. Fuckin' *caveman* territory... Actually, no. Strike that. The cavemen weren't that stupid.'

I shivered. London's spring doesn't seem very spring-like to us antipodean types. Cold air and cigarette smoke were blasting in through the open doors. I decided there wasn't much point me staying inside, and stood and stepped out onto the balcony to join Donovan.

I leaned on the railing upwind of his smoke. 'It's not exactly my favorite question, either,' I said. 'I never know what to say. If you said, *well, I'm a revolutionary*, they'd look at you funny... Like, how the hell do you make a living from *that?'*

Donovan put on a high-pitched, old-lady voice. *'Ooh, got a*

good pension plan then, has it...? Good prospects for promotion...?
Comprehensive health insurance...?'

I laughed and peered out across the rooftops into a light fog, through which I could see the top of the London Eye – the massive Ferris-wheel that sits alongside the Thames river – in the middle distance. Its edge was dotted with bright lights that shone through the fog.

'So what *do* you do when you're not being a revolutionary? I asked. 'What do you do to put food on the table?'

'Always being a revolutionary, mate. And I never do anything to put food on the table. Rather *starve* than work for a living.'

'You don't work at all?'

'I sometimes do stuff that *happens* to put food on the table. Like photography. 'Cause I *like* it.' He coughed and spat over the rail. 'I like it, so I do it. What about you?'

'Mmmm, well. I don't really think of myself as a revolutionary. I don't have any grand plan to change the world. I think it has to be an individual thing.'

Donovan peered at me sideways. 'So you ah, work for a living?'

'No. No, shit no. We're definitely on the same page there.'

There was a long silence. I figured Donovan was hesitant to ask any more because he'd kind of verbally painted himself into a corner. So I offered, 'I was a teacher, but it ah... It didn't work out so well.'

He smiled. 'Sounds like a story.'

Donovan was right – it was something of a story – but not one I liked much to share around, because it represented a recent wound that still felt a bit raw.

As a young guy I'd trained to be a teacher, because I always had a major problem with the education system as a whole, and I naively thought I could help to change things from within.

In New Zealand there's a Unit-Standard system that students are measured against. I never believed that any two people should be measured with the same ruler, because we're all different, and it seemed to me that it was the *system* that failed the *student*, rather than the other way round.

So I started drawing up alternative Unit Standards for my seriously "failing" students, with objectives and criteria that suited their individual strengths. I didn't want to see these kids thrown on the social scrap-heap with a permanent aversion to learning. And hey, whatever I came up with, how could it be worse than a "fail"?

Now, really, I wasn't fooling myself – I knew I'd probably be in for some flak. But I was unprepared for how vehement that flak would be.

Seventeen year-old Rydell was the son of Grant Mautz, a local city councilor who fancied himself as a bit of an entrepreneur. Rydell's grades were getting worse because he clearly couldn't see the relevance in the stuff he was studying, so I drew him up an alternative plan. The first sign of a problem was a summons to a meeting in the principal's office, with Mautz senior present, and also a local moderator for the certification authority.

It was a prickly meeting. Councilor Mautz felt it was my job to ensure that young Rydell passed the official Unit Standards. With my meaningless alternative teaching material, I was giving up on his son and failing in my job as a teacher. The principal, and the local moderator both agreed, and they were very concerned to learn that I was pulling the same foolish stunt with several other students. I was to stop my meddling and do my job.

I have to admit, I got pretty angry at this point, and said some stuff I probably shouldn't have. I left the office half an hour later without a job, and with an impassioned promise from Mautz that he'd do everything in his power to make sure I never taught again.

Donovan lit his third cigarette and took a long drag. He eyed me then nodded with what looked like approval. 'Tough choice. Principles... or food on the table.'

'I don't mind going hungry now and then,' I said.

Donovan gestured out across the foggy cityscape, and around to the cozy upmarket apartment behind us. 'Well. Here we are. Not exactly starving.'

I laughed. 'Not really, no.'

'Oh,' said Donovan, 'Before I forget... Di's due back later on. She won't mind you staying, but it might be better if you crash at Ax's tonight. Just so's I can give Di the heads-up.'

'Um... *Ax?*'

'You know – Akemi.'

That's how I learned that the apartment wasn't, strictly speaking, Donovan's. He was a guest there himself. Diana – a freelance fashion-shoot coordinator, and the apartment's lease owner – was hardly ever there.

So I was going to be farmed out elsewhere for a night. I didn't mind too much, but I was a bit dicey about being an uninvited guest at Akemi's.

'You sure she won't mind?' I asked.

'Are you kidding? You saw how she was flashing the stuff.'

'Flashing the stuff...?'

'Aw, don't tell me you didn't notice. Maybe you blipped out and got the amnesia thing...'

'You mean the leg up on the chair? The panty-flash?'

'Yeah, mate. The panty-flash.' He counted off on his fingers. 'And the little looks and the blushing and the giggles and the pouting.'

'Aufff... No. No, I don't think so.' I turned see Donovan giving me one of his *what-the-fuck* looks. I'd known him for all of thirty-six hours, but the look was already familiar.

'I seriously wonder about you mate. Like, I'm not sure if you're kidding around, or if you're a sandwich or two short of a picnic.' I laughed. Donovan shook his head. 'Nah, I mean it. She likes you. I can't believe you didn't notice.'

It's true. I'm not much chop when it comes to women. They certainly seem to find me attractive at first. Then I open my mouth, and after that, I'm interesting at best.

Yeah, from a conventional perspective, I'd have to be one of the least heroic protagonists in the history of storytelling. From another perspective, it's a different matter. I can say, without bashfulness or modesty, that I'm true to myself. I have my principles, and I live by them one hundred percent. In my view, that's what really counts. That's where *true* heroism is.

What's heroic about that? Well, the heroism isn't in the truth itself. It's in the *doing what it takes* to be true to yourself. That stuff is hard. It takes real courage. It's a daily, colossally-demanding challenge that few are willing to take up to any great extent. But me? There's no alternative. I *have* to.

You see, a long time ago, I made a promise.

*   *   *

Principal Redmaine stood before the assembled senior school.

He spoke slowly and grimly into his microphone: 'From today, it will be the individual student's choice as to whether or not they stand for the singing of the national anthem.' There was a whoop and a swell of eager clapping. Grinning, I turned to my friend Boz and slapped a high five.

Two months earlier, myself, Boz and three other friends from year 12, had been summoned to the principal's office for staying in our seats while the rest of the school stood and sang the national anthem. I spoke up for the group.

'Jumping to our feet when we're expected to is the mindless response of an automaton, and not – we believe – a genuine show of respect. Neither is it respectful of the school to expect such behavior of us.'

'You're entitled to your own opinion, certainly, but we have rules at this school,' Mr Redmaine replied with a meaningful arch of his eyebrow. 'Rules that you, and your parents agreed to abide by.'

Next to me, Boz asked, 'Which rule says we have to stand for the national anthem?'

Redmaine grunted and took a book from a shelf behind his desk. Leafed through, then read out loud. 'Students are required to show respect for their teachers, other students, school property, for the school itself, and the school's standing in the community.'

We didn't agree with the interpretation. We got permission

17

to stage a ballot across the entire school – junior and senior students, and all staff – and we won. The school board reluctantly recognized the majority opinion, and the policy requiring students to stand was changed. Or more accurately, it was clarified: there was never any official requirement to stand. People stood because everyone else did.

This all happened right before the summer break, which runs December through January in New Zealand, and coincides with the end of their academic year. Still impressed with ourselves after our little victory, my group of friends and I shunned the usual beach/ parties/ movies/ general-vacation stuff, and got together almost daily to plot our next challenge to the system.

Winning our first battle had been a bit of a coup. It had gained us some social credibility, and as a result, our numbers had swelled to twenty-seven by this point. But only a core eight of us were hard-out enough to turn up to all the meetings.

One Tuesday afternoon, we dubbed our group *IRE:* 'Individuality Recognized in Education'. The name felt good, and it boosted our confidence even further. We were ready to brew up some decent trouble.

*   *   *

Donovan and I rode the London tube for twenty minutes, then the train came up above ground and clattered through a suburbia that grew more and more down-market. The usual graffiti: some creative, some ugly. Shady types with hoods up, strutting. Oily hulks of cars, either abandoned, or ought to be. The sun was weak and low in the sky, flashing orange through the landscape of trees and buildings.

Donovan put a foot up on an empty seat. He was sitting opposite me in a carriage that was about half-full. 'Capitalism,' he said, 'Is dead in the water. Some massive changes are on the way. Like Thatcher's Britain on fuckin' *steroids*...'

A wizened little old lady with skin like a walnut and a large floppy hat was perched on the seat next to us, a well-worn leather purse on her knee. I saw her wince in reaction to Donovan's swearing.

'Old Thatcher got bad press, but all she really did was face up to reality.' He continued, and shrugged. 'Like, coal was suddenly a redundant commodity, so what was the point of keeping tens of thousands of coal miners in work?' He shrugged. 'Someone had to pull the lever. She just happened to be the one in the big seat.'

I glanced at the walnut lady. Donovan was harping on in a loud Australian accent, about something that happened when he was a sprout of a kid, living comfortably thousands of miles away. About hard times experienced by some of the people on this very train.

'Well, yeah,' I said. 'But it was the *way* she did it, wasn't it. You can't just pull the rug out from under people and expect them to be happy about it.'

'What, so you reckon keep them in jobs until they get used to the idea...? Mate. Forget it. The only thing that'll get them off their arses and thinking for themselves is a rude shock.'

The walnut lady's eyes swiveled slowly in Donovan's direction.

'Well, I dunno,' I said. 'But there has to be a kinder way than just demolishing everything wholesale. That's what bothers me most about revolutions. It's why I don't call myself a *revolutionary*. Real change can't be brought about by force, or by politics. It has to start from the inside out. With the individual.'

Donovan shrugged. 'Revolution is revolution. Doesn't matter where it starts. But it has to start somewhere. I don't plan on sitting on my hands, waiting for a revolutionary movement to appear spontaneously out of nowhere. We'll be waiting for fuckin' ever.'

When the walnut lady stood up and turned to Donovan, I was bracing myself for a good telling-off, but she offered her hand to Donovan, and as he shook it, she said in a cultured accent, 'This is my stop. Good luck to you. I hope you're serious about doing something...' She paused and gave a crinkly smile. 'Not *all-mouth-and-no-trousers*, like most people seem to be.'

As we stepped out of our train station and onto the street, we were narrowly missed by two kids in puffer jackets, going like the clappers, pulling a cart with an ancient dog strapped onto it. Donovan and I shared a grin and started walking.

Around the next corner, a guy with a bruised mouth lurched into our path on a squeaky pair of crutches. I wondered if we were about to be rolled by the world's clumsiest mugger, but instead of a weapon, he brandished a small plastic bag with what looked like a turd in it. 'Hashish?' he rasped.

'Ah, no, thanks.' Another plastic bag from another pocket.

'Weed?'

'No.' Crutch guy produced three more options, all of which we refused. He grinned, showing a recently-smashed set of teeth. 'Okay, no problem, lads.' Then squeaked back into the shadows on his crutches.

Akemi's building wasn't the worst of the bunch, but neither was it a cheery prospect after St. Pancras. She answered the door with a sort of stunned look, and though she took the chain off, seemed reluctant to invite us in. But Donovan barged through and gave her a hug, then started telling her about the battered drug dealer we'd met outside.

'Oh, that's Molly,' Akemi said absently.

'Molly? You mean *Morrie*,' said Donovan. 'Molly's a girl's name.'

'No, I think he said Molly.'

Donovan shot me an amused look. 'Right.'

The apartment was a dingy bedsit with a single grimy window. There was a queen-sized bed covered in clothes at the far end of the room, a sink with a narrow bench, a tattered floral sofa, a red plastic chair and an ancient box-like TV. And that was it, apart from a jet-black cat lying curled up on the sofa.

I handed Akemi a bag of groceries I'd bought on the way and said lamely, 'Hope you don't mind me staying over.'

'No, of course it's okay,' she said, plopping the supplies on the bench. 'Don't worry.'

After Donovan had gone, I bought us some dinner at a Cambodian takeaway on the next block, and we ate it back at the apartment – Akemi on the sofa and me on the plastic chair. I'd gone to sit next to her on the sofa, but she stopped me. 'No, there is a bad place. Howdy did a chanda on it.'

'A chanda...? Oh, a *chunder*.' Aussie/Kiwi slang, probably ex Donovan. 'Your cat threw up on the sofa...? Lovely.'

She smiled. 'Yes. I don't sit there.'

The Cambodian *Char Kuay Teaw* was good, and it cheered me up a little. Akemi was dressed in jeans and a sweater four sizes too big. No makeup. No blue wash in the hair. Way shorter without heels. Not as pretty as the first time I saw her, but I liked her better that way – softer, less breath-taking.

Miaowing outside the door: Howdy the chunderer. Akemi let him in, and he swished around our legs as we ate. A big chunk was missing out of his right ear. 'My room is really *crap*,' Akemi said around a mouthful of food. 'It's so embarrassing.'

'Oh, look, it's not that bad. I'm just happy to have somewhere to sleep.'

She dangled a gravy-laden noodle for Howdy, who pulled it from her fingers and ate it on the carpet. 'Evelything in London is expensive,' Akemi said. 'But I like it. So I stay.'

'What's so bad about Japan?'

She slumped in her seat. Took a deep breath and said, *'Evelything.'* She started eating again, and I wondered if I'd got all the answer I was going to get.

'... Plessure,' she continued at last. '... Duty.' She looked up at me, chewing. 'I'm thirty-one, so I *must* get married. I *must* have children. And when the children are old enough to leave, I *must* look after my old parents until they die... My life is not my own.' A paw swiped gently at my foil dish. I pushed Howdy down. *'Howdyyyy...'* she called in a nasal, cartoony voice. She offered another dripping noodle. 'I went to university and I studied hard,' she continued. 'But for *what*...? Just to be evelybody's slave?'

I nodded, swallowed food. 'It's like that everywhere... Maybe not so extreme.'

'Is it selfish to live how you want?'

I gazed at her. 'No. Of course not.'

After dinner we watched TV together until maybe eleven – me still on the plastic chair – then Akemi disappeared into the bathroom. She came out again dressed in a knee-length powder-blue teeshirt. 'You want to sleep?' she asked.

'Um... Sure thing. I'll take the sofa.'

'No. The chunder. Remember?'

'Oh, yeah, the chunder.'

Akemi smiled bashfully and pointed. 'We can both sleep on the bed. There's enough room... I *plomise* I will not attack you.' I laughed. A bit loudly. She cleared the jackets and various clothing off the bed, carefully folding and piling them on the plastic chair, then looked me up and down. 'You going to sleep in your *clothes*?'

I lay back-to-back with Akemi, peering up at the window sill above the bed on my side. The blind was down, but a sliver of light from the street-lamps outside showed through. Crisp summer sheets on the bed. I was wearing just my undershorts and was cold.

Akemi didn't move for a long time, and I thought she was asleep. Then suddenly she spoke. 'I'm not Donno's girlfriend.'

Donno. Short for Donovan, I guessed. I lay there for a beat, trying to cook up a response. '... Hmm.'

'I can't trust him.' She coughed. 'He smokes.'

'Yeah.'

'You don't smoke.'

'No.'

I felt her turn over behind me. '*Evelybody* knows smoking is so *bad* for you...' Her breath was warm on the back of my neck. 'But some people still do it. Even when they know the risk. It's so crazy. I can't trust them because they don't care if they get sick or die.'

'I hadn't thought of it like that.'

'If it's a friend, it's okay. I can't tell them what to do. It's their choice. But a lover... How do I know the *other* stupid choices

23

they made? How do I know who they had the sex with before?'

'There's um... There's condoms,' I suggested half-wittedly.

She snorted. Silence for a long time. *I have to turn around and face her*, I thought. It took me forever to work up the courage, then at last I took a deep breath and spun between the sheets, *swish*, like a spring-mechanism triggered.

Now we were face to face. In the dim light from the window, I could see her eyes were closed. I waited, but she appeared to be asleep.

*   *   *

Traffic noise from outside. I opened my eyes to find the room full of light, and Akemi's side of the bed empty.

I figured she was in the bathroom, and got dressed, banging around a bit to let her know I was up. Stopped to listen, but there wasn't a sound. The bathroom door was partially open, and I carefully angled myself so I could see inside. No one there.

I decided she must have gone for milk or something, and busied myself looking around the apartment. I found a small trash can under the bench. Stepped on the peddle, and the lid popped up. They say you can tell a lot about someone from their rubbish, but it was just full of food scraps and what looked like pieces of red melted wax.

There was a very used-looking acoustic guitar standing in the corner of the room, chipped and grease-stained from many hands. It had a frayed strap with what looked like an American Indian pattern. I picked the instrument up and strummed a clumsy sequence of the only three chords I know – *A, D, G* – at least, I think that's what they are. It had a nice, warm tone.

I set the guitar back down and moved on, looking closely at

the two solitary pictures on the walls:

Minimalist sunset in red, white and black – print number 97 of 500.

Sixties French-style cartoon of a black cat on a street.

Which reminded me – there was no sign of Howdy the cat, either, with his weak stomach and his raggedy ear.

It was nearly ten-thirty when she came back. She had that stunned look again. 'Did you eat some breakfast?' she asked.

'No. I was waiting for you.'

'Oh... Sorry.'

We can go and get some now. My treat.'

She bit her lip. 'Mmm, I already ate. But thank you...' She hustled forward into the room and pulled an item of clothing from the pile on the plastic chair. A uniform of some kind. 'I have to go. I have work, from eleven.'

'Oh, right. What sort of work you doing?'

'Why?'

I shrugged. 'Just wondering, I guess.'

She tucked strands of hair behind an ear. 'Waitress. At a restaurant in Brixton.'

'Okay.'

'Okay. I'll see you later.' She stuffed the uniform in her bag and headed for the door. On impulse, I leaned in and kissed her temple. She stopped and looked up at me. Smiled – a brief, but sweet smile. 'Bye,' she said, walking out the door. 'Oh... Don't let Howdy inside the room – he will do shit and chunder everywhere.'

My schoolfriend Boz Holicova came from a Balkan immigrant family. He had a long dark fringe that he was constantly flicking out of his brown eyes, and a rumbling, low-pitched laugh. Girls found Boz very attractive, and he knew it, but he was quite grown up in many ways. Mature about a lot of things us native Kiwis were still too young and inexperienced to understand. He'd seen a lot of nasty stuff as a kid, during the Yugoslavian conflict, but didn't like to talk about it.

Boz told his folks he was out fruit picking during the summer break, because he knew they would object to our scheming, and then turned up to every IRE meet with his nineteen year-old girlfriend in tow. We were all gutted when Boz's parents discovered the fruit-picking lie, and he was grounded. We had to make do without him until the new school year began in February.

But then Boz was back on board with a vengeance. I was pleased, because he was a really smart guy, and good company. The guys in the group were awed that Boz had a girlfriend that was a good two years older than us and quite pretty, but she was another secret Boz worked hard to keep from his parents.

After a long summer of intense plotting, we had something major up our sleeves. IRE were going to target the two-strand winner/ loser ethic the school had embraced more and more during the years we'd been there. We felt that the pressure to *measure up* was ludicrously high, and the school's approach was based on cruel double standards.

On the one hand we were told we were individuals and must treasure our uniqueness, but on the other, we were treated as if we were all exactly the same. Each "unique individual" was measured against the same ruler and expected to achieve the same results. And the underlying message was that if we didn't, we'd be doomed to a life of loserhood. It was *their* way or the *spare* way. The inconsistency, and the narrow cruelty of the message was unacceptable to us.

We had a list of changes we wanted made. We wanted the words *winner* and *loser* to be banned outright: never again to be uttered by a staff member. We wanted the disturbingly frequent prize-giving ceremonies cut back to one per year, and attendance of that to be optional. We wanted guidance counseling to include supportive and non-judgmental treatment of the increasing number of students who didn't know what they wanted to do with their future, and didn't want to be pressured to make a choice that might be hard to change later. Some of my smartest friends were in this category, including Boz. We also wanted the school to stop putting pressure on staff to achieve high pass levels, because this encouraged a factory approach – and we were *not* production-line products.

But most of all, we wanted a deliberate shift in emphasis: the fundamental purpose of learning was to understand more about the world and about ourselves.

Not to get a job and to put food on the table and be a *winner*.

IRE's first meeting with Principal Redmaine didn't go well.

I'd undemocratically decided that all thirty six of us – new-year's recruits included – wouldn't fit in the small office, and named the eight-member delegation by myself. It was clear from the moment we stepped into his office that Redmaine was unhappy. He sat squarely and straight-backed in his seat while Boz read out the statement of intent, and our list of demands. When he'd finished, Redmaine peered around our faces for what seemed like forever, then said, 'All right. I'll take it to the board.'

Meeting over.

The date of the next board meeting came and went. We'd expected to be summoned to Redmaine's office for some kind of official response to our demands. Good or bad. But that Sunday night, my mother and father sat me down and told me they'd had a call from the year-thirteen dean.

My Mum and Dad had always been supportive of my various antics, or at least willing to stand back and give me the benefit of the doubt. But this time they were a bit concerned. I showed them our list and explained the reasoning, and they ended up pretty much agreeing with me. My Dad made some suggestions, though: 'You've got to put yourself in their shoes,' he said. 'Speak to their logic whether you agree with it or not.' He went through the list with me and took the opposing view as an exercise, which was very helpful. I felt encouraged, and went to bed happy.

But the next day was a depressing day. Calls had been made to parents of all the listed members of IRE. There'd been family meetings around dinner tables. Laws laid down, and ultimatums made. We had a membership crisis on our hands.

Boz was subdued, but determined to carry on. The pair of us walked around the school grounds at lunchtime, collecting up IRE members who hadn't woosed out on us completely. We begged, belittled, and made bold promises. When the bell rang we did a headcount – all told there were nine of us. Skipping the afternoon's lessons, we sat among piles of fragrant grass clippings at the edge of a football field and made our plans.

The following day we drafted a notice announcing a petition, with the list of our demands attached, made a thousand copies and distributed them around the school. We decided not to bother asking permission, figuring our scheming would be squashed straight off if we did. We planned to present a big stack of signatures to the board. Put them on the spot again, like we had the year before.

We high-fived and shouted gung-ho slogans, and I chose to ignore the feeling in the pit of my stomach that something wasn't quite right about it all.

*   *   *

After a breakfast of coffee and a muffin at a café, I took the tube back up to St. Pancras. But I was reluctant to just turn up on Diana and Donovan's doorstep.

I wanted to call ahead and check I was good to go. Donovan had written Akemi's mobile number, along with his own, on the back of an old supermarket receipt for me, and it struck me that with my stay in London extended, I'd be better off with some kind of connectivity beyond the free WiFi at Starbucks and McDonald's. I ducked into an Orange shop on The Strand, and came back out with a local plan that gave me unlimited UK calls and texts, and a good whack of data. My phone pinged to tell me I had new emails, and I sat down on a bench to look at them.

There was only one message of immediate interest: A fellow speaker at WARF called Jimmy Planck was asking if I was still in the UK, and if I was, could I go speak to his eco-group in nearby Bristol. I vaguely remembered giving my email address to a guy while we were waiting outside the venue, but nothing about what was said.

I quickly tapped out a reply, saying I'd be happy to talk to his group, and hit *send*.

Then I switched apps and drafted a text message to Akemi:

Hey! This is Reagan. Thnx heaps for having me stay over yesterday. You were excellent company.

The reply came back seconds later:

You are welcome :-)

I guess I was hoping for a little bit more. I used the new call plan to give Donovan the heads up, and ten minutes later, Donovan himself let me into the St. Pancras apartment.

Diana – his friend/ partner/ landlady – was a short, bubbly Australian. Attractive in an unconventional way: wide face with piercing blue eyes and a large, animated mouth. Loud and husky and refreshingly straightforward.

'I hear you're one of Donno's revolutionary mates,' she said. 'You're welcome to use the guest room until the terrorist squad comes knocking...'

I stammered, 'Well, I er...'

'... And then you can move in permanently. Could go a bit of excitement around here... Hahaha!'

Apparently she and Donno had met in London two years before at a photo shoot, on which Donovan was a photographer. They'd had a short fling until Donovan went down to Spain – where he'd stayed until recently when his invite to speak at WARF arrived. He'd decided it was a good time for another move, and was now back in London and looking for photography work.

Donovan had got hold of a DVD copy of the other night's WARF event and he chucked it on so Di could see it. Whoever authored the DVD had helpfully added a menu with the guest speakers' names, so each was easily accessible. Donno selected mine.

I was a bit nervous. I scrunched down in my seat.

'Look, Di...' Donovan said, pointing at me. 'Yul Brynner... *The King and I*...? *Magnificent Seven*...? Haha!'

Di rolled her eyes and smiled at me.

'Ladies and gentlemen... All the way from New Zealand... REAGAN JAMES!'

The sound quality of the video was pretty bad. On the screen, I stepped up behind the mic – Brynner kicking in big time. Beside me on the couch, Donovan shrieked with laughter.

Di looked pained. 'Donno, shut the fuck up, will ya?'

'Oh, look..' replied Donovan. 'If you're feeling sorry for the bastard, just you wait.'

And yes, to be perfectly frank, I was good. I was very good. As I watched, I could see that something alchemical was driving me, something that enabled me to verbalize my deepest convictions. And verbalize them in a way that struck a chord. A way that spoke directly to the truth that was already there in the audience's hearts. And I wasn't aware of that ability in my day-to-day life, because it never raised its head when I was relaxed.

Watching the DVD in Di's living room, I was still nervous. But not badly so, I guess, because I was still conscious enough of Donno and Di to be aware they hadn't made a sound for some time. Their eyes were riveted to the screen.

My "spot" ended, and while the audience were clapping, Donovan stopped the DVD. He shared a long look with Di, then they both turned to look at me. An odd look, like I was a stranger.

I said, 'Let's see your one then, Donno.'

Donovan cracked a slow grin. 'Don't think so, mate. Ladies present, and suchlike.'

'His style is a bit more, uh... *subdued* than yours,' suggested Di.

Donno snorted a laugh. 'She means I'm fuckin' boring.'

'Uhuh, well...' Di hedged uncomfortably. 'Different style of presentation... But your ideas are definitely in the same ballpark.'

Donovan turned in his seat so he was facing me. 'Tell you what... rather than sit through ten minutes of me yabbering on, I'll give ya the thirty-second version. Yeah?'

'Okay.'

'All right then. My title was, *Evolution of the True Individual.*'

He held up a finger. 'Evolutionary Stage one: *The Misfit*... Doesn't function well in conventional society, and suffers for it. Okay...?'

'Yep.'

'Stage two: *The Willing Misfit*... Still doesn't fit into the social picture, but is generally happy *not* to. Becomes aware that conventional reasoning is limiting. Begins to find alternative ways to reason and to function.' He raised an eyebrow. 'With me so far? Superb. Here's the important one...

'Stage three: *The Willing*... No longer wants – or needs – to be subject to conventional social reasoning. Willing to be fully responsible for his *own* reasoning, and for his entire *life*... and willing to share that life again with the wider group.'

He stopped and spread his hands. 'My spot. In essence.'

I leaned back in my chair. 'Hmmm. The *Willing*... Yeah, I like that. Not a misfit anymore, because *fitting in* becomes a redundant issue.'

Donovan leaned forward, nodding. 'So, then.'

I shrugged. Smiled. 'What?'

'Exactly. *What*. What are we gonna do about it?'

Behind him, Di stood from her chair. 'I'll leave you guys to it, then.'

We said our good-nights, and she headed off to bed. I picked up where we left off: 'Like I said. I'm an individualist first and last. I don't...'

'All *mouth and no trousers*, are ya?'

'What?'

'You heard. Why bother doing WARF and shit like that if you're not invested in making some kind of impact? It doesn't stack up.'

I felt my face coloring. 'Call it an ideological difference if you like. I figure I can make an impact with individuals who are ready for it.'

'Fine. Fine. But you've gotta *reach* the buggers first. You can talk till you're blue in the face at your *WARFs* and your *EROs* and your *SIRs*, but you're only reaching a tiny, *tiny* fraction of the population. The ones who're motivated enough to get off their arses, and to shell out the dosh to come listen to what you have to say. *Fuck-all* people, basically.' He nodded, his eyes hard. 'You gotta think bigger and you gotta think wider, or you might as well not bother at all.'

*   *   *

On the day we'd named for the school-wide petition, each of our seven remaining IRE members – we'd lost two more by then –

set up a stand at spaced intervals around the school grounds.

They were waiting for us. A bunch of teachers swooped and shut down the petition before we'd even started. The seven of us were suspended for a week for staging a disruptive action in the school grounds, in observance of the exact same rule that Redmaine had quoted to us late the previous year: disrespecting the school and everyone in it. Apparently.

I was outraged, but wasn't intimidated or disheartened – I believed we had truth on our side. The other IREs didn't take it so well. When I called Boz, his parents repeatedly told me he wasn't home or wasn't available. Late in the week, I got a call. It was Boz.

He was in a bad way. His parents had decided to move him to another school. He'd stood up to them, and they'd responded by grounding him for the rest of the school year. All nine months of it. And he thoroughly believed they would follow through. 'Boz,' I said, 'You're seventeen. You're legally old enough to leave home... You can get a benefit and go out on your own. Do your own thing, man.'

Boz couldn't see that this was an option. He hung up on me while I was urging him to get out and go independent. Or perhaps his Mum or Dad cut us off. I don't really know.

But the worst was still to come.

On my first day back at school, Principal Redmaine announced to the assembly that Boz had died. When I went to see Redmaine after, he had no further information to give, and the phone at Boz's house was busy. A paragraph in the newspaper the next day said Boz had hanged himself at his home.

I spent the rest of the school week in bed, sick with grief and regret. On the Saturday, I was blobbing out in the conservatory when I heard a knock on the door. My mother showed an attractive middle aged woman into the room and introduced her as Mrs Holicova. Boz's mother.

Mrs Holicova had a fixed, vacant smile on her face and she wouldn't look directly at me. My mother left us alone to make some tea or something, and when she was gone, Boz's mum spoke quietly to me, all the while picking pieces of fluff from her skirt.

'I have lost my son,' she said. 'I've had pain in my life before, but this is truly the worst.' At last she looked up at me with far-away eyes. 'It's your fault he died, and I will never forgive you.' She took a deep breath, then got up and left.

I knew Mrs Holicova's reasoning was warped, but still, the weight of the accusation was terrible. When my dad came home, the three of us talked about it for hours, and although my parents were largely on my side, I could sense a hesitation. In hindsight, maybe it was just because they could identify with a parent's terrible loss, but they didn't seem to wholly support the way I'd behaved. It was the first time I'd really felt cast adrift. Forced to stand in my own sense of reason.

An awful night that night. No sleep; anxiousness and self doubt poisoning my blood, my muscles, my mind. But sometime before dawn it all clicked into place, and the picture that crystallized was this:

I couldn't rely on anyone else's approval to validate my actions, or to share the burden of my personal integrity. It was down to me and me only; wholly *my* responsibility.

I could hear the first birds singing outside. Peering up at the dark wooden boards that ran across my ceiling, I made a solemn promise.

I promised, in Boz Holicova's memory, that I would always be true to my highest principles. No matter what the cost.

Then I turned over and went to sleep.

3

For better or for worse, Karl Donovan convinced me that the
two of us should get together and brew up some trouble. He got
me with his *all mouth and no trousers* accusation.

And he was right about that. Since Boz Holicova's death back
in high school, I'd been cooking up trouble aplenty, but not
doing a thing about it. At least nothing that roused more than an
angry outburst from a controlling parent.

Donovan was an abrasive, insensitive guy with a mess of
annoying habits, let's not beat about the bush. But his
convictions appeared to be his own – meaning he'd arrived at
them through careful thought – and he seemed to be thinking
along very similar lines to me. This was not your everyday
occurrence, believe me. I'd pretty much given up on meeting
someone else who saw things anything like the way I did.

So, yeah. I'm willing to consider the possibility that I was
seduced by some deep need for common ground. For
endorsement of my own far-out, seldom-appreciated notions.
Someone who actually agreed with me for once.

*   *   *

'Eggs and bacon all right?'

I fought myself awake. I was face down on the bed in the
guest room at Di and Donovan's apartment, and Donno was
standing in the doorway with a fish slice in his hand.

I blinked. '... Nnneggs...'

'No eggs...?'

'Mm? No... Um, *yes*. Eggs and bacon's great.'

Stumbling along the hallway a few minutes later, I heard a musical laugh from the kitchen, and stopped. It was Akemi's laugh. No mistaking it.

I ducked into the bathroom to check myself in the mirror. Not the best I've looked, but not the worst either. I stole a swig of mouthwash from a shelf by the sink. Checked my breath and made my appearance.

'Mor-niiiing,' rang the happy chorus as I walked in. Akemi, Donno and Di were seated around a small breakfast table, spread with a pretty check tablecloth and laden with seriously yummy-looking food. Di pushed out a chair behind a huge white plate with a lot more on it than just eggs and bacon – there were enough tomatoes, toast, sausages, and basil pesto to feed a small family. It was beautifully, painstakingly arranged, like a picture from a magazine.

I sat down, ogling the plate. 'Bloody hell,' I said. 'I'm not sure I want to ruin this.'

Di laughed, and explained that she'd been learning food arrangement for her job, and she hoped I didn't mind being a guinea pig for her studies. 'Oh, I'll probably get over it.' I said, and tucked in. The food was great, and I'd happily inhaled the first few mouthfuls before I noticed that Akemi was wearing a dress that revealed quite a lot of her breasts.

After that, the food lost its taste. Ridiculous, I know, but I couldn't help it. I tried zoning out Akemi's boobs and concentrating on the conversation, but that didn't help either.

They were laughing about something that happened a few weeks back, when Di had come back from a shoot to find a strange pair of panties in the washing machine. She'd confronted Donno with them, and he'd explained they were Akemi's. Next to me at the table, Akemi laughed like a lunatic and spilled her coffee. I felt myself blushing.

Donno picked up the ball at this point. 'I'd invited Ax to town for a drink, and she turns up wearing that miniskirt of hers – the one like a belt. Yeah, you saw it the other night – but no panties.'

Akemi chuckled heartily, 'Evelything in the wash,' she said.

'Yeah, so I bought her a pair so she'd be halfway-decent...' Donovan beetled his brow in mock exasperation. 'And then she crashes here for the night...'

Akemi raised an interrupting finger. '... In the *guest room*.'

'... And where does she chuck her panties when she takes them off? In *our bloody washing basket!* Jeez. Tryin' to get me in the shit with the missus, ain't she!'

Akemi laughed again. 'You bought them,' she shouted, 'They were *yours*!'

Donovan balked. 'Mine...? What do I want with a pair of ladies' panties...? What are you saying...?'

I did my best to join in the hilarity, but it wasn't really happening. I was still working at the plate of food when Donno and Di stood up and excused themselves – something about a meeting about a job – and left, saying to leave the dishes. They'd see to them after.

I heard the door close. The food tasted dry in my mouth, so I took a sip of coffee.

Akemi asked softly, 'Why does my body make you nervous?'

My throat constricted. I felt a two-pronged panic attack hit me, BA-BANG.

The first wave was, of course, my shock at being confronted head-on about something so scary, by the very source of my fear; second was the dread that I was going to go into choking, spluttering spasms right there in front of her and spit my breakfast all over her and the tablecloth.

But I surprised myself. With a superhuman feat of control, I focused all my attention on my throat muscles, and managed to swallow. I even got out a weak smile.

'Because, ah... it makes me stupid,' I said.

She looked puzzled. 'My body makes you *stupid*...?'

I took a deep breath. '... Sex, ah... destroys my sense of reason,' I continued. 'Makes me stupid enough to... You know, probably do dumb things like go without a condom...' I coughed and nodded. 'Hypothetically... And, well, frankly, that kind of stupidity scares the shit out of me.' I looked up at her, and my breath caught in my throat again.

Her cheeks were blotchy red. Eyes misty. Lips parted.

She turned slowly in her seat and reached down. Pulled her dress up and gathered it around her waist. I guessed all her underwear was in the wash again, because she wasn't wearing any today, either. She parted her legs.

'Lick me,' she breathed.

We lay together on the bed in the guest room sometime later, worn out and breathing hard. Akemi's naked body was hot and shiny with sweat, and felt delicious against mine. She snuggled into my neck.

'Was it so bad?'

'Terrible.'

I smiled and let my mind drift... A woman like Akemi. So sexy. So desirable. Hard to believe I'd had sex with her. I sat up with a start.

'Shit.'

Akemi scratched her forehead. 'What...?'

'I told you. I told you I'd lose control'

I felt Akemi's hand on my arm. 'Hey. It's okay. I'm taking the pill. I get them from my friend.'

'We did it *without a condom!*'

'Don't worry. I trust you.'

'Um...' I snorted a dark laugh. 'You trust me because I don't smoke.'

'I trust you because you're honest.'

'You've known me for all of, what, three days?'

'It's enough.'

'Enough for *you.*' I turned to face her. 'What about *me?* Am I supposed to trust *you?* With you flashing your stuff everywhere?' Her face darkened and she reached for her dress. I shrugged emphatically. 'How do *I* know where you've been and what you've done and who you've done it with?'

She pulled on the dress and walked quickly out of the room.

*   *   *

'Mate... what the hell'd you do to Ax?'

Donovan knew something was up, but he'd graciously waited till we were out of Di's hearing and walking in the general direction of the Thames river before mentioning it.

It was a real spring day at last. A lot of high cloud about, but the sun doing its best to peek through and warm our faces. At Russell Square it seemed like all of London was out and about, making the most of the weather. Bus brakes squealed, car horns blared at cheeky jaywalkers, and groups of Asian women swung selfie-sticks like daleks.

I thrust my hands down into the deep pockets of my coat, and told Donovan about the condom thing, tactfully leaving out the stuff about smokers.

'Jeeez. She let you do her without a condom?' Donovan blurted. 'She never let *me*.'

I stopped walking. 'She told me you weren't in a relationship.' He shrugged.

'We're not.'

I gazed at him, then shook my head. 'Well, it doesn't matter now, anyway.'

'Oh, come on. You're not gonna just leave it like that...'

'I texted her. She didn't reply,' I said lamely.

He made a face.

'What?' I asked.

'You really are one emotionally stunted bastard.'

We clattered down some steps to the riverside promenade by King's College. Our chief purpose for the walk had been to nail down a few strategies for our *Willing* campaign, but we'd walked mostly in silence since the thing with Akemi had come up.

Standing by the gray water of the Thames, we could see all the way up to London bridge in one direction, and the London eye in the other. It was an impressive place to stand. Difficult to walk and talk – unless you were a local, maybe, and the vista was already burnt onto your eyeballs. So we sat on a bench near a big stone lion. A very imperious-looking thing, crouched low on its haunches.

Donovan took out a cigarette and lit it. He breathed out

smoke and nodded towards the lion's statue. 'We need to kick things off with a flash and a roar.'

I was deeply suspicious of things that flashed and roared, but I kept that to myself for now. 'Di had a few ideas on that score,' he continued. 'But first we need to build your profile.'

I sighed. 'How?' This was pushing my buttons. *Build your profile. Get a good CV Together. Sell yourself like a product.*

'First, we should look at changing your name. Something weighty and mysterious to go with the Brynner thing. Like say, *Brock Veuling...* or *Anderson Ure...* It'd reinforce the image, and it'd also help to protect you. Give you a layer of security.' He gave a meaningful look. 'We shouldn't underestimate how important that'll be later on.'

I shook my head. 'I want everything to be above board and out in the open.'

'Right.' He snorted and peered at the tip of his cigarette for a moment. 'So. You gotta write a book,' he continued.' And you gotta write it in your inimitable grab-em-by-the-curlies style.'

'I can't.'

'*I caaan't,*' he mimicked. 'Jesus, what's the matter with you, man? You wanna do this, or not?'

'These are all *your* ideas, not mine.'

'Uhuh. I seem to recall you saying you were *in*.'

I colored. 'Why don't you do it yourself? You do *grab-em-by-the-curlies* without even trying.'

A slow smile. He leaned back on the seat. 'Wouldn't work, mate. It'd come out more like *grab-em-by-the-curlies-and-twist-until-violent-reaction-forthcoming.*'

He took a puff on his cigarette and let the smoke slowly curl up into the air. 'Remember that dickhead at WARF? Terry...?

Yeah, well. One Terry, I can handle. But not fifty of 'em.' He breathed a long sigh. 'That's me, I guess. I'm either fuckin' *boring*, or I'm fuckin' *insulting*. No middle ground.'

He shrugged. 'I'm a bruised man, Reags. Maybe the world hasn't been as kind to me as it has to you. I can't pretend I love everybody when I don't.' He blew out smoke and peered up at me. 'Answer your question?'

'Sorry. I'm in a foul mood. It's the Akemi thing, I guess.'

'Yeah, we better sort that out later on.' He pointed his cigarette at me. 'So tell me why you can't do the book.'

'Well, you *know* why... I don't do *grab-em-by-the-curlies* when I'm not freaking out.'

'Right. You gotta be freaking out. So...' He pointed his cigarette at me again. 'We do a tour of all the conferences and forums and bowling clubs and women's group meetings and whoever-the-hell else will have you... So you get to wank it up large with your Brynner on...' He nodded, warming to his subject. 'We video it, and we transcribe it. Then we repeat the process as many times as it takes. We call it the *Jerk-it Circuit...*'

He grinned and spread his hands. '... Not so hard.'

We got off the tube at Akemi's stop, and walked in stiff silence, like we were on a mission. Which, of course, we were: *mend rift between Japanese crazy-woman and emotionally stunted bastard, so stunted bastard can recover normal functions and perform revolutionary role effectively.*

It didn't feel great.

The guy with the squeaky crutches lurched out of the shadows again, then stopped as he recognized us. He gave a wretched grin and started his retreat, but Donovan called him back. 'Hang on a sec there, mate... *Morrie*, right...?'

44

'Molly.'

'Yeah? Seriously?'

Molly shrugged. I hung back, scoping the street, while a sly exchange took place between them, and soon Donno joined me again. He passed me a small plastic bag with a turdy-looking thing in it.

'What the fu...? I don't want it.'

'It's not for you, idiot. It's for Ax. Making-up present.'

'Uh-huh. Likes *hashish*, does she?'

'Yes, mate,' he said tersely. 'She does, But she can't afford it, so it's a bit of a treat.'

Akemi blinked at me, then turned away without a word. Stepped back into her room, leaving the door open. Donovan frowned and gestured frantically for me to follow her inside. I hesitantly entered, and heard the door click shut behind me. Donno had left us to it.

Akemi was standing at the bench, mangling some cat food in a bowl, while Howdy did his two-legged act, trying to reach up and swipe some.

Today, Akemi was dressed simply but stylishly: long red eighties-style cardigan with hard-out shoulder pads, stovepipe jeans and sneakers. I could see she was wearing a little makeup.

I sat on the couch, then quickly stood again, remembering Howdy's chunder spot. My eyes roamed around the room, came to rest on the guitar in the corner.

'Nice old guitar. You play?'

'Yes.' She put the bowl of food down for Howdy and turned. 'You?'

'Not really. Three chords.'

She nodded. 'I can play something. If you want.'

'Well, yeah. Absolutely.'

Her pout still very much intact, Akemi walked slowly over to the guitar. She slung the frayed strap over a shoulder. Stepped out into the middle of the room and checked tuning for a moment, plucking strings in sequence. Then she deliberately planted her feet and squared up to face me.

She started plucking an up-tempo riff, very dexterous, very melodic. Then the riff turned into a jangling, upbeat strum. It was very good, but pretty loud in the small space of her room.

And then she started singing. In Japanese, I guessed. Her voice had a much bigger power and presence than I could've imagined, looking at her tiny shape. Foghorn force and clarity; disciplined control and finesse. It all added up to something very impressive, but completely inappropriate for a tiny room in a block of apartments. I wasn't surprised when the banging started on the wall, but Akemi took it as her cue to play and sing even louder.

I did my best to stay composed and give Akemi my full attention, but soon there were loud thumpings coming from both sides, and then on the door as well. At last she strummed the final chords and ended the song stylishly with a prolonged trill and a wooden *thump* on the guitar body.

The banging stopped, but voices continued to mutter on the other sides of the walls. Akemi spun towards the door and performed a stiff-backed bow. 'Thank you for put up with my song,' She said loudly and clearly. 'I'm sorry. *Very fucking sorry!*'

She dumped the guitar on the couch – on the chunder spot, I noted – and sat heavily beside it. There were beads of sweat on her brow.

I pulled the red plastic chair over and quietly sat down

opposite. 'Wow,' I managed. 'That was really, uh... *loud*.' Akemi wiped her brow and smiled. Plucked the guitar back up from the couch. 'Quiet is better?' She started to play again: this time a slow, melodious riff.

I shrugged, kind of relieved. 'Yeah, now and then.'

'I played in a band in Japan,' she said, looking somewhere distant past my shoulder. She talked as she played, as if the music was a soundtrack to her words. 'We made a contract with the big Japanese label called *Fuckluck*, and we recorded an album.' Her eyes found their focus on me. 'It was our dream come true, you know? Our friends and our families always said to us we are being foolish and irresponsible, to play in a band and waste our time. At last, we could prove they are *wrong*...' Her eyes lost their focus again. 'But it was big fucking disaster. We did some tour and we sold CDs and we thought we are doing well. But the record company, um...' She stopped strumming and uttered something in Japanese. '... They did a trick to us... *Big expenses,* they say. *No plofits.*'

She raised an amused eyebrow, then started strumming again. She began to sing. Quietly this time, and in English:

> *Not my kind*
> *But I don't mind*
> *I wait when you're late*
> *Fret when you forget...*

A sad, tender song. When she'd finished, she said, 'I wrote that two years ago. For Donovan.' She looked me in the eye. 'I think maybe I was in love with him.'

'Okay...' It stung a bit to hear that.

'I knew he was not a person for me,' she continued. 'But I was

um, you know... *implessed* with him. The way he told the truth.'
She gave a coy smile. 'Truth is very exciting for me. But...' *BOM* —
She thumped her guitar. '... As I said before. I couldn't trust him
as a lover.'

I couldn't think of anything to say, so I pulled the plastic
baggie out of my pocket and handed it to her. 'Present,' I said.

'Oh!' Her eyes opened wide.

'... From Donno,' I added. Her face fell.

'Oh.'

'He said you liked it.'

'Well...' she grimaced. 'Not really. It was, uh... something we
did together, you know?'

'Um... Not really.'

'Reagan...' She looked me in the eye again. 'I am not a slut.
Since I came to London three years ago, I had the sex with three
men. *Three*. Russell was first one. He was bad. Very selfish...
Then Donovan. Then *you*.' She nodded to emphasize the point,
then started quietly plucking her guitar strings again. She sang
directly to me, calmly and sweetly:

> *Too... true*
> *Too... blue*
> *Too vain in your comfortable*
> *Values and principles*
>
> *So... far*
> *We... are*
> *Two leads in your tragedy*
> *Craving some empathy...*

A bit mushy and melodramatic. Not to mention critical. But

hey, who am I kidding? I was very pleased to realize that Akemi had written a song about *me*.

Sometime close to midnight, I texted Donovan from Akemi's bed:

> All good. Staying over. See u tomorro

An answer came back a minute later:

> Sly dog

*   *   *

The first stop on our Jerk-it Circuit came very close to being *big fucking disaster*. To borrow some of Akemi's terminology.

It was an international eco-conference called *Bristol Future Fair*, and all the invited speakers were big guns. Well-known politicians, writers and world-recognized eco-experts.

Except me. Which I found out shortly before I was due behind the mic.

Donovan and I had borrowed Di's old Volkswagen beetle and driven to Bristol that morning. We were met at reception by Jimmy Planck – the guy who'd emailed me about the gig – then given a program and hustled straight into the conference room. The audience numbered maybe four hundred, including invited speakers. They were dressed to impress: suits and slinky skirts and shiny shoes.

When we analyzed my spot later on, we wondered if it was the small size of the audience that did it. Whatever it was, it gave us a bit of a fright. You see, we'd been taking it as a given that *the Brynner* would kick in when I stood up to do my thing.

The guy on the program before me – a US senator – finished his spot and sat down while the audience applauded. I took my place at the mic. Introduced myself and looked around the faces in the audience, willing the Brynner to descend and envelop me and make me a halfway-decent speaker.

It didn't happen. Donovan was sitting at the back with a video camera on a tripod. He gave me a puzzled look.

I launched into things as best I could.

'Most of our best efforts to fix our eco-problems are nothing but a waste of time,' I began lamely. I was too close to the mic and the sound system squealed feedback. I backed off a bit and continued.

'For sure, some of us are working hard to isolate and address the problems. But it isn't going to work, because we're making huge assumptions about life and how we should live it...'

I stopped for a moment, very aware that the audience that'd been so upbeat until a few moments before had gone very quiet. Scanning the faces, I saw some were faintly irritated. I took a deep breath. *Engage, engage.*

'I guess you guys are familiar with the old Volkswagen beetle...? Yeah? The older model had it's engine in the *back*, right...? Not in the *front* like a conventional vehicle...?'

I got some murmurs of agreement.

'Yeah, well it's a good example. If you drive into your local garage in your older model Vee-Dub, and your mechanic pops your hood looking for your engine, you go, *uh-oh*, right? Does this guy know what he's about? He's assuming the engine will be in the *front* like most other cars.

'This is what we're doing with our eco-problems. We're popping the hood and we're fixing a broken picnic basket we find in there, or stitching a hole in a blanket... Stuff that's *never going to help the car go any better.* We're making assumptions and we're looking in all the wrong places...

'Our biggest assumptions are connected to *lifestyle.*' I figured I needed to get things moving a bit, so I took the mic from the stand and took a step closer to the audience.

'Okay, I want to introduce the concept of the *Armchair Greenie.* This is a person who calls themselves *green.* Who buys fashionable *green* products. Who recycles, and who carefully pays their carbon tax after their holidays abroad... But this Armchair Greenie is actually just a massive hypocrite, because they keep on living a fundamental lifestyle that *causes*, and *perpetuates* all our ecological problems...

'The Armchair Greenie expects a certain level of comfort and convenience, and won't accept anything less' I said, and raised my hand. 'Who here has a dishwasher...?'

Mutterings from the audience. A hesitant hand here and there. '... A clothes dryer? Air-conditioning unit...? An outdoor barbecue...? Motor mower...? Swimming pool?'

Restless shuffling. I was losing the audience big time.

A woman near the front stood up from her seat. She was wearing black-framed power spectacles and had a yellow pass around her neck: conference staff.

'Mr James. Could you uh, perhaps tell us about your *credentials?*' she asked, and gave a tight little smile before sitting down.

Could you tell us about your credentials...? Are you qualified to talk to us about these matters...? Several of my buttons were being pushed. But as I started formulating a snippy, reactionary answer, I felt something wash over me... The Brynner at last. Hopefully.

51

'Okay, well, I haven't written any bestselling books,' I began. 'I'm not a high-profile politician. *Or* an eco-expert...'

Nervous shifting about and looking at the floor.

'... So I don't have the dazzling credentials my fellow speakers have. But I do have some left-of-field ideas occasionally, so maybe I can offer an alternative perspective...'

A chunky digital timer on a board near my feet told me *07':14"* was left of my allotted ten minutes. I shrugged. 'And I'm running out of time. Better get cracking, eh? Okay...' There was a large white board behind me with some marker pens stuck to it by magnets. I grabbed a marker and wrote

OVER-POPULATION

large on the board.

'All right. Over-population. Often quoted as a major cause of our problems. But. Have you ever driven, or ridden in a bus, across country? In the UK? On the European continent...? China, Russia, America. Anyplace? What do we see between cities?' I spread my hands. 'An awful lot of *room*, right? Miles and miles and miles of green open fields. Trees. Nothing.' One or two heads were nodding. 'It's like that all over the world. Everywhere. Look at Google maps. You'll see what I mean. A NASA guy did the calculations. We occupy only *one percent* of the total land area of the planet.' I held up a finger. *'One percent!*

'We definitely have to change the way we live... But we have to stop looking at this like *population* is a chief cause of our woes. It's *not*. There's plenty of room, and plenty of resources for us all... *if* we live responsibly.' I turned and crossed out *OVER-POPULATION* on the white board. *Squeak, squeak.*

'We have to look right past that little myth, because it's part of a whopper smokescreen that's masking the bigger issues. For ages now, we've been looking at the smoke instead of the fire.

'Like I say. I'm not going to say that ecological issues aren't real, but they're a secondary problem. A *symptom.* An indicator of *larger, core* issues that lie deeper down. Issues that need to be addressed *first.* Or we're just dealing with the smoke.

'So. If that's the smoke, what's the *fire*...? What's the real issue here?' I turned to the board again, and wrote

PROGRESS

I underlined the word twice for emphasis, then turned back to the audience and said, 'Progress, in our personal everyday lives, generally means the improvement of of the lifestyle we've worked hard to achieve. *If we're not moving forwards, we're moving backwards.*'

I paused and shook my head. 'I don't know about you, but I don't think that's a very meaningful kind of progress. It makes us more and more focused on material things; less and less adventurous. Less and less interested in genuine personal growth.' I patted my chest. 'Progress in *here.*' Now I had the audience's attention, but I could see some of them squirming in their seats and shaking their heads. I shrugged.

'Sure, we can say it's a matter of opinion: *Well, hey - my clothes dryer and my motor mower and my car and my swimming pool are the fruits of my hard work! I've earned them! They don't cause any direct harm to the environment! They're just drops in a vast ocean!*'

'But are we really being honest with ourselves...? After all, millions and millions of households across the planet are thinking the exact same thing. They're all just as reluctant to give up what they've worked hard for. If each of them is a drop in the vast ocean, then all of them together actually *create the sum total* of that ocean, don't they?'

I stopped and took a moment to gage the audience's mood. They'd stopped their shuffling and most were looking at their feet. '*What,* then? A change of lifestyle? Should we simplify? And would that voluntary simplification be a step backwards...?

'Or would it actually be a step *forwards?*'

I ranted about simple living for the rest of my ten-minute spot. Managed to wrap up quite tidily when I saw the digits counting down through ten seconds, and finished feeling, well... sort of okay about it all. The audience didn't exactly go wild, but their applause was a notch or two better than polite.

Donovan didn't think so. When I took the seat next to him, he hissed, *'Well, that was pretty fuckin' useless, wasn't it.'* People were looking at us, so we went out to talk in the lobby.

Donovan snorted and thrust his hand in his pockets. 'I coulda done that myself,' He muttered.

'I don't know what happened,' I said, still feeling fairly bullet-proof. 'When that woman stood up and asked for my credentials, I got a bit pissed off, and things seemed to improve. But it was, um... different.' I shrugged. 'Sort of comfortable. Halfway between normal and Brynner.'

Donno wasn't impressed. 'Like I said. Could've done it myself.'

And his mood didn't improve when he learned that, as a supernumerary, he wasn't invited to the after-function drinks. When he tried to bluff his way in without a pass, a guy in a security guard's uniform stepped in front of him and pointed towards the door. Donno said he'd find something better to do and stumped off towards the town. Not a great start. But later on, things definitely took a turn for the better. For me, at least.

Jimmy Planck grabbed me as I was taking my first sip of Chardonnay, and pulled me to one side. Jimmy was a tall, thin guy with round glasses and a cultivated four-day beard. 'Great, man,' he said out of the side of his mouth. 'Just what I was hoping for. 'This lot can get really bogged down in their self-serving rhetoric. Your left-of-field stuff was just what we needed to wake 'em up.'

I told him about our *Jerk-it Circuit* plan – without actually calling it that, of course – and he enthusiastically promised to sound out some of his connections in the conference circuit. Just then I looked up to see the senator approaching, glass in hand. Jimmy did the intros, and threw a mock salute as he headed off towards the drinks table.

The senator was from Florida, and his name was Grant Bourne. Bourne was an interesting blend of hard and soft. A politician's solid jaw, but compassionate, almost effeminate eyes.

'You're a communist, then?' he said with a grin.

'Actually, no. I don't believe in -*isms*, but even if I did, I don't think communism can realistically be imposed on a society. You can't wave a magic wand and make people generous. The only way it could work is for individuals to spontaneously start living that way.' Bourne nodded.

'Hey, I like that. Can I use it?'

'Sure. I'll give you my address and you can send me the royalties.'

He laughed. 'A capitalist, after all.'

'Nope. Not a communist or a capitalist, or an anarchist. But we're gonna have to start thinking pretty soon about alternatives, because capitalism is about to spit the dummy.'

'How do you figure that?'

'Online mega-stores.'

'Online *mega-stores...*?'

'The big online stores that sell everything cheaper than everyone else.'

'Yeah, like Amazon, right?'

'Like Amazon. I'm no financial expert, but capitalism is based on the ability to make a profit, right? Online mega-stores have the lowest possible costs. They buy cheap, at high volume and sell for a small profit, but it adds up, so they do fine.'

'Okay...' He was nodding, but I could see he was planning his escape from the commie lunatic.

'Yeah, so that spells the end of capitalism, because no-one will be able to compete with that,' I continued. 'Small to medium business will shrivel up, and so will most of the jobs. We'll have to find different ways to do stuff.'

Bourne smiled. 'I think you may be right, my friend. But I don't think it's gonna happen in our lifetimes... Aha!' Suddenly Bourne raised a hand and called across the room. 'Jo... Josephine...!' My response died on my lips.

A tall, voluptuous woman walking nearby turned and smiled. She stepped in to join us. 'Reagan,' said Bourne, 'I'd like you to meet Josephine Bourne. My wife.'

'Jo,' she corrected in an English accent. 'Hello, Reagan.'

I'm not sure if it was the wine, or the heady buzz of social interaction, but I felt a stirring in my trousers as our eyes met. She wasn't beautiful in a conventional way, but her soft brown eyes, and her bow-shaped lips were striking. Her dark hair was worn piled up on her head. Simple, matching jewelry on ears, neck and wrists. She was a good ten years my senior, and easily one of the sexiest women I'd ever met.

'I'm very impressed,' said Jo, 'with the way you managed to completely change your delivery style to suit the audience here today.' The senator looked puzzled.

'You guys meet somewhere before?'

'No, not really. I saw Reagan speak at WARF last month.'

'Oh, you were at WARF,' I said, the penny dropping. 'Yeah, well. To be honest the delivery style wasn't part of the plan.'

The senator waved to someone across the room. Leaned in, resting a hand on my arm. 'Good talking to you. Catch up later on?'

'Sure thing. Good to meet you, too.' He disappeared into the crowd.

Jo looked me up and down. 'So, tell me your plan,' she said.

'My plan?'

She gave an *oh-come-on-now* smile. 'How are you going to do it?' she asked. 'How are you going to change the world?'

*　　　　*　　　　*

'I don't believe it,' said Donovan. We were sitting on the bed in the motel room booked for me by the conference. I shrugged.

'It's what she said. Based on what she's seen so far, up to fifty thousand pounds, and more later if she approves.' It was a struggle not to spontaneously start doing cartwheels around the room, but I knew exactly where Donovan was coming from.

'Gotta be a catch,' he muttered. 'She must want something.'

'She said not.'

'Fuck,' said Donovan.

'There's a way we could check. See if it's legit... She told me she was sponsoring Herbert Drus.'

Herbert *'Air-bear'* Drus. World-renowned SIR revolutionist and rude bastard. But I needed his advice. The only way I could get in touch with Drus was through the saturnine WARF organizer Bill Sykes, and Bill's reply email made it clear that he couldn't give me the Frenchman's contacts. I had to go through him.

I wasn't keen to question Jo Bourne's integrity in an email that could potentially be read by God-knows-how-many people, but there wasn't much choice. Anyway, Drus's reply came a few days later:

> Reagan
> Yes, you can trust Josephine Bourne.

Chatty guy. At least he came through.

By this time, I'd already been contacted by Jo about another matter – an invite to speak at another conference. One of the speakers on their program couldn't make it – could I step in as a last-minute replacement?

This one was a forum about new approaches to education, and it was happening up in the northeast of England, in Newcastle. I was a bit nervous about how I'd go Brynner-wise, but I was really keen to talk face to face again with Jo Bourne. For multiple reasons.

Donovan was pleased about the speaking opportunity in Newcastle, and he didn't seem worried about my performance. I thought maybe he'd been reassured by the positive reaction I got in Bristol. I'd find out later this assumption was wrong.

But I'm getting ahead of myself a bit. The day after the eco-conference in Bristol, we arrived back in London shortly before lunchtime. During the drive over, I'd arranged by text to meet Akemi at her place at five and take her out for dinner somewhere. But Donovan was called away to a meeting about a photo shoot, and I was really looking forward to seeing Akemi, so I ended up outside her door a couple hours early.

I knocked. Waited.

Standing there in the corridor, I pulled out my phone and texted Akemi.

Hi! I'm early. What you doing?

I hit *send*. There was an unmistakable PING sound from inside the room, followed by a faint shuffling noise. I knocked on the door again. Nothing.

That struck me as pretty weird, but I shrugged it off and left. I drank coffee for a while at a Starbucks, thinking little paranoid thoughts, then came back later at five, like we'd arranged in the first place.

This time Akemi opened the door with a big smile, looking hot without even trying. We kissed – long, deep and wet. I was happy again. Didn't mention the three-o'clock-knock episode, in case she thought I was cramping her style.

Holding hands, we walked down the road to *Maharajah's* Indian restaurant – which happened to be the namesake of my favorite Indian establishment in Petone, New Zealand. The handsome young waiter picked up on our new-lovers' vibe, and smilingly seated us at a quiet corner table.

I got what I always get when I eat Indian: Chicken Madras. It's tough to match the Petone *Maharajah's* Madras, but I reckon they fair nailed it here in London. Then again, I was on a real high. Boiled dog on crackers would've tasted good right then.

Akemi said she liked Indian, but wasn't all that hungry. Picking at her food, she asked, 'How do you feel to have the *second person* inside?'

'Second person? You mean the *Brynner?*'

'Of course.' She did an exaggerated freak-out look, eyes wide, mouth open. Breath-takingly cute. 'You have *more?*'

I chuckled. 'Ah, no, I don't think so.'

'I wouldn't like it,' she said, taking a noisy bite from a large poppadom. 'It would be scary.'

'Well, the Brynner's not like a whole different person... He's really just an aspect of *me*. A more full-on expression.' I shrugged. 'I guess I'd be worried if I didn't trust him, if I thought he might do something I didn't agree with. But he never has, so it's not a problem.'

She gave a smirk. 'He's quite sexy.'

'Yeah, he's my inner *sexy.*' I smiled and waved my arms wide. 'So anxious to be expressed that he bursts forth... Oh shit...! *Shit!* Sorry...'

I'd knocked a whole tray of food from a passing waiter's hand. I sprang to help clean it up.

Embarrassing. But the waiter was very gracious.

'That wasn't very sexy,' I said when I was back in my seat.

Akemi peered at me through her false eyelashes and smiled. 'Self-expression is always sexy.'

We talked for a while about how Japanese society didn't encourage individual expression, and how the western part of the world is better at it, but not by so much as people like to think. Akemi told me about her challenges living in England as an illegal. Finding work was tough, of course. When she *could* find it, she was generally treated like shit, and promises were routinely broken. Who was she gonna complain to?

She had no health cover of any kind. She'd been to a medical center once, but walked back out the door when they asked to see ID. It was tough, she said. But worth it. Better than a safe, fully-insured existence in Japan.

'Can't you do some music stuff here in London?' I asked. 'That'd be a good way to express yourself, surely. *And* earn some money.'

Akemi screwed her eyes shut and shook her head.

I decided not to push it.

*   *   *

During the following week, I prepped for my spot at the conference in Newcastle. Education had always been a favorite beef of mine, so I enjoyed the work. It also took my mind off Akemi. Helped me to avoid a whopper temptation to shut myself in a room with her and go like bunny rabbits, 24/7. By now, the birth-control pills Akemi's friend gave her had run out, and we were using condoms, but it didn't make much difference to our passion levels.

It was Thursday night, and Donno and I were all set for our trip up to Newcastle the following day. I took my phone out, meaning to text Akemi, and stopped.

'Hey... why don't we take Akemi along with us?' I suggested, as if this was the first time I'd thought of it. 'Could be fun.'

Donovan was fiddling with his phone charger. He paused.

Pushed the plug into the wall socket. 'Nah, she'll have work.' He turned and gave a meaningful look. 'Busy night, Friday.' I felt some faint twinge of dread, but shrugged it off.

'Right.' I turned to leave the room.

'She told you what she does for work, yeah?' Asked Donovan. I stopped.

'Yeah. Waitressing, right?'

'Nah, mate. Her *main* job. Waitressing keeps Howdy in cat food.'

I took a deep breath, and sat down on a kitchen chair. 'All right. What is it?'

'Oh... You mean she didn't tell you?'

'Nope.'

Donovan rubbed his chin thoughtfully. 'Maybe she should be the one to...'

'Just cut the crap, will ya, Donno. What's this *main job?*'

'Well, she's a fem-dom. I believe *dominatrix* is the more common term.'

I lay down on the bed in the guest room. My head was a *confused clutter of contradictions, conflicts and conundrums*. It hurt.

I always found alliteration clumsy in a literary context, but it's a life-saving mental game for me. The habit goes back to my teens, when I'd lie awake at night re-hashing the day's conversations and events and worrying myself half-silly. I started making up daft little alliterative sentences to distract myself, and to steer all that spare energy in a different direction. To *curb my catastrophically crazy creative concoctions.* The more worried I was, the more complex my alliterative adventures.

It didn't seem to be helping me much tonight. Daa – daa...

Dominant diva daring to delve deep down into dark,
dangerous depths with, mmmm...

Multitudes of malevolent masturbating monsters.

It killed me to think of Akemi's hard-won intimacy, given out so freely and so carelessly. Crushed into worthless nothingness.

And how the hell could a *domi*-bloody-*natrix* reason that she's a safer fuck than a smoker? I mean, *what...!?*

We'd had unprotected sex. Not just the once. Many times. I couldn't count how many. I cast my mind back over our weeks together. The melted wax in Akemi's trashcan. Saa – saa...

Scraped from the sweaty scrotum of some sleazy,
secretive scumbag.

The unanswered knock; the shuffling sound from inside Akemi's room. Haa – haa...

Horny hooded half-wit hastily hushed by whore.

And as a *stunningly suitable soundtrack to the sad, sorry scene,* Akemi's song *hummed hauntingly* in the background, a four-note sequence looping endlessly:

Too... true
Too... blue...

A sleepless night. When I closed my eyes the dark went

63

beyond black and into deep purple.

*   *   *

'Hey... *hey!*' Donovan snatched the pillow away from my face. 'Gotta be on the road in an hour, Noddy boy.'

I groaned. 'Can't go. Cancel it.'

'Yeah, right. Breakfast's on the table.'

Donovan had to remind me to shave, but I made it to the car on time, dumping myself wordlessly into the front passenger seat while Donovan held the door open. We didn't speak at all on the drive out of London, or on the way up through mid country on the M1. At the comfort stop in Sheffield, we exchanged a few essentials.

'Something to drink, Reags?'

'Nnn.'

'I'm off to the bogs. Need to go?'

'Nah.'

Donovan whistled happily along with CDs from the collection that came with the car: Di appeared to like classics. Old stuff. Nothing more recent than the eighties. Which I usually like, because I grew up on a diet of that kind of music, but today it didn't have much appeal.

My phone pinged. It was a text from Akemi: the second in the inbox marked unread. I recalled the first one arriving during the night. I'd ignored it. I put the phone away again without reading either message.

The old Men at Work classic, *Down Under*, came on, and Donno started shouting along with the chorus. To be frank, he couldn't sing for shit, and he knew it. It was awful. And he

64

appeared to get a kick out of my discomfort.

At last the song finished, and Donno said, 'Whaddya reckon I open for you at the gig, then, Reags?' I rolled my eyes but felt myself smiling. Donovan pointed a finger. 'Oh, *there* you are... Thought maybe you were dead!'

I took a deep breath. 'I dunno if I can do the gig, Donno.'

He looked at me, amusement in his eyes. 'You'll be 'right, mate. You'll be 'right.'

We arrived in Newcastle early. A pretty place. Like a lot of European cities, it's kept a lot of its historical stone structures. But Newcastle's town was already quite familiar to me because I'd been there once before – twelve years before, to be exact – as part of a little side-trip away from my French home-stay.

I don't believe that culture should define a person's identity, but I do recognize its influence. I think it's down to us, as thinking individuals, to decide how we *use* that influence.

A lot of New Zealanders are English, Scots or Irish by heritage, and some more recently than others. My mother was born in Newcastle and emigrated along with her wider family to New Zealand when she was still a kid.

My visit to Newcastle thirteen years before had quite an impact. Shortly after my arrival, I'd asked a local something about the weather, and when he replied in a strong Geordie accent, tears came. I cried.

Why? Why the hell would I *cry?* I thought about it for a while, and figured out that the diverse cultural influence in my early life had been a lot stronger than I'd realized. At that time, Adults in New Zealand still related to children with a kind of lofty disdain. Children didn't know anything about the world, so they weren't worthwhile listening to. But my Geordie relatives were always warm and engaging and listened to me like I mattered. I looked forward to visits with them. I'm pretty sure this is why the Geordie accent triggers an emotional reaction in me even today.

We checked in to our Ibis hotel in Gateshead and dumped our bags in the room. There was a safe in the wardrobe with a push-button panel on the front, like in all the other Ibises I've stayed at before. The keys to Di's Beetle had a weighty leather key folder dangling from them which Donno didn't like to carry around, so he dumped them in the safe and reset the combination. 'What's your birthday, mate?' he asked without looking around.

'Ah... September ninth, eighty-one.'

'Nine... nine... eight... one... *Enter*. There we go.'

We left the hotel and walked across to the conference venue, which was only two blocks away on Mill Road. I was growing more conscious of my sorry state. Less and less keen to have a conversation with Jo Bourne while I was is such a frame of mind. I nervously scanned the lobby as I signed in at the front desk.

The conference name was announced on the board in plastic letters: *Learning for Tomorrow*. It was a dull, starchy name, which I suspected would reflect the general tone of the event. Another bunch of academics suggesting more band-aid fix-ups instead of the dramatic grassroots changes that were really needed.

We were in a room called the Tailforth Suite. The suite was starting to fill up, and Donovan and I were setting up the video gear at the back, when I caught Jo Bourne's eye across the room. She was wearing a long, dark-green dress that bunched in and accentuated her hourglass figure. Her hair was up again, but arranged this time in tidy swirls about her head.

Jo smiled and started to move towards me. I felt a knot in my throat. There was an urgent beckoning from someone outside the door, and Jo did a theatrical direction-change and raised a hand in apology. I could hear the swishing of her dress from across the room as she walked out. Saved. For the moment.

We were all seated, and the opening fluff began. A bony, tanned woman with short blonde hair swung into an upbeat welcome, which seemed to have the effect she was aiming for. The audience whooped and clapped and said *oohhh* and *ahhhh* on cue. Which I found encouraging in some ways, and really not in others.

I could see Jo sitting near the front, over to the left side, smilingly observing, but not joining in the hoop-la. I could still get up and leave. I could give the girl at the front desk an excuse and a message. But Donovan seemed to be reading my mind. He gave me a punch on the shoulder. 'You'll be fine, mate,' he whispered. 'Just leave the fuckin' white board out of it.'

One small mercy – I wasn't too far down the schedule, so I wouldn't have long to wait – but that forty five minutes was tough. When it was my time at last, I got to my feet. Started the walk up to the stage, and somewhere along the way, I faded. I can track what followed because of Donovan's video.

Donno was panning his camera with me as I approached the stage. My step seemed to take on more purpose and more spring, and by the time I stepped up behind the mic, I was the full Brynner.

4

'What are the first things we learn to do...?' I asked the audience. 'When we're really small. What do we learn to do first...? Mmm? *Sing...? Eat with a knife and fork? Jump on a pogo stick...?* Well, probably not, right?' I got several responses at once. 'Yeah. To *walk...* and to *talk,* you reckon?

'Cool. Well. Those are pretty hard-out things to learn, wouldn't you agree?' I pulled the mic from the stand and took a step upstage. 'I mean, we're as impressed as hell when little Tabatha or little Timmy get up and take their first steps, aren't we. Proud as anything.

'But I suspect it's more the proud parent in us than anything else. We're just taking it as a given that they'll learn this stuff eventually, right? Sooner or later they're gonna hop up and start walking. Sooner or later they're gonna open their mouths and talk. Well, sooner rather than later, we hope.

'But think about it. This is major, *major* learning.' Looking down at my legs, I started a slow walk across the stage. 'The *balance* and the *muscle control* and the *spacial awareness* needed to walk...' I stopped and pointed at my head. '... The trillions of *aural and visual cues* that have to be recognized and correlated before we even *start* speaking. It's breathtaking.

'And what we don't appreciate is that they do all this off their own little bat. If that's not *awesomely successful self-directed learning,* tell me what is! I mean, come on... They're just little mites! Without a single qualified professional standing over them, coaching them, testing them, examining them, they manage the whole lot by their tiny selves. And with great success, by and large. Amazing.

'Right. So they've got the walking thing down. Big tick. They've got the talking thing down. 'Nother big tick. But wait. This is where things go crazy.

They're happily getting on with their massively effective learning technique – the one that successfully got them walking and talking, right? – And they're all curious and enthusiastic and asking loads and loads of questions, *why is this like this*, and *why isn't that like that...* and we say, *STOP...!!!*'

I shouted the word into the microphone and gave the audience a bit of a fright. There were sharp intakes of breath and embarrassed giggles. But I wasn't done with my shouting yet.

'*... STOP WITH ALL THE QUESTIONS ALREADY...!*' I jerked a thumb towards myself. '*... WE ARE GONNA GIVE YOU ALL THE ANSWERS YOU NEED, SO JUST SHUT THE HELL UP AND LISTEN, OKAY...?*'

The audience was completely hushed.

I nodded. 'This is how we begin the process we call education. The stunningly-effective process that turns a stunningly-effective, self-directed learner into a *moron*.

'How does it do that...? It tells a kid their random questioning is not relevant, or welcome. Shuts them in a room for most of their waking day, for at least ten important years of their life. Blasts a massive amount of barely-relevant information at them, and then tests them on it; makes 'em feel like their whole future is on the line if they can't regurgitate the whole lot, verbatim.

'But this is the real kicker right here: It sets them up so they're almost completely dependent on *other people* to tell them about life. About the world. About *who they are* as individuals. About how and when they should do stuff. It's a gruesomely effective sausage-machine that takes in brilliant young children at one end, and churns out irrevocably stunted grown-ups from the other...

'Wow.' I shrugged. 'And we wonder why we find it harder and harder to learn stuff as we grow older.'

I was sitting back in my seat before the Brynner lifted and I came back to myself. Donovan was looking at me with a happy smirk, and the other members of the audience were still clapping. Clapping loudly and turning in their seats to look at me.

This time the conference's security was pretty relaxed, so Donovan could probably have come to the after party if he'd wanted, but he chose not to. He stomped off to town by himself, because we'd had a fight about Akemi. Or more accurately, about Donovan being a manipulative shit, and using Akemi to steer me in whatever direction suited him.

I guess you've probably worked it out for yourself by now. Over the days and weeks following the Bristol eco-gig, Donovan had thought good and hard about what went wrong. He'd decided my relationship with Akemi – which he happily admitted he'd engineered in the first place – was taking the edge off my revolutionary abilities, so he purposefully sabotaged it. Fucking wanker that he was. Combing his hair in the men's toilet at the venue, he argued that the dominatrix thing was true and I should know about it anyway.

In a way I could see his point, but I resented being used like a puppet. I also resented his apparent belief that he was running the show, and I was just hired help. Hired help that would respond to whatever combination of carrots and sticks he chose to administer. He didn't like that one bit. And in hindsight, I can see I was a bit out of line there. Also in hindsight, I feel pretty bad that Akemi's feelings didn't get even a moment's consideration from either of us.

In spite of the ill-feeling, I was in fairly good shape when I went back to the venue's bar alone. It was a long, shallow room, wrapped around two outer walls of the third floor. On the one side, there were views out to the river Tyne and the clam-like Gateshead Millennium Bridge. The weather had cleared and it was shaping up to be a stunning evening, with late sunshine filling one end of the room.

Interestingly, the more relaxed type of conference-member seemed to gravitate towards the sunny parts, while the serious ones lurked in shadow. I saw Jo Bourne herself standing by a window in full sunlight. From where I stood, the evening sun was right behind her and she appeared to be glowing.

I took a glass of wine from a tray and headed over. Jo saw me coming and touched the arm of the woman she was talking to: a tall, thin blue-blood, in her late fifties, I would guess. Short blonde hair and large, hooded gray eyes.

'Liz Lochlan,' announced Jo. 'Meet Reagan James.'

Liz's handshake was firm and dry. She gave a toothy smile,

'An interesting little talk today, James.'

'Oh, thanks. It's Reagan, by the way. Reagan James. Don't worry, everyone gets it back to front.'

'I saw you speak at Bristol, too,' she said, without acknowledging my correction.

'Oh, you were at Bristol?'

'I was. You have some very challenging ideas.' Then her expression changed to serious and she drew herself up. 'And I must tell you, I'm concerned about this *Armchair Greenies* business. You're belittling the efforts of humble, hard-working people.'

I nodded. 'Yes, that's right,' I said. 'I'm glad the message got across.'

Liz looked startled. She took a moment to collect herself, then nodded slowly and walked away.

'Wow,' said Jo in a low voice. 'That was original.'

'Pardon?'

'The way you handled Liz. I don't think I could stand up to her like that.'

'I'm not sure what you mean.'

She gave me an odd smile. 'Seriously...?'

'Um.. Yeah.'

Jo shook her head. 'Reagan,' she said. 'You're a very interesting guy.' She took my arm and led me across the room. 'Come and meet my friend Andrew,' she said.

We stopped next to a gray-haired bloke in his sixties. He had dark pouches under his eyes and the kind of hang-dog expression that comes from a lifetime of disappointment.

'Andrew Symes, meet Reagan James, our traveling revolutionary.' I shook hands with Symes. Out of the corner of my eye I saw Jo strike up another conversation nearby.

Symes squinted at me. 'So tell me, Reagan... You're proposing some serious upheaval. Once we've chucked the whole caboodle on the scrap-heap, what do you propose we do instead?'

'I don't have a structured plan yet, but it'd be based on self-directed learning.'

Symes nodded. 'You know that in Finland, they've been using self-directed learning for a while now, and they're finding an awful lot of their graduates are not in the least bit interested in working.'

'Oh, really...? No, I didn't know. But it doesn't surprise me.'

'You don't think that's a bit of a problem? Generations of

young people leaving school without a way to feed and clothe themselves?'

I held up my hands. 'Don't get me wrong – I'm not suggesting a sudden blanket changeover. Most people are not ready for it. It'd be a disaster.' I heard the swishing of Jo's dress somewhere behind me and had to work hard not to look. 'But I think we need to bring it slowly into the mainstream approach to learning. And we also need to take a whole new approach to the idea of employment and working. Our current idea's based on a society made up of *sheep* and *shepherds*. Self-directed people will be able to imagine more than just those two choices. A *lot* more.'

I basically did a long, dry rant. What Donno would call *fuckin' boring*. When I'd finally finished, Symes threw a quick glance at his watch and nodded. 'Very interesting. When you have a draft proposal together, shoot it through to me.' He offered his hand and we shook once more, then he nodded and left. I watched him as he nodded more farewells, then walked out the door.

A swishing sound, and Jo appeared at my side. 'How did that go?'

'Well... he listened. Didn't say much, just wanted to see a proposal.'

Jo raised her eyebrows. 'I'd say you did quite well, then.'

'Why? Who is he?'

'Oh... Sorry, I thought you knew. He's the Secretary of State for Education here in the UK.'

I didn't actually believe that Symes wanted to see my plan, and I doubted it would be much help if he did. But I have to admit I was seduced to some degree by my brief injection into a world that's closed to most of us. There were some seriously interesting people at the event. Admittedly, few of them shared my vision completely, but there was a surprising number who wanted to spitball the ideas I'd floated. Also present was a well-known college professor who advocated radical changes to learning methods, and who I recognized from some great TED clips I'd seen on YouTube. I'm not sure he agreed with all my ideas, but he was quietly encouraging.

'I think we'll see a gain in momentum in the next decade or two... It's the X-gens who are slowing things down,' he said. He was referring to the generation of school-leavers in the 1990s who threw their toys out of the cot, and spent their twenties on the dole, surfing, or aimlessly wandering between polytech courses. 'They're doing the old knee-jerk thing – pushing their kids hard to achieve, achieve, achieve, because they *didn't*, and it didn't work too well for them.'

It was after twelve when we got back to the hotel, because Jo had needed to stay on until everyone had left. She'd invited me to her room for a talk, but I stopped by my own room to use the toilet and freshen up – which in this case, meant splash cold water in my face and gaze into the mirror for a bit. I was disappointed that Donovan wasn't back yet, because I wanted to blab about the amazing evening I'd had. But alcohol and lack of sleep, combined with the sneak-peek I'd had into the Movers-and-Shakers' club, was making me light-headed. It all seemed fantastic and unreal.

I knocked on Jo's door, which opened to reveal Jo with a phone to her ear. She sat me down while she finished her conversation. I watched her for a bit while she swished around the room, talking into her phone, then I started to feel a bit awkward.

I'm not normally one of those numbos who just *have* to take their phones out and fiddle whenever they have a spare second, but that's basically what I did. I remembered there were two unread text messages from Akemi in my in-box, and fired up the app. I opened the first message.

> Have a great time in Newcastle tomorrow. Wish I was going with you! Axxx

Tomorrow? It was only yesterday she'd sent the message, but it seemed like ages ago. I pressed on the the second one.

> Is everything okay? Maybe you didn't get my text. Have a great time. I miss you
> ヾ(＠︿－︿＠)ﾉ Axxx

Jo ended her call and turned to me with her hands on her hips. 'What do you say to getting the business done with first,' she asked, 'and then relax a bit...? Maybe have an *apéritif?*'

I slid my phone back in my pocket. 'Sounds good to me.'

'Good. Just a moment...' she opened a wardrobe door, revealing a small safe – identical to the one in our own room. She spun the dial and cracked the door, then pulled out a thick brown parcel, which she handed to me. She sat down opposite while I opened the package.

It was a standard manila envelope that had been folded and wrapped around its bulky contents: a single white envelope, standard letter-size, and five thick, shrink-wrapped wads of hundred-pound notes. Jo yawned and smoothed her hair. 'I like to deal in cash. Hope you don't mind.'

I was speechless for several moments. '... Wow. No, I uh... I don't mind at all.'

'Keeps everything tidy, I find.' She indicated the money. 'That's fifty thousand. It's technically a gift. No strings attached. What I get out of the deal is the chance to participate in *real change*. That's all. Sound okay?'

'Sounds, um... fantastic.'

She smiled. 'There's an envelope in there, too. Do you want to open that now?'

'Oh... Sure.' I tore open the envelope and pulled out a single folded page. It was a letter with a fancy, old-fashioned logo on the top, underscored with a ribbon containing the words *Société Internationale des Révolutionnaires*. The letter itself was in English. My eyes flicked down to the bottom, where someone called *Simon Duchesne* had signed their name. The body of the letter began:

M. Reagan James is cordially invited to speak at the one-hundred-ninety-seventh annual meeting of the Société Internationale des Révolutionnaires (SIR), this year to be held at the Château de Sable in Nice, France

Jo took a sip of her drink. 'Herbert Drus recommended you as a late addition to the lineup.'

'*Drus...?*' I took a deep breath, blinked and shook my head. Jo leaned forward in her seat.

'Are you okay?'

'Ah, yeah. It's all a bit hard to believe.'

She laughed. 'So I take it you'll be going.'

'Um... *Yeah.*' Fairly heavy emphasis on the *yeah*.

Jo smiled and gently plucked the invitation from my hand. Standing from her seat, she tore the page into little strips, then swished into the bathroom. I heard the toilet flush and a moment later she reappeared. 'Ready for that drink now?' she asked.

'Definitely.'

Jo took a bottle of wine from the fridge and fussed with some chunky juice glasses, wiping them with kitchen towels. 'No wine glasses, I'm afraid.'

'Mmm. I'm not fussy,' I said, and leaned back in the chair, looking up at the ceiling. Frankly, my head was spinning. I'd been invited to speak at SIR. That exclusive, secretive club for the world's elite revolutionaries. And Herbert Drus himself had recommended me.

'You remember my husband Grant?' Jo's voice.

'Mmm? Yeah, of course.'

She handed me a sturdy glass tumbler, filled to the brim with wine, then said, 'We had our first real fight in ages soon after the Future Fair eco-conference in Bristol...' Gathering her dress, she sat down and took a sip from her own chunky glass. '... Can you guess why?'

'Erm... No, not really. Why?'

'Well, first I got rid of the dishwasher at our home in Wimbledon...'

'Oh.'

'... Then I went through the glossy eco magazines I had subscriptions to. All the glossy advertisements for expensive clothing and furniture. The beautiful pictures of cultivated gardens and gorgeous houses... And for the first time, I saw them for what they were, and who they were appealing to.'

'Armchair Greenies.'

Jo nodded. 'Armchair Greenies. I canceled the subscriptions, of course...' She turned the glass in her hand. 'But then the real upheaval started. I ordered the swimming pool filled in at our Florida home, and Grant hit the ceiling.'

'Wow.'

I've made all sorts of little changes since then. Oh... ' She made a little gesture with her hand. 'Grant has taken it in his stride, like he always does. He's a dear.' She straightened in her seat. 'The point is, I didn't do all that on a whim. I'm not that easily influenced... Unless it's by *truth*.'

When I got back to my room it was two thirty. Still no sign of Donovan.

I stripped and jumped into bed, but was surprised to find I wasn't the slightest bit sleepy. Lying on my back looking up at the ceiling, I felt the first traces of doubt creeping in...

Where was all this going? I was setting myself up as a purveyor of truth, and people were really buying into it. People I admired and respected were recommending me and singing my praises. Giving me money, even.

But could I be so *sure* about truth? What if the *truth* I blabbed on about was just *my* truth, and not genuinely anybody else's? What if, at some point down the track, I changed my mind? Came up with a whole bunch of *better guesses?* It'd happened before, many times. Could I just turn around and tell everyone, *sorry, I've been talking shit all this time. How about I just start over?*

I felt a growing dread in my chest and it was difficult to breathe. Without thinking, I opened my mouth and said, *Oh, Boz.*

I froze.

Boz....?

I had to move. Sometimes shifting perspective physically

frees me up mentally. I jumped out of bed and hurried over to the window, from where I had a view out across the hotel's car park. Not a pretty view, but good enough for my purposes. I leaned against the sill and touched my cheek to the cool glass of the window. My breath quickly misted over my view to the outside.

I'd already been aware already that the thing with Boz's death – and his mum's accusation that it was my fault – had been a major factor in my reluctance to join up with Donovan. To let my trouble-making go beyond just talk. No matter how I rationalized it, I *had* ended up assuming some of the blame for my friend's death. And I was afraid that my efforts might just lead to causing more hurt, for myself and anyone else involved. But I hadn't realized how deep that went until now.

My breathing eased, and I stood back from the window, feeling much better.

Sudden, miraculous recovery, right? A bit weird? This is how it happens with me. I have regular crises of integrity. I go off the rails. Fall off the horse. It lasts a few minutes, a few hours, or in rare cases, days. Until I can see where shitty logic has been tripping me up, and POFF. Suddenly I'm okay again and I get back up into the saddle. Like a dislocated bone slipping back into place, the reasoning becomes clean and clear again, and I can relax. Yes, it might seem strange, but my rational integrity is that important to me. And it's fairly fragile.

I was back in bed again and was just drifting off when I heard a ping from my phone.

It was a text from Donovan:

> Just giving you heads up. Need you to pick me up
> at Newcastle General hospital, Westgate Rd, after

you check out tomorrow. Going in to surgery at 9.
Got a bit banged up, but okay.

I got maybe two decent hours of sleep before I got up, scraped
my stuff together, and used my birth-date combination to open
the safe and grab the car keys. Then I checked out of the hotel
and headed over to Newcastle General. It was a sprawling series
of ancient brick structures with a shiny modern glass section
grafted on. Google Maps made my trip as far as the front door
very simple, but finding Donovan was a mission. Nobody had a
Karl Donovan on their list, and he wasn't answering my texts.

The fat packet of money I'd got from Jo Bourne was safely
zipped into the side pocket of my tote bag, which I carried on
my shoulder. I wasn't going to leave it lying around. I was
trudging along another stark white corridor, thinking about
going back out to the car to wait, when I heard a shout from
behind. It was Donno.

His right arm was in a sling, and the left side of his face was
swollen. A blood-red eye made him look particularly gruesome.
'Righto,' he said with a subdued smile. 'We can get out of here
after we settle the bill.' he nodded towards a bald security guard
standing behind him, who hooked a thumb on his utility belt and
avoided my gaze. 'They're a bit worried I might do a runner, I
think.'

The security guy led us back along the corridor in silence. I
figured Karl had found himself more trouble than he could
handle, but I didn't want to hear about it. I was too tired and too
annoyed. We stopped at a desk where a studious-looking young
woman was tapping away at a calculator. She saw Donovan and
handed him a sheet of paper with an apologetic smile.

'It's really an awful shame you don't have insurance,' she said
in a soft Geordie accent. Donno's eyes scanned the sheet. Did a

double take.

'All right. Well. I'm just gonna have a chat with my friend, yeah...? I'll um, I'll be back to sort you out in a minute.'

The security guard leaned against the desk and watched as Donovan clutched my arm with his free hand and guided me to a seat. He sat down next to me and leaned in.

'You get some money last night?' he asked in a low voice.

'What?'

'From that chick, what was her name...?'

'Sure, I got some money. Money for living expenses.'

Donno held up the sheet of paper and said, pointedly, *'Living expenses.'*

I barely had time to scan the bottom line of the document before he snatched it away again. '

'Eighteen hundred pounds...!?' I gasped. 'What the *fuck?'*

He made a face and said lamely. 'Look, I'm sorry, all right...? It's more'n I thought it'd be.'

It was an unsettling experience to see Donovan looking so pathetic.

Not keen to flash big bundles of cash about, I went to the toilets to get the money out of my bag.

The roles were reversed on our drive back down to London. This time Donno was the one in the dumps, and though I wasn't exactly cheerful, I felt like I had solid ground under my feet. Window down and heater up full blast, Donovan sat brooding in the front passenger seat, and smoked. I wondered if Di would be happy about her nice leather upholstery soaking up the fumes.

It was my first time behind the driver's wheel for months, and it felt pretty good gliding smoothly along the A1, past the

Angel of the North statue and on through beautiful open green country. I remembered people telling me when I was younger that it's a weirdly comfortable feeling visiting the places of your heritage. I decided I'd have to agree.

5

Akemi opened her door, leaving it on the chain. She stared out at me through the six-inch gap like I was a stranger. I hadn't been given the stunned-mullet treatment for weeks, but here it was. For a moment, I wondered if she was going to close the door in my face.

'Sorry I didn't answer your texts,' I said. 'I didn't know what to say.'

Her look said, *what the hell are you talking about?*

'I thought we should talk face to face,' I continued. 'Donno told me about your other job.'

Her expression tracked through furious, to puzzled, and finally to resigned. She nodded. 'Wait,' she said, and closed the door to take it off the chain.

It was a moody atmosphere. The only light in the room came from a bedside lamp and the TV, which had its sound turned down. We sat in our customary places – she on the sofa, me on the red plastic chair, my tote bag parked on the floor beside me. Yes, I'd brought along the money I got from Jo Bourne, still zipped into the side pocket. I was starting to feel a bit paranoid about it.

Akemi's face was lit intermittently by the light from the TV. Her battered guitar was lying next to her on the sofa. On the chunder spot.

'What did Donovan say?' she asked.

I shrugged. 'That you worked as a dominatrix.'

Akemi sighed and leaned back. 'I did. It's true. But I stopped.'

'Oh. When?'

'About, um... three months ago. Before I met you.'

'Donovan was lying, then.'

'Yes. Well... Maybe he didn't know.'

I nodded. 'Did you have sex with them? With your clients?'

'No,' she said with sudden ferocity. 'I made the rule. No sex. No touching.' She cleared her throat. '... But there was one man. Every time, he made a big plessure for the sex. He said he will give me five thousand pounds for the sex. Just one time, and with a condom.' She shrugged. '... So I did it. I thought it will finish then. But next time, he said he will give *ten* thousand for the sex with *no* condom.'

I squirmed in my seat.

Akemi took a deep breath. 'But, I said *no fucking way...*'

'Glad to hear it.'

'... I said give me *fifty* thousand and I will do it.'

'Oh, shit. *No...*'

She raised a hand. 'No. Wait. Listen... I was sure he will say *no... fifty thousand pounds is too expensive,* and he will give up. But he didn't... He said yes. Of course, I was shocked. I went to the bathroom and...'

'Stop.' I cradled my head in my hands. 'I don't wanna hear any more...'

But she wasn't going to spare me the details. 'I went into the bathroom for a long time,' she continued. 'And when I came out I said *no, I can't do it*, and he hit me. He hit me very hard in my stomach. I did the chunder on the couch. Not Howdy. It was me.'

We both looked at the spot on the couch.

Anyway, that's when I decided.' She nodded, her focus

distant. 'That's when I decided I will stop.'

The last thing on my mind was any kind of sympathy. I sighed and leaned forward. 'So it's over? You're done with being a dominatrix?'

'I don't know...' She gave me a hard look. 'Maybe.'

'Maybe...?'

She clenched her fists and screwed up her face. 'Fuck...! Yes, *maybe*. I have some saving money now, but what can I do when it finished?' She threw up her hands. 'It's so fucking *expensive* to live in London!'

I shook my head. 'There has to be some other way...'

'Tell me!' Her eyes flashed. 'Tell me the other way and maybe I will do it. It fucking piss me off... It's just a *job!* Why is so different to be the waitress? To do *any* job for money? *Why...?* I don't even *touch* them. Not usually. It means nothing!' She looked pointedly at me. 'Evelybody put the plessure for me to stop. I stopped for Donovan during one month, and then I started again,' she shrugged. 'And so we broke up... *Fuck!'*

She breathed slowly out, like she was deflating. We sat in silence for a long time, as I tracked through feeling sorry for myself, to anger at Donovan, to second-guessing myself, and finally to some remorse. I reached out and took Akemi's hand. Squeezed it.

'I'm sorry,' I said quietly. 'You're right. You should do what you want. And I'm sorry to hear about what that guy did.' She eyed me for a minute, and then seemed to relax. She squeezed my hand back.

We slept in her bed. Sex first. It was nice, but I was trashed. I remember a slight hesitation before going in without a condom, but then I figured it wouldn't make any difference: in for a penny, in for a pound.

Next I knew, Akemi was waking me up with a kiss. It was ten in the morning and the room was filled with light. She was on her way out to her waitressing job.

I grabbed her hand and pulled her back onto the bed beside me.

'No!' She giggled and slapped me playfully. 'There's no time...'

I kissed her, and said, 'I'm going to France.'

'What...? When?'

I shrugged. 'Today, I guess.'

It was a tougher job telling Donovan about my new plans. But not for the reasons I'd expected.

On my way back up to St. Pancras on the tube, I'd racked my brains for a way to break it to him gently. Or at least to wriggle out of things without too much strife.

Donno was out smoking on the balcony. Still brooding, I supposed, over whatever it was that went down during his *neet on the toon* in Newcastle. I said hi, and then snuck into the guest room, where I quickly packed my things into the tote bag. As is always the case when you spend a bit of time somewhere, there was way too much stuff to take with me. I made some quick, brutal decisions and ended up with a large plastic shopping bag for the trash.

I pulled the money out and extracted one ten-thousand-pound brick. Then from the already-broken brick, I counted out another two thousand, which I sealed into the envelope from my SIR invitation. I wrote on it,

To Di
With thanks and salutations,
Reagan

Di was away on another job. Donno's idea of living expenses was a bit too flexible for my tastes, so I didn't want to leave him with the two thousand pounds I'd earmarked for his partner. She'd put up with me for weeks and housed me and fed me, with little contribution from me so far. I was glad I could give her a reasonable whack of cash.

Confirming that Donno was still out on the balcony, I slipped out and posted the envelope into the letterbox. Di was always complaining that Donno didn't clear the mail while she was away, so I figured the money was safe there.

Taking a deep breath, I stepped out onto the balcony. I held out the brick of cash to Donovan.

'What's this?' he asked.

'Ten grand.'

He turned away. 'It's yours, mate. I don't want it.'

I leaned on the rail next to him. 'I'm going to France. Dunno when I'll be back. I figure you should have...'

'I don't want your money.'

This was not going the way I'd planned. I didn't know what to say. Donno gave a rueful smile.

'It's okay, mate. I know why you're jumping ship.' He put his cigarette in his mouth and presented his good hand. '... Together or apart, doesn't matter. We'll be fighting the same fight anyway.' We shook hands and leaned together on the rail, looking out at the view.

'Everything okay with you, Donno?' I asked.

'Yeah, mate. Spiffing.'

'What the fuck happened in Newcastle?'

'Not much. Tangled with the wrong yobbo.' He made a face. 'Bastard had a bunch of mates over on the pokies. Four of 'em. When I was down, one of 'em stomped on my elbow a couple of times.' He gave a dark laugh. Stubbing his cigarette out against the railing, he flicked it away, and said, 'Ya know, I finally worked out the difference between me an' you.'

'Yeah?'

'Yeah, mate. Me...? I just wanna be *clever.'* He turned and pointed with his good hand. 'But, you... You ain't lookin' to prove anything. You really wanna *help*.'

I left him on the balcony, and dumped the 10K-brick on the kitchen table on the way out.

I'd seen – and been irritated by – several versions of Donovan. Donovan *insulting*, Donovan *manipulative*, Donovan *irresponsible*. But Donovan *feeling sorry for himself* was the hardest to take.

Later, I would find out that Donno was not a man to give up so easily. For now, I felt pretty bad leaving him like that. But I had a bus to catch.

*   *   *

I was about to find out that the whole playing field had changed. And not in entirely pleasant ways.

I rode a bus from Victoria Station down to Dover, where I was supposed to catch a ferry for Calais, and then hop back on the same bus and continue down to Paris. The whole trip was on a single twenty-nine euro ticket.

There was a passport control station at Dover, which was the UK's point of entry to the *Schengen* area – a practically border-free territory which includes countries like France, Germany, Spain and Holland, but not the UK. I wasn't expecting any problems, because I'd done my homework back in NZ before I left.

The government website told me that New Zealand passport holders have it fairly sweet. Because of a bilateral treaty, we can enter the Schengen area without a visa, and stay as long as we want, as long as we don't work. So when the mustached passport control officer started messing with his computer and cross-referencing data on his screen with my passport, I was a little confused.

Finally he handed back my passport and said in a French accent, 'I'm sorry sir, you cannot enter the Schengen area.'

PART TWO

1

I leaned forward, thinking I must have heard wrong.

'I'm sorry...?'

'You cannot enter the Schengen area today, sir.'

I held up my passport. 'But I'm on a New Zealand passport. What's the problem?'

'Your name is on the no-entry list,' he said crisply.

'Why...? What list?'

The officer's mustache twitched. 'One moment, please sir.' He reached down to push what I guessed was a concealed button, and a few seconds later I was joined by another uniformed officer, who signaled for me to follow.

We entered a small, starkly-lit room with a table and two chairs. This wasn't looking too good. I started to think I was in some rare kind of trouble I hadn't been looking for. But the officer who'd just joined me was an easy-going type who seemed as puzzled about the situation as I was. We sat at the table facing each other.

'I'm sorry. I wish I could help,' he began in a cultured British accent. 'But we don't have any information about the list. We just police it. If you're on the list, we can't let you go through.'

There wasn't much more to say, really. I walked back through the people waiting in line, who seemed pretty eager to get out of my way. I guessed the refusal of entry marked me as a dodgy character.

Outside, I stumped around the bus terminal, trying to figure out what to do next. The no-entry list thing was weird. What would single *me* out as being an undesirable? Whatever it was, it meant I might have trouble getting to the SIR forum in Nice.

Which started me thinking.

I was still in the UK, so my local SIM card still worked. I texted Jo Bourne and told her what had happened. A few minutes later her reply came:

> No need to worry. I'll see what I can do. You should assume all communications are being monitored. Look for a hotel in Dover but don't book in yet. I'll get back to you soon.

Monitored? What the hell was I getting into here?

I sighed and looked beyond the bus terminal buildings, up to the chalk-white cliffs that surrounded the Dover terminal. A cold, spare-looking place. I could hear whistling, whipping wind above the sounds of the crashing surf. Was I going to be spending a night here?

I pulled up Booking.com on my phone's browser, and started to trawl through the options available nearby. I'd tracked down a few fairly pleasant-looking options, when the phone pinged again. Another message from Jo.

> Problem fixed. For now. You have maybe a 24hr window to enter France. No-entry listing might be back in place after that. Pls confirm successful entry.

It was no problem sorting out a ticket for a later sailing, though I had to pay for a phantom vehicle the ticketing system assumed I had with me. This time, I breezed through passport control without a second glance.

Weird. It got me to thinking that I was standing at the edge of a different world. How easy was it to add – or remove – a name from a no-entry list at a European border? Not very, I was sure. Not for anyone I knew. Or at least for anyone I *had known* until now. With all the paranoia about terrorism and undesirable immigrants, these were tricky times. A no-entry list had to be serious stuff.

So I was grateful to be on my way again, but I obviously wasn't going to make it to Paris that night. I used the few minutes of UK cell coverage I had left to book myself a hotel in Calais.

Once safely sailing, but still in the coverage area, I texted Jo Bourne.

> Whatever you did worked. Am on ferry now. Thanks!

She replied:

> You're welcome. Stay alert.

*   *   *

Calais was a pretty town, but I don't think I was capable of paying it the attention it deserved. Walking up a cobbled street on the morning after I arrived, I was getting more and more paranoid about the £36,000 in cash I had in my bag. Talk of *communications monitored*, and of *staying alert* hadn't helped me much on that score.

Though I was cash-rich, my bank accounts in NZ were almost empty. The transport and accommodation I was booking online required some form of electronic payment, which meant paying by credit or debit cards.

I holed up in Starbucks, where I drank coffee and scoured the net for info on transferring cash money to an overseas bank account. Then I tracked down a Western Union agent in Calais and gave them thirty thousand of my pounds, which they kindly transferred into my bank account in NZ and made some electronic funds available again. All at a healthy profit, of course. But what I lost on transfer fees and exchange rates, I made up for on flexibility and the relief of offloading all that cash.

Next, I exchanged five thousand more of the pounds for some euros, and made my first purchase on the continent: a French SIM for the phone.

At last I could relax. I spotted a pretty little boulangerie with an opulent display of its wares in the window. Bought some lunch, and sat at a table outside to eat it. It was a reasonably warm day, but not quite warm enough for the plan that had been slowly forming in the back of my mind.

I was going to go off-grid for a while. Camp out in a forest somewhere. My seven weeks in the UK had been intensely social, and hugely enlightening. But also very demanding. Exhaustingly so for a person like me who generally likes his own company. I needed some serious time out – both to recharge my batteries, and to get my shit together for my spot at SIR.

My memories of camping in the past fell clearly into two categories: *cold and horrible*, or *warm and enjoyable*. I really needed to go somewhere warm. During my exchange visit as a teenager, I'd visited the southern French town of St Tropez with my host family. It had been a lot warmer than the Rural Poitou-Charentes region where my family lived up in the north west.

I opened up google maps and switched on the satellite layer. Did a trawl along the length of Mediterranean coast between Nice and Marseilles, looking for a substantial forest close to a town. Somewhere wild, but not too far from civilization. I found what I was looking for on the outskirts of a coastal town called Fréjus.

In hindsight, my search methods were a bit dodgy – when choosing an incognito camping site from satellite imaging, I'd guess the hit/ miss ratio must be pretty unfavorable. But the forest in Fréjus actually turned out to be perfect for my needs.

I arrived there on a bicycle with a pack full of quality camping gear, all of which I'd bought locally – and very cheaply – at a huge sports and outdoor store called *Décathlon*. Taking into account the time I'd be spending in the forest, the four-hundred-euro spend-up was a cheap alternative to most other kinds of accommodation on offer. The bike was the most expensive thing on the list, but it turned out to be a good purchase, because it was a daunting hike to the nearest Géant Casino supermarket every day for food and bottled water and the occasional bit of human contact. I also enjoyed bike rides up and down the beach-side roads.

The twenty three days in the forest were not exactly full of high drama, but the experience was profound. Mysterious. I'd go so far as to call it a kind of rebirth. It was early June. The days were warm and sunny enough to comfortably sit naked in a clearing and give myself a sponge bath and wash my hair in a basin of cold water. But the nights were still pretty cold. I slept in a two-man tent, with three layers of summer sleeping bags – started out with just the one, but bought a second, and then a third – because as the days passed, I grew less inclined to tough it out.

Each night, in the wee hours, I had a visitor. A visitor who I guessed wasn't fussy about what he ate, because each morning I'd discover my previous day's poo that I'd carefully buried had been dug up and tidily disposed of.

I thought at first it sounded like a dog, and each night I lay quietly in the tent, listening as he snuffled and shuffled around my campsite. But during a conversation at the Géant shopping center with an easygoing local, I learned that forests in France were full of wild boars. The young guy insisted I was in serious danger. *Les sangliers* were known to attack. My instincts told me otherwise, but I filed the information away.

One night I was up late reading an e-book on my tablet, when I heard my visitor's feet crunching carefully through the undergrowth nearby. The footsteps stopped, and there was a deep menacing growl. The hairs on the back of my neck sprang up erect. I stopped breathing and listened.

The footsteps continued – *crunch, crunch, crunch* – circling the outside of my tent. *What's up...?* I wondered. *He's never growled before...* As I looked around the tent I could see that the canopy was lit up by the glow from my tablet. I guessed my visiting sanglier saw *me* as the visitor. A scary and unwelcome visitor who glowed in the dark, and who was sitting in the middle of *his* patch.

I hit the button on the tablet and the tent went dark.

Still, the footsteps continued – *crunch, crunch, crunch* – around to the back of my tent and closer to where I lay propped up on my pillow, staring into the pitch black. Now the crunching was joined by a *shnuffle, shnuff, shnuffle* as my visitor sniffed and began tentatively pushing his nose against the tent. I jumped back, away from the tent's wall. Despite my conviction that wild boars were not innately vicious, I was getting pretty scared. In my mind, I could picture the small black eyes, and the long, curling white tusks.

My eyes were adjusting now, and I could see the bottom of the tent flaps push upwards with each experimental thrust. I sat, stock-still, holding my breath for what seemed like ages. And finally the sanglier gave up and went off. In search, maybe, of the supper I'd left buried for him nearby.

The most mysterious aspect of my stay in the forest was the phantom choir. It was pretty normal for me to wake up multiple times during the night, then drift off again. The second or third night, I woke with the feeling that something was different. I emerged more fully from sleep, and lay listening. The wind was up, and with each gust I fancied I could hear voices. Many voices, singing in unison. A substantial choir, with meticulously arranged harmonies. Low-end bass voices. Mid-range voices. High-end sopranos. The more I listened, the clearer it became. There was a melody. An indistinct four-bar phrase that repeated over and over and over, chanting:

> *La-la-la-la-la-la-la; La-la-la-la-la-la-la...*
> *La-la-la-la-la-la-la; La-la-la-la-la-la-la...*

I checked my watch. 1:45am. The forest was a long way from the nearest residential area. Had a local choir come all the way out here to practice? In the *middle of the night?* Maybe it was some black magic ritual? I remembered that movie *Blair Witch Project* and felt a faint shudder.

The music continued for a long time without changing, which also seemed pretty weird. I must have stayed awake for about an hour that first time, listening and wondering, but then I drifted off again... To awake two or three hours later and discover that the choir was *still* going. Definitely weird. I listened again and found I could pick out each individual harmony.

The next night was a calm night, lit by a three-quarter moon.

No choir that night. I was figuring choir night was a one-off, when a few nights later, it struck up again. Same deal. Repeating four-bar phrase with distinct harmonies, continuing over and over for several hours. I can't be certain, but I think that night was a windy night too. That might've been a factor.

Whatever it was, the phantom choir was a regular thing. I'd say three days out of each week, I'd wake to its sound and happily listen for a while.

La-la-la-la-la-la-la; La-la-la-la-la-la-la...
La-la-la-la-la-la-la; La-la-la-la-la-la-la...

As the days went by, I felt less weirded-out by it, and more comforted. It had a surety to it. Many voices, one sound. Like every small part of the forest was singing its own unique song, and effortlessly fitting in with the whole.

I'd quite purposefully gone off-grid, but ironically, for the first few weeks in the forest, I was anxious about staying in touch with the outside world. With Jo Bourne and whoever else might be contacting me from SIR. During the whole time, I think I must've got less than ten emails in total, but I nursed my phone like it was a lifeline and checked my emails constantly.

I also had a sense of urgency about prepping for my spot at the SIR conference. The only real, immediate pressure was to come up with a subject title for my spot a week before the event. Which wasn't in itself a big thing. But it would set in concrete what I'd be talking about, so I couldn't just chuck them any old half-assed idea. Strangely, each time I set my mind to thinking on it, I felt a massive lethargy descend, and I put it off.

Late in the second week, though, I started really relaxing. I left my phone switched off, and checked my emails only once a day – sometimes even less frequently – while plugged in at an e-comms station at the Géant shopping center. But now, sitting in the clearing next to my tent with sunshine warming my face, I could forget the outside world almost completely.

And with the pressure off, the first fragments of my SIR spot also started to click into place. On the day of the one-week deadline, I emailed through the title for my spot:

The Willing.

I did feel a momentary tug at my conscience – after all, the term was originally Karl Donovan's. I tried several times to think of an alternative, and never came up with anything better.

But I didn't expect any trouble from Donno – he hadn't exactly been champing at the bit when I saw him last. And he didn't strike me as the covetous type. Once he said to me, *ya can't copyright the truth, mate.* And I think that's true.

Having said that, I also knew – deep down – that my use of the term would mean Donovan had a vested interest in whatever developed. There'd be times later when I'd wish I tried a little harder to find an alternative.

2

The *Château de Sable* was an ancient stone building perched on the side of a hill above Nice. The sweeping views down to the blue Côte d'Azur sea, and the rambling, sprawlingly substantial quality of the surrounding houses, gave the area a *fuck-off-I'm-rich* atmosphere that I found kind of intimidating. Rich or poor, I'm not usually fussed, but this hilltop suburb had an exclusive, other-world feel about it that places like Beverly Hills *try* to attain, but never get beyond the trying. Dotted along the lush-green hilltop edge, the traditional burnt-browns and oranges of the Mediterranean-style houses were interspersed with massive castle-like structures rendered in stark white and blue.

Using google maps, I'd bused and walked up from the town, having read that Nice's taxi drivers were spectacularly untrustworthy and best avoided. I was an hour early, but as I approached, the Château's car park was filling up with expensive-looking cars.

There were men and women with cameras standing around the entrance, taking snaps of the arriving guests as they went in. I noticed that some of the guests were geared up in hats, sunglasses and face-scarves that completely obscured their features.

No wonder SIR had such a mysterious image – these guys were really working hard at it. It seemed to me like a foolish pantomime. Then, as I neared the main entrance, I noticed the calculated method of the camera people. These guys were not paparazzi out to sell pictures and put food on the table. They worked methodically, swinging their cameras robotically from one guest to another. When my turn came to run the gauntlet, I felt weirdly violated.

Inside, a jolly plump woman stood behind a low wooden table, with a hand-written sign saying *Bienvenue* sellotaped to it – but no mention of the conference by name. The woman's name badge said *Marianne*.

'Ah, Bonjour Monsieur Reagan!' Marianne said with a big smile. She knew who I was. *'Bienvenue.* Welcome.'

After a quick greeting, I said, 'it's er, *James*, actually. Reagan James.' I was being pedantic because I didn't want to go through the next few days being called James Reagan. It'd happened before.

'Oh, *pardon!* Mister James!'

'No problem. A lot of people get it back to front.' I nodded towards the front entrance. 'What's with the cameras out there? They don't much look like media.'

Marianne made a face. 'They are police. Every time it is the same.' She took a stack of papers from the desk and handed me them one by one. 'This is your schedule... this one, venue information... And a confidentiality agreement. If you could please sign the agreement and give it back to me today.'

'Okay, sure. *Merci, Marianne. Bonne journée.'*

'Et vous aussi, Monsieur Reagan. *Bonne journée.'*

I let that one go. There were some bench seats nearby, and I sat down, leafing through the papers she'd given me.

The schedule was the most laid-back affair I'd ever seen: twelve speakers over three days, starting 10am each morning; two speakers before a 12:30 (provided) lunch; then two more in the afternoon, to finish at 4pm. All interspersed with liberal breaks for coffee.

That meant four speakers per day. Wow. After the exhausting ten – or even twelve – speakers per day I was accustomed to, this was luxury. My spot was on day two, first up after lunch – in keeping with the preference I'd named in a questionnaire emailed to me while I was foresting it in Fréjus. Which all meant I could relax a bit today.

I scanned the confidentiality agreement next. Mine was in English.

> *REAGAN JAMES*
> *agrees not to discuss by name, any SIR conference*
> *guest, nor to repeat any matters or material*
> *discussed...*

'Ah, Reagan... There you are!'

It was Jo Bourne, with Herbert Drus in tow. Definitely in that order. Jo's relaxed, radiant smile was a sharp contrast to Drus's prune-like gloom. She was wearing tan slacks and a loose white top, and her dark hair was loose about her shoulders for a change. When she moved, her breasts swung in a way that showed she was bra-less, which I had to work hard to ignore. To be fair to Drus, the part of the Mediterranean gentleman sat well on him, with his crisp turquoise shirt, white trousers and leather loafers. I glanced down at my own clothes – simple white shirt and jeans – and felt a little shabby.

I stood to trade a two-cheek kiss with Jo, then shook hands with Drus, whose face wrinkled – surprisingly – into some semblance of a smile. *'Ça va?'* he asked.

I nodded. *'Ça va bien, merci. Et toi?'*

Beside me, Jo did a double take. *'Tu parle Français?' Je savais pas!'*

'Yeah, well. A little. Bit rusty, though.'

As we moved through into the conference room, I told Jo

and Drus about my year in north-western France as a teenager. The seating in the room was stock-folding type, which is often chosen because you don't want your audience to be *too* comfortable and fall asleep on you. Certainly this lot didn't need to skimp on costs like that. To one side there were two long tables, one of which sagged under the weight of many bottles of wine and two large urns; the other, under the weight of many fine-looking dishes of food covered in cling-wrap.

Drus and Jo greeted other guests. Introduced me to some, but not to others, and soon we were settling into our seats. All up, I guessed there were fifty, maybe sixty guests. A compact affair. All the hats, sunglasses and other disguise stuff had gone, and our fellow guests were dressed like they were out on a classy picnic. Very Mediterranean.

A tanned, handsome guy of maybe forty stood behind the mic and introduced himself as Simon Duchesne, whose name I recognized from my invitation letter. He had sun-bleached brown hair and a long, smooth face framed by a pair of carefully-shaped sideburns. Gesturing towards a large screen on the wall behind him, Simon spoke to us in French:

'Mesdames et Messieurs. Bienvenue à la cent-quatre-vingt-dix-septième conférence de la Société Internationale des Revolutionnaires.'

After a very slight delay, an English translation appeared on the screen. There was a low murmur of approval and some light clapping. Beside me, Jo whispered enthusiastically, 'This'll be a real game-changer.'

'Ladies and gentlemen,' Simon repeated in English. This time a French translation popped up on the screen as he spoke. 'Welcome to the one hundred ninety-seventh conference of the International Society of Revolutionaries. As you can see, we 'ave a new translation system. It is not yet, 'owever...'

But then a howling siren drowned Simon's words. An ear-piercing shriek that couldn't be tolerated for very long. Jo and Drus shared a vexed look, and we all covered our ears and hurried for the exit.

When we were assembled in the car park, a uniformed policeman parked himself in front of us and spoke in a loud voice. Confident but apologetic. In French. Something about a bomb – I could only make out part of what was being said. When I turned to Jo and Drus, I saw they were fuming.

The policeman finished his piece, then stumped off towards a cop car parked up on a grass verge. Simon waited till the cop was well out of earshot before making his own announcement. We were on the move. He started handing out pieces of paper, and the guests began to disperse. Some climbed into cars and started to drive away, as a pair of black vans turned into the car park, blue lights flashing on top. A small squad of men in dark uniforms jumped out of vehicles and hurried over to join the police officer who'd spoken to us earlier.

I had only a patchy idea what was happening. One of Simon's handouts finally made its way into my hands: it was a map. At last, Jo took my arm and steered me towards a tatty old Toyota sedan.

We tore down a hillside road in loose convoy with other guests' cars, Drus driving, Jo in the front passenger seat, and me in the back. There was a tense silence in the car, but once we reached the bottom of the hill and turned onto the coastal road, Jo seemed to relax a bit. She turned around in her seat and gave me a subdued smile. 'We're on our way to the back-up location in Beaulieu-sur-Mer.' She glanced at her watch, and spoke rapidly to Drus in French. Drus grunted a reply.

'Last year we lost nearly half a day,' Jo continued. 'Standing waiting in the car park, while the bomb squad searched the building, used a robot thingy to extract the briefcase they found in a cupboard, then blew the thing up on the hillside.' She shrugged. 'A hoax, of course. But we learned from the experience. This time we were prepared.'

'A bomb hoax? Who would do that?' I asked from the back seat.

'Police.'

'Police...?'

'Well, not your garden-variety PC Plod. A branch of the anti-terrorism squad. It's a team of five, apparently. Working out of an office in Paris. The local police and bomb squad are just doing their job.'

'Seems like a lot of trouble to go to, just to knock a few hours out of your schedule.'

'Oh, there's more to it than that. It's an erosion tactic. What they aim to do is shut down all our venue options, by establishing a security threat. By slowly fostering a general reluctance to associate with... Oh, my God...'

Drus swore in French. We were swinging into a car park that was an identical scene to the one we'd left only minutes before: two black vans with flashing blue lights blocking the way, and uniformed men hurrying between the vehicles and a broad Mediterranean-style building. A cop ran into our path, waving for us to stop, then plopped several road cones in the road to prevent access.

Jo groaned and briskly rubbed her brow. Several other vehicle-loads of SIR guests had also arrived and were parked haphazardly about the edge of the car park. Jo straightened in her seat. Nodded. 'Right. Okay.'

We joined the gathering guests in a corner of the car park and Jo herself made the announcement. We were relocating again. This time, to Jo's house in Antibes. An hour's drive west.

The house was set into a wooded hillside. A big, rambling place, but a bit of a squeeze for the sixty-or-so guests. During our drive over, Jo had used her phone to call a swarm of people and set up things like catering and seating and extra parking space in a neighbor's yard.

It was an old house, but recently renovated. Again, typical Mediterranean stonework, but with a sharp-cornered, exaggerated solidity imposed on the structure. Recently added with little grace. Husband Grant's work, apparently. A broad gravel yard out front provided enough parking for about twenty of the cars, and the other ten or so had to make do parking on the other side of the small forest that separated Jo's lower section from the house next door.

By now, I was convinced that Jo Bourne was more than just a signed-up member of *la Société Internationale des Revolutionnaires.* Even Herbert Drus waited for her to make key decisions. And it was easy to guess why: apart from her money, her power, her connections, she had a real go-getter attitude. Combined with a passion for truth and integrity, and her settled self-assurance, that made her what people generally consider to be prime-leadership material.

But it seemed to me that she had something even more important: despite those qualities, she didn't *want* to lead. She had an innate understanding that leaders attract *followers.* And there were already far too many of those in the world.

After all the fuss, we did actually end up losing a half-day, but Marianne and Simon Duchesne (they were a couple, it turned out) had quickly sorted out a new schedule, which had us go straight into lunch. We all took a plate and a plastic chair and sat eating and talking in the sun, in the purposefully-overgrown garden around the back of the house.

I'd noticed the Aristocratic Liz Lochlan among the guests at SIR – the lady who took me to task over the *Armchair Greenies* business – she was talking heatedly with Jo about the bomb hoaxes. Jo took my arm and steered me to one side. 'Be nice to Liz,' she said. 'I've been working on her, but she's a tough old bird.' Jo then took me over and re-introduced me.

Liz gave me a thin-lipped smile and nodded. 'Good, yes. I believe in second chances. I'm sure we'll be able to work together.'

When we finally got cracking with the real business, it was one o'clock. The talks were conducted right there in the garden. The translation system was still locked down at the Château in Nice, so I had to make do with my sketchy understanding of French.

It was at this point in the game that I realized none of the other speakers was there to present fresh revolutionary theories, or discuss ways to overthrow governments. They were giving status reports on programs already in place somewhere in the world. The programs all had interestingly odd names, like *Wenn-Denzler* and *Parapolite* and *Rotodyne*. There was an experience-based education program. One research and development support fund for alternative energies, and another for alternative lifestyles. It seemed they'd all been going for a while.

Puzzled and a bit disappointed, I wasn't sure how I fit into this picture, but during one of the breaks, Drus reassured me. 'Each year we look for new blood,' he said. 'Someone with fresh ideas and a considered, realistic approach. This year that is *you*.' He put his hand on my arm and looked me in the eye. 'Here, we are not in the business of *talking* about change... We are in the business of making change *happen*.'

I got talking with a dark-skinned Belgian woman called Sandrine, and learned that each speaker's program usually required between two and four sponsors. If everything went well, my chief sponsor was to be Liz Lochlan. That didn't sit well, but I decided to keep an open mind. Sandrine talked freely about money, telling me that SIR's programs cost between two hundred thousand, and five million euros a year to run.

We finished the day's business at about seven in the evening. It was starting to get dark. Jo asked if I'd stay and join her and a few others for a drink, but I was tired from struggling to keep up with the French presentations, and nervous about my spot the next day. I needed some time alone to sort myself out. Simon and Marianne Duchesne were given the job of driving me back to my hotel in Nice.

It was an awkward forty minutes in the car with the Duchesne couple. He was smolderingly silent, and she was on the edge of tears the whole way. I figured they must have had a fight, and I used the time to go over the material for my spot.

But the reason for the icy atmosphere came clear when we assembled for the second day of SIR business, at Jo's house the next morning. Simon waited until everyone was seated and ready, then made an announcement.

Marianne wouldn't be joining us today, he said in a somber voice, because she'd gone to stay for a while at her mother's house in Strasbourg. He'd discovered the day before that she was keeping the anti-terrorist squad up to date with our movements, and providing names and private details of SIR's guests.

It was a weird way for the day to start, but once we got underway things went smoothly. The translation setup had been released from the château, and it was cranked up and seemed to be working pretty well.

I was up first after lunch, having skipped the rich-looking spread for lack of an appetite. I was pretty nervous, but not worried so much about the Brynner. It happened, or it didn't. This crowd didn't need a fizzy, challenging performance. And at any rate, I'd been warned to keep slang and colloquialisms – especially of the Antipodean variety – to a minimum, to prevent the translator program from spitting out something confusing in French, or from spitting the dummy altogether.

The translation technology would also provide a bit of a bonus. It would help me get past an annoying problem we have in the English language: gender-neutral grammar.

Don't get me wrong: gender-sensitivity is crucial, but it plays havoc with our spoken language. It either complicates things horribly with its clumsy *he-or-she/ him-or-her/ his-or-hers*, or it forces the use of plurals – *they/ them/ their* – and I wanted to talk specifically about the *individual*. I was going to be using a lot of straight *he*s and *him*s to keep the message clear and I didn't want sensitivities about gender issues to get in the way. Thankfully, when I tested the technology out earlier in the day, it seamlessly translated the English *he* into the gender-neutral French *on*.

At the microphone, I introduced myself, and waited for a moment to see if the Brynner would descend.

It didn't. Simon evidently thought I was checking to see if the translator thingy was working – he gave me a thumbs-up. I nodded, took a slow breath in, and began.

'We strive for *Certainty*. We strive for *Comfort*. We strive for *Convenience,*' I said. 'These are the three *Cs* that've become the pillars of our everyday lives. We plan our lives around them. Work most of our waking hours to achieve them. But we know deep down that they're rotten things to base our lives on. We know in our hearts that they're empty and meaningless.

'I propose a new kind of life that's *not* empty and meaningless. And I propose a new type of person that can realize that life.

'I'll call this new type of person *the Willing*, because he's *willing* to take responsibility for his own life on his own shoulders. He's *willing* to decide for himself who he is. He's *willing* to accept a simpler, less convenient, less certain lifestyle, and he's *willing* to share that with others. He doesn't need leaders, and he doesn't need followers, because he's his *own* leader. He's his *own* follower.

'It seems such a simple concept. And yes, actually – it is. But if it's so simple, why do so few of us live our lives this way? I suggest it's because we're confused about our ideals. We've become very superficial. We're more concerned about evidence than we are about real substance. The way we look and behave *externally* has become more important than who we are in our hearts.

'We tend to define *Responsibility* by behavior. By attitude. But our actions are secondary in importance. First and foremost, responsibility must be a conscious, *internal* ownership of all our choices.

'We measure *Integrity* by words and actions, when first and foremost, it should be an internal observance of our highest personal principles.

'We define *Identity* by a social yardstick, rather than by what we see in our own hearts.

'... And all this is the reason we believe that an external influence like politics can actually make a difference. Why we think we can legislate for change. But *Willingness* is not something that can be imposed by politics, by law, or by any kind of social influence. We can't just wave a wand and make a person willing. He has to arrive at a willingness *within himself...*'

I went on to describe how a core aspect of the *Willing* concept was nurturing of the uniqueness in every being. As you can see, it was very dry compared with any Brynner-fueled performance, but on the whole, I felt pretty good about it.

During the break, I relaxed and had a glass of wine and talked. It was a hot, early-July afternoon and most of us gravitated to the marquees that had been put up that morning. After a glass or two I was talking volubly in my bad French. Which was a bit of a coup for me: I'm usually so anal that I'd rather shut up than risk making mistakes.

We wrapped up for the day just a little over schedule. Everyone was on their way home, and this time I said yes to staying for drinks.

It wasn't a very cheerful atmosphere. I could barely keep up with Simon's depressing description of Marianne's treachery, and couldn't contribute anything worthwhile to the conversation anyway. Drus, Jo, Sandrine and Liz discussed the possibility of turning things to their advantage: maybe using Marianne's email account to feed bogus information to the anti-terrorist squad.

Liz's French grammar was better than mine, but the way she grafted her plummy English accent onto a whole other language was pretty grating, and frankly, hard to take seriously. Eyes flashing and cheeks reddening, Liz got quite passionate about taking on the anti-terror authorities, but in the end, Jo was worried it could all blow up in their faces. She did an expert job of calming her snorting fellow-Englishwoman down.

Simon left early, and I started to wonder who'd be dropping me back at my hotel in Nice. We waved goodbye to Sandrine, Liz, and then finally, to Drus. Jo asked if I'd like to stay over – may as well, she said, seeing I'd be heading back here first thing in the morning anyway. There was loads of space at the house. And I was done with prep, wasn't I...?

I was feeling pretty mellow, and it seemed like a pretty good idea. We snacked on some leftover food, then jumped in Jo's car and headed down to the beach.

It was a nice evening in general, but the beach at Antibes was a stunning place to be. It was well past sunset, but the clouds in the sky to the west were still lit up salmon-pink. Jo had chosen us a spot she knew that was usually pretty-much deserted. We climbed over a concrete sea-wall and stood in the sand, looking out across the sea. I got a rare feeling that I was witnessing something so indescribably beautiful that I'd never forget it.

Beside me, Jo dropped her trousers and stepped out of them. Started pulling her top up over her head. 'Don't have a problem with nakedness do you?' she asked absently. As if it was unlikely I would.

'Uh. Sort of. Yes... Yes, I do,' I stammered. She stopped.

'Oh.' She pulled the top back down. 'I don't have my swimming costume, you see.'

This would usually have been the point where I'd clam up. I didn't know what to say, so I should keep my mouth closed.

Better to stay silent and be thought a fool than to open my mouth and remove all doubt. This was a very familiar scenario, believe me.

But I was really tired of dead ends like that. I wasn't prepared to let it happen again today. Even striking out big time would be preferable to yet another dead-end that *could've* gone somewhere interesting, if I'd just let it.

'I'm sort of... distracted by nakedness...' I managed. '...I wouldn't mind at all, seeing you naked, in fact I'd *love* to. But I wouldn't be able to um... to function normally.'

A smile slowly spread on Jo's lips, then she opened her mouth and laughed loudly. She threw her arms around me and hugged me tight. 'Oh, dear, dear Reagan,' she purred in my ear. 'You poor boy,'

She was attractive with clothes *on*, but seeing Jo with her clothes off was such a dizzying experience, my brain just froze up. Seriously. Her breasts were heavy and very mobile. Waist small but tummy deliciously swelled. Hips and bottom broad. I felt less self-conscious without my shorts than with, so I joined her naked in the water and splashings and silly games quickly turned into touching, caressing, kissing.

Yep, the stories you hear about sand getting in all your most private places when you have sex on the beach are true. But I was having too much fun to notice until we were in the shower back at Jo's place later on. We'd had to run back up the beach to get a condom from her bag – lucky she brought it up, otherwise I think I'd have stumbled stupidly into more reckless unprotected sex.

Later on, we were lying in the dark on her king-size bed, her head resting on my shoulder. There was just a touch of light from the moon. I said, 'I guess you have a pretty flexible relationship with your husband.'

She looked me in the eye, wary. Then she relaxed. 'Yes, that's accurate.' She lay back on her pillow. 'Grant is from an old naval family. They say a sailor has a girl in every port, and with Grant that was certainly true. I was furious when I found out... Well, I wanted a divorce. I wanted him out of my life...' She cleared her throat. 'But Grant was just finding his feet politically, and it was my money that got him there. We had a pre-nup, so if we divorced, he left with nothing, and his career was finished. I could see I had him where I wanted him...

'But then I didn't want him to be disempowered and small. I liked him, and I respected him. I realized it was down to me to be a bigger person. We agreed no more sneaking around. Everything in the open.' I felt her shrug. 'And so, yes. It's very flexible now. It still stings occasionally. But I deal with it.'

We lay there for a while, and I felt something loosen. I felt a rare desire to share something more of myself. 'I was married once,' I said. I saw an eyebrow lift in surprise.

'Really?'

I chuckled. 'Is it so surprising?'

'Well, no.' She cleared her throat. 'Well, yes, actually. You don't seem like the marrying type.' She pushed herself up onto an elbow and looked me in the eye. 'I don't mean that as a criticism.'

'No, it's okay. It's not news to me. Believe me.'

'So what happened?'

'With the marriage...? Well. It didn't work out.'

She chuckled. 'Obviously.'

'Mmm. She was pretty young. Actually there was a minor

scandal because we got married a few months after she left school.'

'She was a student?'

'Yeah. She was um... what they called a slow-learner, so she was actually nearly twenty when she left. I was twenty seven. She was very sweet and engaging, and the things that made her less socially functional made her very attractive to me. She was so uncomplicated and honest. And intelligent in unusual ways.

'But the bruises she'd picked up made her really hard to be with. Her parents reminded her constantly that she was *handicapped*, and a real bother to them... To be fair, though, I can't have been a model partner either.'

Jo peered through the dark at me for a while, then said, 'You know, I think you might be some sort of *savant*.'

I felt the muscles in my neck and jaw contract. I guess she saw the change in my expression. 'Oh, look,' she said. 'I'm not being critical. I think you have a very rare gift.'

The term *savant* is typically associated with the word *idiot*, as in *idiot savant,* from the French for 'knowing fool'. I guess that explains my sensitive reaction. But I knew Jo was just being honest with me and forced myself to relax. 'I guess I'd agree it's a gift. Yeah... Mostly.' I concentrated on my breathing for a bit, while Jo stayed propped up on her elbow, silently watching me until I picked up where I'd left off.

'My dad called it *hyper-sensitivity*. He didn't like the terms people generally like to use, like this *syndrome* or that *syndrome*. Everyone's different, so it doesn't make sense to try and lump any two people in the same category.'

Jo nodded her agreement.

'My dad was a hyper-sensitive too,' I continued. 'So he was a real help when I was growing up. He and mum never treated me like there was something wrong. Dad said being hyper-sensitive can be a real gift if we learn to use it. We don't always understand what other people understand because we have a concentrated focus – like a beam – that we train on one aspect of life at a time. While other people are glossing over everything and seeing just surface aspects of a larger picture, we're seeing a massive amount of detail in whatever it is we're focused on...'

As I spoke I grew super-relaxed. My mouth seemed to be blabbering on by itself and my voice sounded distant – like someone else's. Jo's was a warm presence pressed up against me. The feel of her body and her smell, combined with the memories of my dad, gave me a floaty sense of ease. At some point I drifted off into a sweet, dreamless sleep.

*　　　　　*　　　　　*

I sailed through the last day of SIR presentations under a marquee in Jo's garden, with either a glass of wine or a coffee in my hand most of the time, listening, talking and enjoying. Jo had dug out a colorful orange shirt for me to wear, and a pair of leather flip-flops. I caught sight of myself in the bathroom mirror and was absurdly pleased with how I looked – even less dressy than before, but comfortably flamboyant.

Simon's mood had improved. He played the DJ and cranked up some cool seventies disco music during the breaks, and I even spotted Liz Lochlan boogieing down with some of the guests. Drus had well and truly latched on to the Belgian girl Sandrine, and his face was uncharacteristically mobile, so I guessed things were going quite well for him too.

I thought Simon Duchesne was a bit drunk when he leaned over my shoulder and topped up my wine glass till it overflowed. But when he spoke he seemed clear-headed enough – which I was glad about, because drunk people rarely make much sense.

'I like very much what you 'ad to say yesterday, my friend,' he said, fixing me with an intense gaze and nodding slowly. 'Everything is choice, *hein*? We understand our choices, and the world is ours.'

'I agree choice is very important. Is it *everything*, though?'

'Oh, believe me, it is. It *is*... Tell me,' he said, his eyes narrowing. 'Do you remember before you were born?'

'Before I was born? In the womb, you mean?'

He shook his head. '*Non, non.* Before that. Even before you were flesh and blood.' He shrugged. 'But of course, it makes no sense to use the words like *before* and *after*, because in that domain there is no time.'

I was starting to re-think my estimation of his sobriety. 'No. I er, don't think so. Do you?'

'I *do*.' he proclaimed. 'I remember before I was born like it is right *now*, because it *is* actually right now...' He tugged at one of his sideburns. 'And 'ow can I possibly remember such a thing...? I remember because I am willing to take responsibility for all of my choices. *All* of them...' He thrust a finger, pointing to the ground at his feet. '... Including the choice to be *alive.* To be *'ere*.'

I'm quite happy to explore possibilities. After all, the human mind is limited, and it's only reasonable that a whole universe exists outside of our intellectual grasp. But I have an aversion to being lectured. To having a pre-packaged idea rammed down my throat. Even if Simon was open to my input, I had nothing to contribute on the subject of pre-birth existence except conjecture, which doesn't make for a fun conversation when the other guy is convinced he knows what he's talking about. So it wasn't long before I made an excuse and escaped.

I didn't talk with Simon again, but on the whole, it was a pretty fun night and drinks continued until about eleven. Again, I stayed behind after everyone had gone, and again I spent some time in Jo's most private garden – if you'll pardon the silly metaphor. It was a lot more relaxed the second time around, and we didn't talk much about my weirdness.

The fourth day of the SIR schedule was to be a discussion day for sponsors only, so I had a spare day to wander about. I got up early and took a short walk down to the station in Antibes, where I caught a train back to Nice.

I'm not really a touristy type, so I didn't have any specific sights I wanted to to see, but I found myself gravitating to the Promenade des Anglais. It's a really beautiful spot. When you step down from the promenade, you find that instead of sand, the beach is made up of small, smooth pebbles. It's a pretty, and comfortable place to chill out and relax.

I took a large bottle of water down onto the beach and sat in the warm sun, rubbing smooth stones between my fingers, and thinking about the Willing campaign. The hows, rather than the whys. *How would I run the thing? How many staff would I need, and how would I recruit them? What other resources would I need? How much money should I ballpark for the whole thing?*

Sometime around mid-afternoon, I headed back to my hotel, which was up the road a bit, near the airport. I felt like talking to someone, and there'd been a cute girl in reception the other day. When I got there I found a different girl on the desk. Smiley, but not so friendly. I went upstairs to my room, to find my key card didn't work. I couldn't get into my room.

Back downstairs, the receptionist took a look at my key-card, hit a few buttons on her computer, then called another staff member over. A middle-aged woman. The woman mutely handed me a business card, which said,

> *Laurent Brouté*
> *Détective Superviseur*
> *6 Groupe, DGSI*
> *7ème étage*
> *814 Rue de Chantilly*
> *75009 PARIS*

'Can't I get into the room...?' I asked. 'What about my bag?'

The woman said, 'I'm sorry sir. They took everything away with them.'

This was really getting ridiculous. I sat down in the lobby and called Jo. It went to message. I left a halting description of what had happened, then waited for about ten minutes, drinking a Coke from the drinks machine in the lobby, and trading the occasional uncomfortable look with the girl at reception. Then, finally Jo called back.

'Brouté is back in Paris,' she said. 'I spoke to him. Is there anything valuable in the bag?'

'I don't think so. No.' All my valuables were in a money belt strapped around my waist.

'Okay. Well. He wanted you to go in and claim the bag at a Nice police station, but I'd say forget it. You're not wanted for anything, but they might want to have a crack at you. Pump you for what you know. Things like that can lead anywhere with the powers those guys have at the moment.'

'But I don't know anything... do I?'

'Apart from info about SIR members, no, not really. Who knows... They might just give you back your bag and tell you to get lost, but it's not worth the risk. That's my feeling... Do you have plenty of cash? Euros?'

'Yeah, I guess.'

'Good. Don't use credit cards, and don't stay anywhere more than one night. In France, that is. Should be okay elsewhere. Oh – and don't try to leave the Schengen area for the time being, unless it's from Calais. Anywhere else, they might pick you up... Okay?'

I sighed. 'Sure. Yeah, okay.'

'Okay... Oh, and remind me to set you up with an HFE.'

'...HFE?'

'A scrambler app for your phone, to stop people listening in. SIR uses one called *Hellfire*. Both of us need to have it or it won't work.'

We made a date to meet for brunch the next day and hung up.

For the first time, I started to have real reservations about SIR. They *seemed* to be perfectly legit. The work they were doing was aimed at improving the world in ways that didn't appear threatening at all. Not as far as I could tell, anyway.

I was ready to accept that the anti-terrorist squad could conceivably just be paranoid. The attention and the resources they were devoting to SIR might just part of a frantic scatter-gun approach to fighting an invisible enemy. But how could I know that for sure? Associating with SIR, even in the minor way that I was, was proving to be a real headache.

As it turned out, matters would come to a head the following day, at my brunch date with Jo.

Jo turned up with Liz Lochlan in tow. We took a table outside a café on the Promenade, and a waitress filled our coffee cups while we waited for our orders to arrive.

Smoothing a sheet of paper on the table before her, Liz balanced a pair of fragile spectacles on her nose. 'The sponsors like the *Willing* concept,' she said. 'Fresh approach. Well communicated.'

She looked up. Her eyes were large through the lenses. 'But we found the implementation plan too ethereal as it stands. We think it needs a mainstream approach, through conventional political avenues.' She took off the spectacles and gave a benign smile. 'I think with a few pushes and a few shoves, I can get you into a constituency in Plymouth. I believe you said your mother was English...?'

'Hold on a second,' I said. 'Um... *political* avenues...?'

'That's right. The only way...'

'Were you *listening* to what I said the other day...?'

'Yes, of course.' She held up her page of notes. 'And we're responding. The only way we can responsibly sponsor a project is if we think it has a decent chance of success.'

Liz turned and shared a long look with Jo, then stood from the table. 'I'll just use the powder room,' she said stiffly, and left.

Jo reached out and squeezed my hand. 'You need Liz on your side. She has a lot of influence.'

'Fine, but *Political* avenues...? My talk the other day was all about how Willingness *can't be imposed by fucking politics*. Was the translator not working properly?'

Jo gold-fished for a moment. 'Well, yes. As far as I know it was. But I think you were speaking English anyway, weren't you...?'

'I don't understand this. I thought you said you wouldn't

interfere.'

'And *I* thought you'd be more flexible.'

'Well. If flexibility means ignoring my principles, no... I'm *not* flexible. I would've thought you'd understand that.'

'Oh, come on. It's a game. You just have to play along for a little bit, and you'll get what you want. Are your principles so rigid you can't bend just a little?'

I ran the whole thing through my mind, like a taste-test: *could my principles bend to accommodate what was on the table...?* I decided hell, no. And anyway, the thought of being answerable to an old boil-in-the-bag like Liz Lochlan made me physically sick.

I said, 'I'm sorry, I've used quite a lot of the money you gave me. I can give you back about thirty-six thous...'

'Reagan, *Stop that,*' Jo spat, with a vehemence that surprised the both of us. 'Don't be ridiculous. I don't want it back. I told you, it's a gift.' She leaned back in her chair and rubbed her brow. 'You don't want to take some time to think about it?'

I had to concede that, one way or the other, it was a good idea to cool off for a bit, no matter how convinced I was. As promised, Jo showed me how to download the *Hellfire* scrambler app for my phone, so we could stay in touch without any unwanted eavesdroppers.

I was just leaving when Liz arrived back at the table. It was an uncomfortable moment. Jo graciously stood for a goodbye kiss on the cheek, but Liz wasn't going to let me get away without a piece of her mind. 'You can't tell me you're *that disabled*, you can't afford people a few basic manners...' she began. Jo looked horrified.

'Liz! For God's sake!'

'Hey. It's okay,' I said, 'I know how stupid people are.' Then I turned and left.

As I was walking away, I cursed my barbed comment about *stupid people*. It'd just made me small.

I left Nice that afternoon in a bit of a funk. Took the train along the coast to St Tropez, to revisit memories of the hot, lazy summer I'd spent there back when I was eighteen.

Sitting in then train, I peered out the window, through the passing trees, to the coast of the French Riviera. Its blue, blue sea. Its rocks. Its pricey real-estate. We passed places I recognized, including Antibes, then Cannes... Then Fréjus. I wasn't sure, but across the rooftops of Fréjus town, I fancied I could see the broad green clump of trees that was my forest.

I felt the pain of loss when I recalled my meeting with Jo and Liz that morning, but there was something else there too: a kind of relief. I realized I was slowly detaching myself from the emotional investment I'd had in Jo's body, the sponsorship, and in SIR's mysterious magic mantle. Despite my best intentions, I'd been seduced by heady potentials. The money, the sex, the social status, and of course the approval. But none of it had ever felt quite right.

There was no denying that I'd profited from the experience. In many ways. I was left with a fairly substantial concept of what I wanted to achieve with the *Willing*, and of how it might actually happen – with, or without SIR's millions. I'd found it in myself to be sexually open with Jo, which was a serious personal victory over my insecurity in that area.

I also had a stash of money left from Jo's initial cash injection. Yes, I would've been flat broke if she'd taken the money back, but I hadn't been bluffing. If I'd thought it was the price of a clean break, I would've returned every remaining penny, without a moment's hesitation.

I'd figured the £35,000, (translated into about 60,000€) would keep things going for a while, but when I took out my phone to make hotel bookings, I saw the room prices were rising steeply. The summer high season was kicking in, and all the cheaper accommodation was already full up. Most places also had a sliding rate that reflected seasonal demand: rooms that were fifty euros per night a few weeks back were now up around the hundred mark. My money was going to drain away quite quickly if I kept living the way I had been in Nice. I'd have to do some strategizing.

My two days in St Tropez were lonely days. There were people all around, but it seemed no one was interested in talking to me. Even the weeks I'd spent completely alone in the forest were less lonely. I knew my frame of mind had a lot to do with it, but I figured it was mainly the social dynamic of the town: a high turnover of rich, largely indifferent guests meant people didn't much expect to connect with strangers.

I suddenly found myself missing Karl Donovan. He'd been an annoying bastard at times, but we'd always talked about stuff with real substance, and I respected his mind. Well, mostly. I sent him an email.

The reply came when I was eating a cheap salad dinner in my hotel room. He wanted to talk. Did I have the internet-phone app *Viber?* It was the only one that worked on his older-model Android phone. I downloaded the app and called his number. He answered right away.

'Hey, Reags. How are ya?'

'Lonely. Disappointed. Apart from that, pretty good.'

He laughed. 'Oh, mate. Good to hear you're still a fuckin'

basket-case.'

'How are things in London?'

'Aha. Well. I wanted to talk on the phone because things have ah, changed quite a lot. I'm not in London any more.'

'You're not in London?'

'No. Um, where do I start... Di er... Di *died*, you see. No pun intended.'

'She what? She *died?*'

'Yeah. Car accident up in Liverpool. First I knew about it, her family turned up at the apartment to clear out her stuff. Bit embarrassing.'

'Shit. That's terrible.'

'Yeah. Anyway, I cleared out of London. Not much point sticking around. Too expensive to find somewhere else to live... And I'm down in Valencia now.'

'Valencia...?'

'East coast of Spain. Excellent place... Nice people. Cheap. Great food. Mate, you should come down for a bit.'

3

I arrived in Valencia by bus two days later, having spent the whole journey freaking out. To my paranoid mind, every new passenger who got on the bus and scanned the faces on board was someone from the anti-terrorist squad who had my description, and was there to take me in.

My Viber convo with Donovan had been unscrambled – I had the HFE app, but Donno didn't. Anyone could've been listening in, and I was expecting, any minute, to be hauled off and detained for an indefinite period. The feeling reminded me of the time I'd had unprotected sex with Akemi. Panic and regret and fear.

In any case, I made it across the border to Spain, and then all the way down the coast to Valencia without being picked up. Donovan was there at the bus station to meet me.

I almost didn't recognize him. He'd lost a lot of weight, and his hair was cropped short. In a wide-brimmed straw hat, T-shirt, shorts and flip-flops, he looked ten years younger. But as soon as he opened his mouth I realized the old Donno was back. Funny, brutally offensive and yet engaging.

His elbow was a lot better, but stiff. As an intro to Valencian life, he bought me a coffee and a chocolate napolitana – a large, moist, danish-type pastry full of custard and chocolate. The coffee was good, and the pastry excellent. Together, they cost a total of 1.85€. Amazingly cheap. We walked along the dry riverbed that traversed the whole of the city, and which had been turned into a long, continuous green garden. Sections of it were wooded with leafy trees, while others were set up as parks and sports areas. It was an amazingly cultural way to use the land, and it also puzzled me that the place could be so green, when local rainfall was so low.

People in Valencia were not generally in a hurry. They would often stop in the middle of the footpath to think, or maybe to get their bearings, and foot traffic would bank up behind them. But no one seemed to mind. They smiled a lot and looked strangers directly in the face, without the usual veil of indifference you see elsewhere. The atmosphere in the town cheered me up almost straight away. And it was good to see Donovan again.

I couldn't get a bed at the hostel Donno was staying at, but found a similar setup nearby. Six people to a room, sleeping in bunk-beds. Communal toilets and showers. Basic breakfast included. All pretty clean. 11€ per night. Wow.

It was mid-afternoon. Sunny and warm. Donno and I sat on the steps in the Plaza de la Virgen with a thirty-eight-cent can of beer each. A broad fountain with a reclining God-like statue at its center splashed and trickled. A string quartet had spontaneously set up and started playing just meters away, and people were stopping to listen, their faces lighting up with pleasure. The music was sweetly atmospheric – soft enough that we could carry on talking. Donovan picked up where he'd left off.

'Yeah, Di was always away a lot, as you know,' he said, letting off a quiet beer-burp. 'I didn't really worry till she was about a week overdue... Oh yeah. Hang on.' He unzipped the bum-bag he had around his waist and pulled out an envelope. It was looking a bit ragged, but I recognized the handwriting on the front.

To Di

With thanks and salutations,
Reagan

'You cleared the mail,' I said.

'Yeah. When she didn't answer my texts and stuff I started wondering.' He handed the envelope to me. 'Anyway. That's yours.'

I hummed and Hahed a bit.

'Look... Her family're obviously loaded,' Donovan continued. 'Stroppy bastards, too. Basically told me to fuck off when they found me at the apartment. Anyway, why give it to them? I'm sure you could use it.'

'What about you...? You doing all right for cash?'

'Yep. Could live in Spain on what I got for a year. Maybe longer.'

I nodded. 'All right then. Thanks.'

I was hesitant to tell Donovan about my dealings with SIR. He knew about Jo Bourne and the money she'd given us, but not about her affiliations, so I told him simply that Jo and I'd had a disagreement and we'd parted ways. Which was true, and it went over fine, but I'd have a bit more trouble explaining the call that came in right then.

My phone rang, and on the screen I was given the option to answer the call with the standard phone app, or with Hellfire. The caller number was blocked, so I assumed it would be Jo Bourne calling.

I swiped the HFE option to select a scrambled call, and entered my four-digit code. 'Hello...?'

'Reagan? This is Herbert. Herbert Drus. Where are you now?'

'I'm in Valencia.'

'Where? Oh, *Valence...*?' He pronounced it the French way. 'In Spain?'

'Yeah, that's right. How about you?'

'Well, I hoped we might meet in Nimes. You know it?'

'Ah... Near Avignon, right?'

'That's right. When can you come?'

I glanced in Donno's direction. He was happily people-watching. 'Can we make it in say, two weeks?'

'I was hoping sooner.'

'Well, I just got here. Is it urgent? Maybe you could come down here.'

I would never have talked to Herbert Drus like this before, but I was fed up with SIR and everything to do with it.

'I'm not sure you will have heard,' Drus said, as of reading my thoughts. 'I'm no longer with SIR.'

'Oh, wow, really...? No, I hadn't heard.'

'I, uh... I had a difference of opinion with them. Actually this was about your *Willing* concept.'

I glanced at Donno again. He was giving me an odd look. I wondered if he could hear Drus's telephone voice over the music in the square. 'Seriously?' I asked. 'How come?'

Drus cleared his throat. 'Well, maybe we should talk about this face to face.'

We arranged to meet in Nimes, but in a week's time. When I ended the call, I looked up to see Donovan, still peering at me with a bemused look on his face. I waited for the questions, but none came.

Instead, he said, 'I didn't realize you did the Brynner on the phone as well.' He grinned. 'Your face was doing all sorts of gymnastics.'

I looked around to check no one was listening in, then took a deep breath. 'That was Herbert Drus.'

'*Herbert Drus*...? What? You're kidding, right?'

'No. I was invited to speak at SIR, and...' I sighed. 'And it didn't go too well. Actually, it was like, *big fucking disaster*.' A thought of Akemi popped into my head, but I thrust it aside for the time being.

Donovan made a face. 'Shit. When were you gonna like, *tell* me about this? It's kind of a major.'

'Sorry. I had to sign a confidentiality agreement. And also I kind of wanted to forget about it.'

I told him about the SIR sponsorship system, my presentation, and the attempt to railroad me into the political stuff *they* obviously thought was a minor detail, but was not at all. Then I told him I'd made liberal use of his term *the Willing*.

He shrugged. 'Yeah, good. *Ya can't copyright*...'

'... *the truth*,' I said in unison.

'Well it's true.'

'Yeah, I was hoping you'd remember that.'

I asked after Akemi and the news was a little worrying. Donno hadn't seen her since before I left London, and she hadn't answered any of his texts.

'She's a big girl. She can look after herself okay,' said Donno, but he didn't look so certain. I felt a little bad that I hadn't contacted Akemi at all since I left London. I was always pretty bad at keeping in contact with people, even before the days of Facebook and twitter and all the other e-messaging options.

I sent her the same message in a text and by email. *Was she all right?*

She didn't reply.

For the first few days in Valencia, Donno and I stayed in our separate hostels by night, and hung out by day. Just the two of us. We found lots of cheap little ways to amuse ourselves. Saw maybe three movies per week, because they always seemed to have some kind of festival going at the local Rialto with English-language movies, and they were two euros a pop. But then I started talking to other people staying at my hostel.

Hostels are amazing places to meet people. Most hostel-goers are adventurous and questioning and love a good discussion – serious travelers, as opposed to hotel-dwelling tourists who prefer a layer of comfort and insulation between them and the places they visit. I started spending more time up on the roof of the hostel, and day by day, people I met joined me, until we had a table of regulars who ate most of our meals together up on the hostel roof. We called ourselves the UN because nearly all of us were from different countries. I got Donno along a couple times, but he didn't seem to click with the group. They were mostly pretty gentle people, I guess. Not really Donno's type.

One of the UN regulars was a laid-back Texan guy called Sam. We called him *Christian Sam*, because he was quite unashamedly bible-besotted in an environment where very few others were. Or if they were, they weren't letting on. The other thing that made Sam especially interesting, as far as I was concerned, was his willingness to question everything, including his religion. And not in a superficial way. I'd always assumed this kind of animal didn't exist.

As I'm sure you've figured by now, I was not a fan of religion. But Donno – for all his talk of clear, open-minded thinking – was a total skeptic. So it was quite fun, one night up on the hostel roof, to see him get his butt kicked intellectually by a Christian.

It was just after sundown, and we were cleaning up the last scraps of our shared meal. Donno had just declared that *belief cripples the mind*, and nobody was sure how to respond, so we sat for a bit in silence.

Opening a can of beer, Sam said to Donno, 'It must be tough, seeing everything through a filter of logic like that... Not accepting anything outside what the human mind can understand.'

Donno was quick off the bat with a predictable answer. 'Not really. It doesn't make sense to me to commit myself to anything I don't understand.'

'So you don't believe in anything.'

'Shit, no. When you stop questioning you can't think properly. You basically *brick* your mind.'

'Okay', said Sam. 'What if I swap the word *belief...* for *trust?* There's a bunch of stuff I read in the bible that was just words to me at first, but I prayed that they'd come clear, and they did.'

I looked at Donno. He was doing the one-eye squint of the skeptic.

Sam chuckled. 'I'm not talking once or twice, here. It happens almost every day. So I've come to *trust* that it's just gonna continue on like that.'

'Hmmm. So, even if you only understand say, ten percent of what the bible says, you're still gonna swear by the other ninety?' Donno asked, crumpling a beer can in his hand. 'That's a lotta trust.'

'Okay, look. You'd trust your Mom to hold your baby child, right?'

'Ah, no. Probably not.'

'Oh wow, really...?' Sam shook his head sadly. 'Well, there is, or was, *someone* in your life, at some point, who you'd trust, right?'

'I guess.'

'Let's say you trust that person to hold your baby... You're basing that trust on a lot of assumptions. What percentage of that person's life have you witnessed personally; consciously and first-hand...? Two percent? Not more than five, even if it's your own Mom. Can you base your assumptions on evidence you've seen from that two percent...? And how do you know what's happened to them since you saw them last? How do you know they're *physically able* to support the weight of a baby in their arms...? That they're mentally healthy and can afford the care and attention required to keep the baby safe?'

Donno gave a crooked smile. 'Exactly my point.'

'Yeah, but are you gonna live that way? In a prison of your *belief?* Never letting anyone else hold your baby because they might be *weak*, or they might be *irresponsible,* because you *believe* more in their *un*-trustworthiness than in their trustworthiness?' He grinned. '*Belief* is *belief,* my friend. Be it belief in the positive, *or* the negative.'

Donno wanted to come with me up to Nimes to meet Herbert Drus. I'd been afraid of that.

'He's a really private guy,' I said, 'And I think he'd be quite pissed off if I turned up with someone in tow.'

'Well, why don't you ask him?'

'Because I think he'd see my asking such a question as proof that he shouldn't trust me.'

'So? What do you care if he doesn't trust you?'

'I'm not gonna be like, *devastated* if he doesn't. But If I'm

135

gonna go up there with that attitude, I might as well not bother going at all.'

Donno made a face. 'Mate, you must have like, the tightest sphincter muscle in the history of the fuckin' planet.'

I waved goodbye to Donno from the bus window at Valencia Station. I planned to come back to Valencia, but I'd made my trip up to Nimes open-ended. This time I'd been very security conscious, and bought my ticket at the station office, rather than online. So the reception that was waiting for me in Nimes was unexpected.

The bus arrived on time at Nimes bus station, and I called Drus, as instructed, French SIM card back in place, using Hellfire.

'Hello Reagan. Are you standing at the front of the station?'

'Yes I am.'

'Okay, walk to your right along Talabot, until you come to Avenue du General Leclerc. Then turn right again.'

I sighed. It was like being in a spy movie.

I hiked my bag up on my shoulder. With the phone still pressed to my ear, I walked along the busy street, and was just turning the corner onto Leclerc when two men in suits stepped out in front of me. I stopped.

The taller of the two held up an ID card in a leather holder, and said, 'We'd like to talk with you, Mister Reagan.'

'It's *James*, I said lamely. Reagan James.'

Just like a spy movie.

We drove in silence across town, to an Ibis hotel. Rode up in the elevator to the third floor, where the taller suit key-carded us into a standard-sized room. It seemed an odd place for an interrogation.

After he'd closed the door, the tall guy seemed to relax. He took off his jacket and threw it on the bed. Clapped his hands together and said, 'Right.'

The other one, a stocky, dark-skinned guy with big square teeth, busied himself at the keypad of the room's safe, while his taller partner held out a hand. 'I'm Inspector Laurent Brouté from the DGSI... And this is Inspector Michel Rollot.' I shook hands with Brouté and shared a nod with Rollot.

'You can call me Laurent, if you like,' continued Brouté with a smile. 'But I think Inspector Rollot is *Inspector Rollot.*' Rollot snorted, and pulled a laptop from the safe. Brouté gestured between himself and his fellow officer. '*Good* cop... *bad* cop.' In his clumsy way, he was trying to lighten things up, but his partner didn't seem to want to play along.

Brouté's face was lightly pocked with old acne scars. He had large eyes that seemed to shine with purpose, and thin lips that didn't get to smile much, but the expressive eyes made up for it. I got a feeling from him that he wasn't motivated by anything underhand.

It was a bit cramped, the three of us in a room dominated by a large bed, and we had to work with the narrow corridors of carpet we had available. Brouté pulled some chairs together and we sat down on one side of the bed, facing each other, while Rollot set up his laptop at a shallow desk on the other side.

'So. Tell me....' Brouté fixed me with his purposeful gaze. 'Did you have sex with Josephine Bourne?'

I was caught off balance. 'I, er... I... I don't think I should answer that.'

Brouté nodded. 'Okay. Now tell me, what do you know about a young Japanese woman called Akemi Yoda who is living illegally in London?'

Yoda, like the Star Wars character. Had to be my Akemi. Too much of a coincidence, surely. But how could Brouté know this stuff?

I took a deep breath and said, 'I probably know her.'

'Probably?'

'I think so. I never got a surname, but I imagine it's her.'

Brouté nodded again. His face softened. 'I'm sorry to ask you these things. It's a technique, you see, to gage your reactions. We ask a few things that we know the answer to, but which you might be tempted to deny. To *lie* about.' He gave a hint of a smile. 'I doubt you would make a good liar, Mister James. That's not a criticism, believe me.'

'How do you know about Akemi?' I asked.

Brouté shared a look with Rollot. 'I can maybe tell you a little about that. She's been known to us for about a year...' he stopped, pursed his lips. 'You know she is a sex worker?'

'A dominatrix. Yes. I know.'

He nodded. 'Let's just say her customer base extends to outside the UK.'

'But she has no papers. She can't leave the UK.'

A tight smile. 'She doesn't need to.'

'Is she all right? Can you tell me?'

He looked surprised. 'I think so... Why?'

'She's been out of contact for um... for more than a month. I've been worried about her.'

In French, Brouté asked Rollot to check a date on his computer. Rollot scrolled through some figures and gave an answer. Quick and efficient.

Brouté turned back to me. 'We have her in London late last

week. Is that enough?'

I nodded, relieved. 'Thanks. That's good to know.'

Brouté pulled rank on Rollot, and told him to scoot off downstairs to the lobby to buy us some Cokes. Everyone drinks Coke in France. Rollot made a face, but left to do what he was told.

When the door had closed, Brouté gave a wan smile and said, 'Do you think you are the first person Josephine Bourne has shared her bed with? Apart from her husband?'

'Well... I guess not.'

'No. And cameras never lie.'

'Cameras? You put a *camera* in her home?'

'*Yes*, there are cameras in her home. Three, we think. *No*, we didn't put them there... Who did? We don't know. Not for sure.'

'But you've seen footage.'

He nodded. 'It's very easy for us to intercept video clips that people send by email. But the cameras? That wasn't us. You have nothing to worry about from us.' He shrugged. 'From *elsewhere*...? I'm not so sure.'

'Why...? What do you mean?'

Brouté took a deep breath. 'SIR are basically amateurs. Clowns, who like to dress up and throw money about and be important. I keep getting messages from them, accusing us of all sorts of things...' He gestured expansively with his hands. '...*intimidation... blackmail... false bomb threats*...' He dropped his hands into his lap. 'Amateurs. A big waste of our time, and usually, they wouldn't even appear on our radar.

'But we think they've annoyed one or more extremist groups who are *not* amateurs. What we can't work out yet, is *which* group or groups... And whether framing *us* for the blame is an intentional tactic, or if it's a happy accident...' He raised an eyebrow. 'Happy for *them*, that is.'

'I see. But why did you want to talk to *me?* My involvement with SIR was just that one conference. I have nothing to do with them any more.'

Brouté reached over and popped open a briefcase that was sitting on the bed. He took out a document and handed it to me. It was a transcribed copy of my *Willing* presentation at SIR.

'At first, we wanted to talk to you for the same reason we want to talk with anybody else associated with SIR... To further our investigation into the parties we think are responsible for SIR's troubles, and frankly, for wasting a lot of our valuable time and resources...'

The door opened and Rollot slipped back into the room. He handed each of us a can of Coke, then popped his own and sat back down by his laptop.

'...But no one from SIR will talk to us,' continued Brouté. 'Because they're afraid of us...' He smirked. 'They think we will detain them indefinitely without charge... and tie up *even more* of our valuable resources.' He indicated the document in my hand. 'But after I saw this speech, I thought we might have found someone who would talk to us.'

'Where did you get this?' I asked. I saw Brouté chew his lip. He answered carefully.

'We've been intercepting encrypted emails sent from someone inside SIR, always to the same recipient. We can crack the encryption easily, so we have free access to the contents of the messages and their attachments. But we can't identify the recipient... The person who actually *receives* the messages at the other end. They're a little bit too clever to be amateurs.'

I left the hotel an hour or so later, without a whiff of a threat of detainment. When I called Drus again – surprise, surprise – he was reluctant to meet with me after my little detour to meet with the DGSI boys. My patience was running a bit thin.

'Herbert,' I said. 'I came all the way up from Valencia to see you. Then I sat in a hotel room being questioned for two hours by the DGSI. Who, by the way, I think are playing it straight. But it really doesn't matter, because you *quit*, right...? Neither of us has anything to do with SIR any more, so how about we just move on.'

Finally, he agreed to meet a few blocks from the station. As I stood waiting, I watched him circle the block twice before eventually picking me up in his old Toyota. Then we started the drive down to his home in Montpellier, which took about an hour and a half going *back* in the direction I'd come from, and which annoyed me a bit, because I could've just got off the bus at Montpellier and saved all the extra messing around. Then again, I suppose Brouté and Rollot would've caught up with me there anyway.

As we drove along the motorway, I tried to engage Drus in conversation, but I guess he wasn't in a talking mood. So I used the time to reflect on how the ground had shifted under my feet yet again.

I felt a strong tendency to trust what Brouté had told me. It jibed with what I'd instinctively felt about SIR from the beginning. I was also a bit puzzled that sneaky messages were still being sent from someone at SIR *after* Marianne Duchesne had been busted. My presentation happened *after* Simon Duchesne announced his wife's treachery and subsequent banishment, and still a transcript of it was sent out on the quiet. I was less inclined to doubt Brouté's word. More inclined to suspect Simon's version of the story...

Which opened up a new can of worms. But it really wasn't my business any more.

Drus's house was a long box-like structure, perched on the side of a hill, with a view out to the Mediterranean Sea. It wasn't a rich man's house, but it was solid and simple in design. A bit worn on the outside, but practical and charming in its own way. Like its owner, really.

Sandrine – the sweet dark-skinned Belgian from the SIR conference – was sitting out on the balcony with a book. I stopped to say hi, but Drus was keen to get down to business and dragged me away from our conversation, and into his study, which I judged to be the largest room in the house. It wasn't so much untidy, as utterly chock-full of books and documents, crammed into every space and piled on every surface. He waved me to a worn leather chair and took a seat opposite.

'I'll get straight to the point,' he said. 'I liked your *Willing* concept. I also admired how you refused to give in to SIR's stupid demands...'

He sat back in his seat and folded his arms. 'I'm not getting any younger. I'm often paranoid, and short-tempered. But fundamentally, I'm *truthful*. And so, I believe, are you.

'Essentially, I want to *share* my truth with the world... Not *impose* it. I believe it to be the same with you.' He nodded. 'I think our ideals are essentially the same, and I'm wondering if we can work together.'

Flattered though I certainly was, I didn't think a team-up between Herbert Drus and me could work. I'd recently gone two rounds in the ring – the first with Donovan, and the next with SIR – both of which seemed to prove that hitching my wagon to anyone else's was a bad idea. But, unlike my last meeting with Jo Bourne, I held off on my decision. It was at least worth looking at the possibilities.

We talked into the evening, sounding out each other's core values. Many times I got the sense that Drus was just as ready to dump me as I was him – if I didn't measure up – which I found encouraging. It showed he wasn't a *believer*. He wasn't handicapped by an investment in any single possibility.

Sandrine was left to fend for herself, which didn't seem to bother her. I saw her from the window coming and going, wearing different clothes each time, a book in her hand. When Drus and I started out on a walk to town for some dinner, I said, 'Should I go get Sandrine?'

Drus asked, 'Why?'

'I guess she'll be hungry too.'

Drus just shrugged and kept walking.

We were sitting, eating at a table in a little seafood restaurant when Drus uttered his next words: 'I'm afraid,' he said.

I'd made the mistake of ordering prawns. I love prawns, but not when they've been left in their shells. 'Afraid of what...?' I asked, trying to pry open my dinner. 'The DGSI?'

Drus gave me a dirty look and carried on eating his oysters. 'Of *love*,' he said at last.

'Of *love?*'

He shook his head. Seemed intensely uncomfortable. 'She's half my age. Technically I could be her grandfather.'

'Oh. You mean Sandrine.'

Another dirty look. 'It's wonderful...' he said. 'And it's terrible. Both at the same time. It makes me feel I'm *less*. And it makes

143

me feel I can be so much *more*… if I can just be brave enough.'

I nodded. I knew what he meant.

I was given the couch in the study to sleep on. It was fairly comfortable, but the night was hot and I had to open all the windows to let in a breeze. The smell of old books and papers was very comforting. I guess it reminded me of my parents' place back in Whanganui.

Drus had gone off to bed with barely a word to Sandrine. Sometime after midnight I heard a quiet knock, and her soft voice. Then a door opening, and clicking shut.

The next morning there were three of us for breakfast. Both Drus and Sandrine had a contented look about them. Drus made an English-style breakfast for us, of which Sandrine ate the lion's share. We made jokes about how such a tiny person could pack away so much food.

It was the first time I'd seen a real smile on Drus's face, and it gave me real pleasure to witness it. His wit was unforced and he was genuinely funny. I got a feeling I was seeing the younger Drus shining through.

Sometime late in the morning a call came through on my mobile, with the HFE option displayed on the screen. It was Jo Bourne.

'Hi Jo. I was thinking about calling you…'

'That's fine, Reagan. I'm actually calling about something, ah… A bit embarrassing. I received a video clip by email, of you and me at my home in Antibes…'

'Oh. Yes, I know about that.'

'…It shows us… You *know* about that…? What do you mean?'

I silently cursed my own artlessness. 'Well, uh... I got picked up by the DGSI and they told me about it.'

'The *DGSI*...? You were *picked up*...?' There was a shuffling sound. 'Okay, I'm going to have to hear about this.'

'What do you want to know?'

'All of it. Go ahead. From the beginning.'

'Well, first you should know something else...'

'Yes, I'm listening.'

'The HFE scrambler doesn't work. Anyone could be listening in.'

'Doesn't *work?* Are you sure? Simon said he really did his homework on that one.'

'Yes, I'm sure he did.'

'Well, we need to talk. Can you come to Antibes for a meeting tonight?'

'I... No, I can't. Maybe in a week or so.'

'I've got a plane to catch tomorrow. It has to be today.'

'Well, I'm in Montpellier...' I turned to Drus, who was sitting across the table from me. Raised my eyebrows in silent question. Drus made a face, but nodded his agreement. 'We could meet here,' I suggested.

We arranged to meet at Drus's at seven. After I put the phone down, Drus had a bit of a spaz about the prospect of unexpected guests, but as the day wore on he appeared to get over it.

On the Mediterranean coast, the summer evening sun seems to sit for ages in the western sky, hovering above the horizon, then to duck quickly down out of sight. The hillside where Drus's house was perched was south-east-facing, so it had great morning and afternoon sun. But at this time of day, the shadows were long and dense. The light that shone through the windows and threw shapes on the walls had a warm orange tinge.

A sound of tires on gravel. I looked out the window to see a dark blue SUV snaking its way down the dusty driveway towards the house. Drus, Sandrine and I stepped outside to meet it. But when the SUV's doors opened, I was unprepared for who climbed out onto the stones of the driveway.

There was Jo, of course. Then there was the combative Liz Lochlan, but there was also Simon Duchesne.

When I looked into Simon's face and our eyes met, I caught a very brief moment of sharp assessment. A flash of suspicion confirmed. And then it was gone. He was relaxed, affable Simon Duchesne again. But it was too late – I'd seen what I'd seen.

It put me in a difficult position. I was certain now that Simon was not what he pretended to be, and *he* knew that *I* knew. But I couldn't start blabbing on about it there and then. If he was capable of such a level of deceit, he might just as well be capable of physical violence. I looked purposefully away from Simon, but my radar was locked onto his presence. So much so, that I was only vaguely aware of what else was going on around me. Jo fussing over Drus and Sandrine. Liz Lochlan's martyrdom at being summoned to a meeting by a young whippersnapper-nobody, and then having to sit in a car for five hours to get there.

As we moved inside, I tried to think of a way to deal with the situation, but Simon moved first. He asked about the toilet and made a joke about being forced to suffer a full bladder all those hours in the car. I wanted to shout something like, *don't let him out of your sight!* But the next moment he'd ducked off down the hallway.

I guess I must've had my Brynner on, because Jo was looking at me with a concerned smile. 'Reagan...? Are you all right? I heard a door, or maybe a window clack somewhere out the back, and hurried over to the window, just in time to see Simon walking quickly up the driveway and away from the house.

'Oh my God...' Jo sat heavily in an armchair, hands to her face. 'Marianne... Poor Marianne...!' Her eyes brimmed with tears.

Liz seemed frightened by the display of emotion. She perched carefully beside Jo and patted her hand. 'It'll be all right. We'll call her.'

'No, she... Oh...' Jo fought for control. 'That... that *bastard!* He was so convincing!' She pawed away a tear and took a deep breath.

'Simon pulled me aside during one of the breaks,' she managed. 'He was crying. He told me Marianne would soon be coming to see me... to tell me that she'd found Simon leaking information to the DGSI. But it would all be a big act, and it was actually *Marianne* who was responsible for the leaks. She was the cleverest liar he'd ever met, he said... Oh *God!*'

After the tears had begun to dry, the spotlight turned on me. Drus and Sandrine moved away to sit by the window and look out at the sunset, while Jo and Liz sat facing me like a pair of inquisitors.

They wanted to know about the meeting with the DGSI inspectors. I told them how Brouté had claimed extremists were to blame for all SIR's problems.

'Well of course they'd say that,' snapped Liz.

I shrugged. 'Would Simon claim the information was being sent to the DGSI if he was *actually working* for the DGSI? I don't think so. He'd try to misdirect.'

Jo frowned. 'That's a good point.'

'Oh, I wouldn't underestimate how clever these bastards are,'

Liz said icily.

I suddenly felt very tired. I rested my head on the soft back of the chair. 'Brouté said SIR were amateurs and wouldn't be on their radar if it wasn't for the extremist connection,' I said. 'It's them the DGSI are after. The extremists. Not SIR.'

'Don't be so *naive*,' Liz said. She pointed a finger. 'What did they have to gain from meeting with *you*...? Excuse me, but a *nobody* with almost no connection to SIR...? *This*...' She closed a fist and gave a satisfied grimace. '...*This* is them at work with their misdirection. And *you* – consciously, or otherwise – are doing their bidding.'

At about ten o'clock I reached my *'nuff*-point. Even Jo was biting her lip and staring into the distance. Liz was going around in logical circles, being more and more condescending and belligerent, and something in me just snapped.

I stood up and said, ' Well, that's me folks. I'm turning in for the night. Thanks for coming.' Jo looked up at me and gave a wan smile, but Liz wouldn't meet my eye. So I just turned and walked into Drus's study and shut the door behind me.

Inside, I stopped and looked back at the closed door. A metaphor. I felt relief and satisfaction, but again some echo of loss.

It was time to move forward.

PART THREE

1

You've might've heard of the rubber-band effect.

It's when you've been holding back on doing something you know deep down you oughta be doing – resisting, procrastinating – until at last you give it up, and *WAMAMAMAM*, you're propelled forward at high speed, like out of a catapult. It's like that moment when the starter's gun goes off, or when the floodgates open.

I hardly slept that night at Drus's. But not because of the evening's dramas – they were the last thing on my mind – I was suddenly possessed. Consumed by the sudden mad urge to concoct a coherent manifesto outlining *the Willing*. Something that would clearly communicate the concept to the world. It'd always been my intention to do that one day, but suddenly I felt ready. I had most of the pieces of the puzzle, and it was time to get cracking.

I was lying on the couch, tossing, turning. This way and that way. After a few hours of feverish mental work, I started to freak out – my head was quickly filling up with whole paragraphs. Whole passages. Big chunks of finished text. I had to start writing it all down, or I worried it might just disappear again, like smoke.

I threw my thin blanket off, quickly tracked down a pen and some pieces of paper and started writing.

The next morning, Drus dropped me outside a hotel. I turned down an offer to stay on at his place, because I needed to concentrate and I needed to be alone. We didn't waste much time on goodbyes, but I could see in Drus's eye that he was sympathetic to the cause. He grasped my shoulder firmly and nodded.

It was an Ibis hotel, and my room was on the second floor. To save time, Drus had given me a thick wad of paper and a handful of ballpoint pens – he had boxes of both for his own use – along with scissors, paper clips and sticky-tape. I guessed he'd done this kind of thing before.

Just underneath the mad rush, there was a sense of stillness. A rightness. I was alone in the room, but each word I wrote made me feel more connected to the outside world. Less a single person, more a part of humanity as a whole.

In the few seconds I took to think on this, I realized this was a major paradox. I was promoting individuality before group, and yet here I was, relishing this melding in with the wider crowd. The deep sense of sharing charged me and motivated me.

I wrote, and I wrote, and I wrote. I stopped to eat one big meal per day, and slept whenever I felt a crash creeping up on me. I lost track of time so badly that a hotel employee knocked on my door one day, and politely reminded me the room booking had ended. I'd thought I still had a day up my sleeve. I booked into a new room and carried on writing.

It wasn't that the manifesto was a massively substantial tome. In fact it was the opposite: I was clear from the start it needed to be short and punchy and engaging, but it took some serious work to achieve that goal. I kept scrapping whole sections and rewriting and rearranging. Cutting out paragraphs and taping bits together. Boiling the information down to its essence. Each day the floor was covered with more piles of papers held together with sticky-tape and paper clips, laid out in barely-coherent order.

152

At last I got to the point where I had a thin stack of heavily scribbled-on, taped-up pieces of paper. The material was tight, but needed finessing. I input the whole lot into a word-processing app on my iPad, and started editing.

*   *   *

I'd been holed up in the hotel for six days. I was utterly trashed, but felt satisfied that the job was done. Finished. I'd written many, many pages of text, but refined the whole lot down to a simple, single-page master. Yep: a two-sided page of text, expressing the bare-bones essence of the *Willing* message. I called Drus and he picked me up.

Back at his place, I collapsed on the couch in his study, but Drus shook me awake, saying he wanted to read what I'd done while I was sleeping. I sleepily pulled out my tablet and sent the file to Drus's wireless printer, then lost consciousness.

I slept through the rest of that day and woke the following afternoon, still pretty groggy. I could smell myself when I got up – mostly the pong of unwashed clothes, I decided – but I had no clean clothing left. I wandered through and found Drus on the balcony. He grunted a greeting.

I plonked myself down in a deckchair, and got straight to the point. 'What did you think?'

He took his time thinking about it. Finally said, 'It's perhaps a little spare.'

'Spare...? You mean, too *many* words?'

'Too *few*.'

That jolted me a bit: in my drive for simplicity, had I trimmed too much, and lost some essentials? I sat for a long time, quietly mulling it over.

I tried to put myself in Drus's shoes, reading the material through his eyes.

Was it possible that his generation could deal with more detail up front...? Maybe they had the patience and the head-space afforded by a simpler life... But then I was fairly certain the age of high-speed connectivity had come along and knocked that on the head. I felt myself calm as I remembered the strange sense of connectedness I'd experienced during those days in the hotel. I'd felt a strange certainty about what I was writing.

I AM WILLING

I am willing to be me
I am new. I am unique

I am willing to own who I am
I am not a nationality
Not a tradition
Not a religion
Not an education
Not a career

I am willing to own all my choices
Not entrust them to a parent
Not to a president
Not to a policeman
Not to a priest
Not to a professor

I am willing to own my physical body
Not entrust it to a doctor
Not to a boss
Not to a parent

Not to a partner

I am willing to own my learning
Not entrust it to a factory-style institution
My learning style is unique to me
What I need to learn is unique to me

I am willing to question
I do not accept and adopt other people's answers,
wholesale

I am willing to stay curious
I do not decide I know, and shut down my learning

I am willing to be wrong and learn afresh
I do not protect my investment in being right

I am willing to stay open
I do not disconnect myself from others

I am willing to be responsible for my own
sustenance
I am not dependent on the group
I give what it suits me to give, and I gratefully
accept what is given

I am willing to see the joy and the wonder in the
world
I do not martyr myself in a dedicated search for the
bad

I am willing to embrace fun and adventure
I do not base my life upon comfort, convenience and

*certainty: these can easily become antidotes to a
meaningful life*

*I am willing to do what suits me, every minute of
every day
I do not base my life on someone else's model of
success*

*I am willing to be me
I am new. I am unique
I can not be classified or measured by existing
standards*

*My essential self is subtle, but it is there from birth,
even if it makes no sense to others in its seed-form
It is a gentle combination of flavors. A blend of
strengths that can be nurtured and brought to a
rich, full bloom
An explosion of self-expression that is supremely
beautiful, whether or not it puts food on the table
Others may help me to define it and maintain it, but
they cannot do so by established strategies,
because I am new.
I am unique*

I am Willing.

2

I took the bus back down to Valencia the following day. I'd made one change Drus recommended: the bit about *not entrusting my physical body to a doctor*. I'd meant to point out the need to *own* our health, but agreed that in its bare-bones form, it was too easy to misinterpret – could be seen as negating the need to ask for expert help when you need it.

Apart from that, Drus accepted my conviction that the text should be left as-is, unedited except for a few tweaks for rhythm and clarity. He also made it clear he was available to help wherever he could, and he started by printing out a few hundred copies of the finished manifesto for me to take with me.

So I was dying to hear what people thought of the manifesto, but the first feedback I got in Valencia was not encouraging. The remaining members of the UN were luke-warm about it. Christian Sam's comment that it was *his right* to define himself by his religion wasn't exactly unexpected, but I was disappointed at the non-committal nods and shrugs and *yeah-not-bad*s from pretty much everyone else. It was tough to hold onto my conviction that what I'd done was any good.

But I was fairly confident that Donno would like it. We sat together on a stone seat in the Plaza de la Virgen, and he read through my manifesto while I tried to focus my attention on the people passing by. I heard a snort and turned to see Donno flip the page over and start again at the beginning.

After his third read-through, he sat for a full minute before tipping his hat back on his head and saying, 'The pill's too bitter, mate. Too hard to swallow. You gotta sugar it a bit, or no one'll wanna know.'

I was seriously disappointed, and for a while I said nothing. Then finally I shook my head and said, 'What d' you mean, *sugar* it? It's not an advertisement for a new type of candy. We're not trying to *sell* something here.'

'No. *No*. Reags, Listen to me, man...' Donno's eyes widened with passionate conviction. 'That's where you're wrong... We *are* trying to sell something here. Or we *oughta* be...' He thrust a finger at me. 'See, you're looking at this like it's a nice wholesome little set of ideals, that a few people around the world might pick up. *If* they're ready and *if* it suits them. But mate, we can't afford to mess 'round. We got maybe ten, twenty years at the outside before things really turn to shit.' He nodded meaningfully. 'What we got here is a fuckin' *emergency*.'

This was it. The point in our conversations where I usually gave up and let it slide. Donno was Donno. Who was I to try and change him?

But I sensed we were at a kind of turning point, and decided not to let it go today. I said, 'You told me once that the difference between you and me was that I wanted to *help*, and you wanted to be *clever*. You remember that?'

He snorted and turned his head away. 'I'm not a fuckin' saint like you are, Reags. I gotta do stuff my way. *Spade a spade*, etcetera, etcetera.'

'Sure, but it's just not gonna work if everything's about people being *wrong,* and you being *right*.' I shrugged. 'If you do actually convince them you're as clever as you think you are, they're probably not thinking for themselves. They're probably the kind given to dumb, blind faith. *Willing* in name only. Same problem you started out with.'

'Yeah well, it's a start, isn't it? Better they have blind faith in something that doesn't fuck everything up.'

I threw my hands in the air. 'Jesus, Donno. I just don't get you. After all your talk about morons being the scourge of the planet, you wanna gather up an army of 'em and make them honorary *Willing* until such time as they see the light. Donno, that's fuckin' *ridiculous!*'

Donovan spat on the ground and then stood up. 'Yeah, well,' he said. 'I'm not so sure your *talking to the truth in people's hearts* is all you think it is, mate.'

'Meaning, what?'

'I mean it seems a bit bloody sneaky to me. A bit manipulative. Bit like your *clever rhetoric*.' He shoved his hands in his pockets and walked away, saying dismissively over his shoulder, 'You go ahead and do things your way, mate.'

I didn't see Donno for about a week. Then he dropped around with some beer and we picked up pretty much where we'd left off. But I was a bit more wary of my friend.

I'd always thought of Donno as secretive, but at some point around that time he started really laboring the point. On more than one occasion I saw people try to swap details with him, but he just waved them off. The five-euro hats he exchanged regularly were a kind of shield. I saw him duck his head and use his hat's brim to hide his face and avoid someone he knew on the street. Whenever someone tried to take a picture, he'd look down and hide his face from the lens, or he'd move purposefully away and out of frame.

Then things took a dramatic turn. I was feeling sorry for myself, and started spending time with people who I wouldn't have gravitated towards before: *younger* people.

I have to admit, the UN Crowd – myself included – had looked on the younger set at the hostel with a kind of disdain. Always hung over. Always looking at their phones. Always in cliquey little groups. Never talking about anything meaningful.

A lot of them were just out of university, or had quit part-way through. Some were trying to get up the courage to quit. They didn't have an established idea of the world yet, and they were still a bit awed, and – frankly – suspicious of it all. They were really good to talk to for just those reasons.

Like they say in the old classics, *there's always a girl.* I'd found this to be the case so far, and it wasn't going to change in Valencia. My first romance in Spain was a smart, very pretty Parisienne called Emiléne. Well, maybe it's more accurate to say *semi*-romance. Anyhow, it was a nice experience and it added spice to the first chapter of my Spanish experience.

Our first conversation at breakfast was stilted. She had zero confidence in her English, and I was way too impressed with her beauty to concentrate properly on my French. She had long blonde hair, a demure, w-shaped feline mouth and big brown eyes: not the type I would generally pay much attention to. Too pretty by far.

And young. Technically I was old enough to be her Dad. A shriveling thought.

Over the next few days, I saw Emiléne around and about in Valencia – having coffee at a café in the Plaza de la Virgen, or seeing off friends at the Estació del Nord – and we'd smile and wave, but wouldn't actually stop to talk.

But one evening, Emiléne brought her dinner up to eat on the roof at the hostel, and I was up there already, talking with

Donno and the few remaining members of the UN.

Us old-fogy UN guys had often joked about going on one of the nightly pub-crawls on offer in Valencia's town. Every evening a young bearded guy with copious tattoos would come up to the roof and give an enthusiastic pitch about how exciting his ten-euro crawls were. Depending on the crowd up there at the time, his patter would either fly, or go down like a lead balloon – and still he came back night after night. I have to say I admired the guy's tenacity.

Some of Emiléne's friends had joined us. The atmosphere was pretty fun, and this time, the tattooed guy's pub-crawl pitch was well received. Anyway, before we knew it, we were all down at reception, standing with a small crowd of hostel folk, ready to head out on the town.

It was a great night. Drinks and food were cheap, and the company was excellent. Donno was already fairly drunk when we started out. He was wandering from girl to girl looking a bit like Indy Jones, with a newly-bought fedora on his head and a three-day beard. I was standing with him when he started talking with a pair of cute Swedish girls. 'Have you ladies ever tried a local delicacy called *Mykok?*' he asked them. I decided I'd rather not be around for the rest of that conversation, and got chatting to Emiléne at the other end of the bar. But I kept tabs on Donno to make sure he was okay, and later in the evening/ morning, one of the girls broke all records and lasted about an hour – the latter part of which, she was wearing Donno's hat. Next time I looked, the pair of them had gone. Together or not, I couldn't say. Maybe *Mykok* was on the menu after all.

Quant á moi – for my part – after a few Spanish beers, my French improved dramatically, and I even found the ability to make silly jokes, which – even more surprisingly – Emiléne seemed to think were funny. Emiléne's English started to surface as well, and we found we could meet in the middle quite well.

The next day, over a late brunch, I showed my *Willing* manifesto to Emiléne and her friends. After some minor help with translation, they got it. And they loved it. It seemed to do the job that I'd hoped it would: speak directly to what they already knew in their hearts. As Emiléne and her friends discussed the material and grew excited about it, I felt my own heart begin to thump.

This is where the game-changing element clicked into place for the *Willing* project. Emiléne's friend, a recent college graduate called Matt, suggested with a mild stutter that maybe a short animated clip based on *Willing* principles would help get things rolling, and hook people in enough for them to pay attention. He was available, and *willing* to take the job on, he joked with an engaging smile.

I wanted to agree, but Matt looked so young. He had long, curly black hair and dimpled cheeks, on a face way too fresh and open and innocent-looking. He didn't so much talk as mutter. The mutter and the stutter sometimes combined to make him incomprehensible – though to be fair, what he did say was usually pretty smart and considered. His ancient converse shoes were full of holes and stank so badly his roomies insisted he leave them outside.

I seriously doubted this barely-coherent, scruffy kid could be capable of the kind of quality required. I mean, hey – *I'd been around the block. I'd made videos with my students at school.* This stuff was hard. I knew what I was talking about.

But actually no, I didn't. Once again, my prejudices had put me wrong. Matt pulled out his laptop and showed me three animated shorts he'd done during his course at the *9Zeros*

School of Animation in Barcelona. I was just blown away. They had such gravity and style and sheer bloody *quality*. The lighting, camera angles and general choreography had the feel of a big-budget Hollywood movie. The animated 3D characters were incredibly life-like: he told me he'd used a new type of motion-tracking program which allowed him to video a live person's body movements and facial expressions, and map them easily onto the animated characters in the computer.

Anyway. I was convinced. I wanted to lock things down before Matt had a chance to change his mind or run away, so I offered him five thousand euros to get to work. He accepted the offer with a wide, dimpled grin. 'Ha!' he muttered. 'My first real j-job!'

Matt had to be back in the States for Christmas, which gave us just shy of four months to finish the animated clip. I figured we'd need every last day of that.

This was really the point where Donno's and my paths really started to head off in different directions. I started spending a lot of time with Matt and Emiléne, and Donno just didn't fit into that picture, so I hardly spent any time with him. I don't think I pushed him away, but I didn't work at maintaining the friendship, either.

Donno didn't think my manifesto was a good foundation to be working from in the first place, and neither did he trust the young, stuttering Matt to make something worthwhile. I could hardly judge the guy for that, having made the same mistake myself.

Shortly after Matt and I teamed up to do the animation, I saw Donno off at the Estació del Nord – the big train station in Valencia. He was off to see a bit more of Spain; first stop, Madrid. I noticed he was smoking again, and that he'd also resumed the associated habits that'd always niggled. Like throwing a cigarette down and grinding it with his foot. And spitting. But Donno was always Donno, even when he was on his best behavior. Which I'd learned not to hold against the guy.

We hugged, and Donno stalked off to catch his train without looking back.

Meanwhile, Matt and I were working on a script for the *Willing* visuals. We stayed on at the hostel we were in, because the common room had a comfortable corner to work in, and it was pretty much deserted during the day: most of the other guests were off sightseeing.

Emiléne had enrolled at a language school in Valencia, and found herself an apartment out near the beach, sharing with two others. The monthly rent there was even better than the hostel rate, which like I said, was already pretty cheap. So she moved out of the hostel, and Matt and I helped her set up her room over a weekend. It put a strange kind of pressure on our relationship, because until that point the only time we'd spent together was in public places, and suddenly she had her own space. A place where we could potentially be alone.

There was a fizz to our relationship and a kind of electricity, but could it be sexual? I was nervous about screwing up the connection we had, and determined to play it cool.

But, hey. I was also horribly aware that I'd *always* related to women that way, and I'd probably missed out on a lot because of it. Forget cool. I made up my mind to come clean, the first chance I got.

Emiléne invited us to a soirée at her new apartment. It was a Saturday. We'd learned by now to buy alcohol before 10pm –

preferably at a supermarket – because even though there are still places you can buy it after ten, you have to look pretty hard. And the price doubles, or even triples. Matt and I carried a case of beer and bags of assorted snacks on the crowded tram out to the beach.

Emiléne's building was a six-story apartment block. It looked like a classy place to live. Nicely painted on the outside. Stylish doors with key-card access. The lobby also looked great, but that's where the illusion ended. When you started walking up the stairs, and your eyes finally adjusted (no lightbulbs) you could see signs of the renovation that – for whatever reason – had been held up for months, or maybe even years. The building was built like a kind of octagonal donut ring, with the rooms all looking inward to a shadowy central space that, to put it bluntly, was a complete eyesore. Glassless inner windows were partially covered in torn plastic, and there was stuff lying everywhere on the floor. Using the stairs, we saw the whole setup was in a really sad state of disrepair. The building's residents had clearly given up any pretense of pride in their collective living space.

We'd happily joked about all this when we moved Emiléne in, but for some reason the desperate shabbiness that permeated the building now mattered to me. Maybe it just seemed worse at night.

An effort had been made to tidy the landing outside Emiléne's door, but there were tattered items of clothing and old boxes lying on the floor further down, and just around the corner, I could see the corridor was filled with someone's furniture. I commented on it to Matt, but he just shrugged. When Emiléne opened the door to let us in, I had to work really hard to leave the dirty taste in my mouth behind.

Emiléne had dressed up and she looked stunning. Matt and I kissed her on the cheeks and dumped the beer and food on the table. As I stepped into the apartment, I could smell fresh paint. She'd obviously put in some hard work, because when we moved her in the week before, the place was pretty dingy. Her face lit up with pleasure when we commented on how nice it was looking.

It was basically a fun night, if a bit confusing for me at times. I was easily the oldest person there, and I found myself growing more careful about what I said, in case I alienated myself with oldster-attitude. Emiléne's roommates were good sorts. One French, one Spanish with French language. Both pretty and both very fizzy and charming. There was a particular song that I guess someone at the party liked, because it was played maybe ten times that night. A catchy pop song featuring a haunting little-girl voice.

Some of the guys had brought along some weed, and they hooked into it straight away. About half of the contingent were out of it by about three, and not capable of making much sense. But Emiléne was still okay, and the two of us ended up out on the veranda, looking down on the street, and at the narrow strip of beach visible to us. Groups of young folk drifted past, singing and laughing. One shirtless, muscular guy did cartwheels and backflips in the road while his friends cheered him on.

The internal pressure to make my move was making me pretty nervous, but the tender, lingering look in Emiléne's eyes was all the antidote I needed. I don't remember how it started. It was like a jump-cut in a movie: we were standing there, and then suddenly we were kissing, without any kind of transition.

Emiléne took my hand and led me to her room, where she stopped and swore. There were two people comatose on her narrow bed and one on the floor next to it. The guy on the floor was lying on his back, snoring, with one leg up on the bed – as if he'd been nudged off and hadn't noticed the impact when he hit floorboards. For our purposes, this was not a happening thing. It was frustrating, but kind of funny too, I guess.

We found some cushions and made ourselves reasonably comfortable, lying pressed together on the floor in the public space of the living room. We managed some fairly intimate stuff between the comings and goings of the other guests, but nothing very full-on.

We hadn't been asleep long when we were woken up by yelling outside in the corridor. Some African or Arab language I didn't recognize. Emiléne stirred and mumbled, *chaque nuit c'est comme ça* – 'It's like that every night.' I wanted to go and look, but she stopped me. Apparently a relative of one of her neighbors had moved his belongings into the corridor, where he was now sleeping, and they fought about it pretty much every night for half an hour or so.

I was smitten by Emiléne, and couldn't wait to see her again. So much so that my mind refused to focus on my work. After a hard weekday working with Matt, I turned up at Emiléne's to find she had guests: two young French guys who were fellow students at Emiléne's language school.

The guys were locking on to Emiléne big time. It was obvious I wasn't going to get any time alone with her that night, and the bits of their French conversation I could grasp were about stuff I'd grown bored with decades before. I decided to bail at about ten, saying I needed to be fresh for work the next day. They scoffed at my conscientiousness, saying *they* had school in the morning, but *they* were gonna spend the night out on the town anyway. Emiléne made a whooping sound and pumped her fist in the air in agreement.

I sat on the tram on the journey back to the hostel, wondering about age differences and the effects of life experience. I felt bad about judging Emiléne for her youthful effervescence, but at the same time I was just plain unwilling to be a part of it.

I had one of those sleepless nights that night, confronting truths about my relationship with Emiléne. Of course there was the difference in age and experience, and also that we had very little in common. But it would've been easier to manage the change if the situation was more clear-cut. If I was certain that I wasn't just avoiding something that could ultimately be good for me. I got up the next day pretty-much divested, but tired and a bit confused.

So this was where my relationship with Emiléne was at, when a Korean lady called Grace took a top bunk in the six-bed room I was in at the hostel. She was thirty-two – almost the same age as me – and had a settled gravity about her. I warmed to her right away, and she didn't keep me guessing about her own feelings: 'I like you,' she said. 'I like you a *lot.*' This was the day after I'd met her, and after little more than a walk together and a shared dinner we cooked in the hostel's kitchen.

You'll have figured by now that it's *eyes* for me. Everything's in the eyes. Grace's were almost black – only when she was sitting in direct sunlight, gazing away from you, could you see they were actually a dark hazel. They were incredibly expressive eyes. They sparkled pleasure, flashed anger, shone approval and utterly *froze* disapproval. With her eyes closed and mouth unsmiling, she wasn't particularly pretty, but the slightest expression lit her up. Made her very beautiful.

I'd never met anyone so frank before. Frank in a way that wasn't brutal or try-hard; though she told me later she'd started out brutal when she was younger, and life had rubbed most of the sharp corners off. Her frankness, she said, was a reaction to the hypocrisy in Korean life.

Grace was smart. Grace was cute. Grace was a *lot* of things I liked, as well as that rarest of birds: an objective thinker. Wow.

I got a text from Emiléne about meeting on Saturday for lunch. It hadn't been my plan to take Grace along to a lunch date with Emiléne, but Saturday came around and we were hanging out together, and it didn't feel right to just ditch Grace and go alone.

It wasn't a fun time. I'm not sure if Eiléne was nervous, or if it was deliberate trouble-making, but she seemed to suddenly have lost the ability to speak English. The three of us had a weird, stilted lunch together, with me playing piggy-in-the-middle, having to translate mostly mundane comments.

Grace went to find a toilet, and Eiléne said to me, 'I have much more to say, you know, when I'm speaking my own language. And when I'm speaking at my normal pace.' I felt my heart squeeze, because I knew she was right. I'd watched her shine when she spoke freely in French with fellow native speakers.

When we waved goodbye, I knew it'd be the last time I'd see Eiléne. It made me really sad. I felt like I'd destroyed some small living thing before it had a chance to grow. I'm not talking about Eiléne herself – she had a potentially great life ahead of her – but the tiny sapling that was our romance had died. Melodramatic of me, perhaps, but it's true.

The pop song with the little-girl voice – the one I'd heard over and over at Eiléne's soirée – echoed in my head for weeks afterward, always with an attendant sting. It took a while to fade.

3

I was worried about working Matt too hard, and limited our working day to 10am ~ 4pm, Monday to Friday, but I actually had to stay on his tail *not* to work past those hours – he was so fizzingly enthusiastic. When we finished talking script stuff, he'd be looking online for new plug-ins and tutorials. I had to sell the idea to him that his work would suffer if he didn't take time out – or worse, he might burn out before we were done.

Actually there'd be no burn-out, but we struck a different problem about five weeks into the actual animation work. On the phone to the States, Matt had proudly told his Dad – an American movie producer called Samuel Greenslade – about his *Willing* job, and how much he was being paid.

Five thousand euros for sixteen weeks' work wasn't a union rate, but neither was it peanuts. Especially in Spain, where living is cheap. Greenslade had asked his son to calculate what that broke down to per week, and told him he was being ripped off.

When Matt related this story to me, he said his Dad was just being a jerk, and I thought maybe the criticism had just bounced off. But from the following day, Matt's enthusiasm levels plummeted. We limped on for the rest of the week like that, and I felt sure his attitude was getting worse. I was worried.

Then he turned up on Monday morning hung over, after a weekend of heavy drinking. I knew it was time for a talk. 'How much money would make you feel like you were being paid enough?' I asked.

'The m-money's fine man.' He waved off my question, but he wouldn't look me in the eye.

170

'So why'd you suddenly lose interest after your Dad said you were being ripped off...?'

Matt stared into the distance for a while, then he got up and strode towards the door, leaving his laptop open on the table.

'Matt...!' I called after him, a tad more harshly than I'd meant. He spun around.

'What!?' he shouted at me, his eyes flashing dangerously.

'What's the problem, man? Where are you going?'

But he was already back at the table. He seized his laptop and flung it to the floor. It made a loud *crackety-crunch* sound that didn't bode too well.

Matt stood there for a long moment, eyes screwed tightly shut; fists flexing. Then his body just seemed to relax and go limp. He dropped heavily into a chair, just as a hostel staff member hurried in – a tall, skinny Spanish guy called Jorge. 'What is the sound...?' he spluttered. 'What happened?'

I stood, then walked over and picked up the laptop. It was cracked clear across its screen, and something rattled inside. 'No big deal,' I said. 'We just broke our computer.'

We went for a walk down to the park on the riverbed, and Matt began telling me random pieces of a story that only made partial sense. Then at last, he said, 'I c-can never do anything right,'

That one statement told the whole story, really.

After our talk, Matt's head seemed to clear a little, and we went into damage control. 'How much was the computer?' I asked.

'Four grand,' came the answer. 'I'm sorry, man. Really. We c-can take it out of my p-pay.'

But I knew that wasn't gonna work. I said I'd pay for the

171

computer and jack up the pay to eight thousand – which brought the rate up to five hundred a week. He made a fuss about it, but I could see he was pleased. All up, I'd be down twelve thousand euros. Almost a quarter of the money I had left. Was it going to be worth it?

But we were up and running again the next day. And over the following weeks, as the completed shots started coming off the rendering queue, I felt more and more certain it *was* going to be worth it.

* * *

I re-jacked the schedule and worked us hard. Whether it was out of guilt or just plain responsibility, Matt stuck with it and worked his ass off. But rest periods were even more crucial than before. Part of making sure we did our best work and stayed focused, was preserving our weekends off. We made a pact not to go near a computer during those two days per week, and to relate only to real people in real time. As far as I know, Matt kept his end of the deal.

We got a really good system going. I was working on my own laptop in a highly-flexible editing app from Sony called *Vegas*. Matt and I would give a finished shot the big tick, then I'd take it and throw it into the Vegas timeline along with the best sound effects and music I could source from the web – which we could use for free because we were a non-profit project. A small benefit but a useful one.

We auditioned about twenty people for the voice-overs, and we got an experienced thirty-four year-old actor from the UK called Lilly, whose breathy voice managed to exude both a warm, sexy presence and a relaxed ease.

My relationship with Grace – if you can call it that – fit easily into our weekly schedule because I didn't have to worry about her. After our strange lunch with Emiléne, we spent two or three days being careful around each other, but apart from that short period, she was a breeze to relate to. One day when we were walking together in the riverbed park, she asked me, 'So, do you like sex?' as if it was the most natural thing the world to ask.

I struggled for an answer, finally coming up with, 'Yes, I guess so. But it scares me.'

'*Scares* you...? Why?'

'Um... I feel like I lose track of what's important. I kinda blank out.'

'You mean your mind switches off?'

'Yeah, that's pretty much what happens.'

'Oh, I'm jealous,' she said. 'I'm the opposite. I can *never* turn my mind off.'

'No, usually I can't either. But sex does it... And sometimes when I talk to a large group of people.'

We sat down on a grassy mound. 'I think,' she said, her eyes closed, 'that like most things, sex is a balance between vulnerability and selfishness.'

I lay on my back and looked up at the sky. 'Sounds like you've had a lot of experience.' She glanced warily at me, but then seemed satisfied I wasn't being judgmental or interrogative.

'No, not really. I'm not very attractive to Korean men. Vulnerability and selfishness are not prized in Korea. I had to work at finding them, and I had to learn to question my motivations and my thinking. I think that's why I can never turn my mind off. It keeps *questioning, questioning, questioning*. All the time. Sometimes it drives me crazy.'

'Like a small child.'

'A small *child*?' She was on her guard again.

'Kids have it right. They ask questions all the time, but adults just want them to shut up.' I looked up at her. With the bright sun behind her head, I couldn't make out her expression.

That night, we booked an Air B'n'B to afford ourselves a little privacy, and had us some seriously fun sex.

It became a weekly thing. Sex at an Air B'n'B on Saturday night, and talking about it through Sunday. Analyzing it and enjoying the memories. Quite apart from the fun and the tenderness, a really important aspect of it was an almost scientific attention to re-training our minds. I learned to consciously observe my mind in its vulnerability, and in its selfishness, during sex.

And Grace? Grace learned *not* to. Or so she said.

Grace left Spain to return to Korea in October. It wasn't a sad goodbye. Not because we didn't really like each other – we liked each other a lot. I saw her off at the airport, and we agreed we'd see each other again sometime, when the time was right.

4

December rolled round, and at last we were ready to have a screening evening. I figured we should vamp it up a bit, and organized with the hostel staff for us to use the common room for a little party. It was quite a decent-sized room if you included the dining area. All the other guests were invited, and by now a lot of them were curious about what we'd been up to, so we ended up with a lot of people crammed into the space.

The screening was set for seven. We'd kicked off early in the evening, and people were already falling over each other and spilling their drinks at five. The staff hemmed and hawed about fire regulations but eventually decided to turn a blind eye.

As people got drunker and noisier I started worrying that the evening was going to be a disaster. Matt was crawling about on the floor on his hands and knees grunting like a pig, while young girls took turns riding on his back, and Jorge from reception was poking his head around the door more and more frequently.

Then the new shift started and Jorge came to join us with a case of beer. His relief – a cute thirty-something called Katia – was disappointed that she couldn't join in too. I realized I was being way too paranoid and forced myself to relax.

Seven o'clock came, and everyone crowded down to the end of the room, where a 50-inch panel TV hung on the wall. I stepped up in front of the screen and raised a hand for quiet. 'Hey guys,' I said. 'We all know why we're here, so let's roll the thing and...'

But I was interrupted by cries of, *'Speech...! Speech...!'*

'All right,' I said. 'Here's my speech...' I composed myself, and everyone went quiet.

I was about to start speaking, when I felt something at the edge of my consciousness. Something I'd begun to think was just a memory: the first tingles of the *Brynner* kicking in. The old familiar warmth. The surge of confidence. Only this time I was fully present and conscious.

I raised a hand. *'To a new world... and a whole new game!'* I shouted.

Everyone cheered. I stood and basked a moment in the happy atmosphere, then turned and hit the space key on my laptop to start the clip rolling.

The clip began with glowing gold captions on black, and a voice over:

> *I am willing to be me*
> *I am new. I am unique...*

As the clip rolled, I watched the faces of my audience: they were fully engaged. The video was doing its job. But then I felt the effects of the Brynner wearing off, and I was appalled to recall my impassioned words a few minutes earlier...

'To a new world... and a whole new game!'

PART FOUR

1

I'm going to fast-forward almost a year now, because this was when things really started moving for the *Willing*.

I was cold. As far as I knew, I was on my way to New Zealand, but I'd scheduled in a stop-off off in London to appear on the well-known Brit talk show *Leighton Farmer.* I was sitting, shivering, in the green room at London Studios, waiting for my call. The heaters were going full blast, but I was chilled down to the bone.

When I'd left Spain it was still pretty warm, and of course, I was headed down to a southern hemisphere summer. I'd packed a few random warm things, but like an idiot I'd underestimated how cold it would be in the UK. I made a note to visit an Oxfam the following day and buy a warmer jacket. Something cheap.

I fingered the diminished bulk of my money belt under my trousers. There was somewhere near five hundred euros left in cash. A quick mental calculation of the balance on my debit card – minus the cost of a flight back down to New Zealand, via Seoul, Korea – told me I could figure on about eight hundred more in electronic funds. Not desperate, but cheap-living in the economically-buoyant Antipodes was way less do-able than in Europe, and I could probably only count on that money lasting me a month at the most. I was flying Korean Air because it allowed me to make a stop in Korea to see Grace. And it was a really cheap ticket.

In spite of my financial situation, I was suddenly a bit of a household name. Not just in Spain, or Europe, but across the entire world. Hence the invitation to appear on *Leighton Farmer.* Matt's animated video had gone viral, and the web was awash with all sorts of discussions about *Willing*ness. What was *great* about it, and what was *terrible.* Its tremendous *potential*, and its dire *danger.* Many thousands of people around the world were standing up and calling themselves *Willing*.

Frankly, this kind of reaction was just what I'd been afraid of: the bullshit self-contradiction of the *oxymoron.* A so-called individualist who's quick to jump on a band-wagon. But I held on to a hope that there were many more who were quietly agreeing with the Willing principles, and getting on with living their lives in their own way, without the need to call themselves anything. It felt bizarre to do a google search for *Willing Manifesto,* and come up with results in seven figures – millions of the buggers – and in pretty much every major Western language, apparently.

For the first few months I'd found it an interesting pastime to read what was being said, but then I came to realize that for every thoughtful, considered comment, there were three really stupid ones, and the ratio seemed to increase week by week, so I stopped looking. It was too irritating and my sleep had begun to suffer: I kept going around in mental circles, formulating futile foils to foolish fancies.

One of these things is not like the others...

Yeah, you probably know the song. It was going round in my head as I surreptitiously scoped my surroundings. I'm used to being the odd one out, but it felt pretty weird to be sharing a room at a prestigious television studio with a bunch of extremely famous people – an actor/ producer, a comedian, a veteran film star, and an eighties band I remembered but was never that keen on. All were household names who I'd seen many times on TV, and all were natural entertainers who hardly seemed to get up a sweat being funny and interesting. They were chatting away between themselves like they'd known each other for ever, but I had nothing to contribute, and it didn't feel right to ask for selfies with them, so I just sat and nodded and smiled.

I'd had a prelim chat with Leighton – the host of the show – so I was fairly comfortable about what we'd be talking about, if a little worried about whether I'd be an interesting watch. It helped that Leighton had – in his words – *quite a large helping of sympathy for the cause*. He'd warned me he was going to be fairly brutal with his questions, because he wanted to play the part of the most hardened cynic in the audience. This, he said, was the best way to engage people's listening. I agreed.

An assistant floor manager gave me my call, and I traded parting good-lucks with the other guests before heading through to the studio.

I was announced correctly as *Reagan James*, and did my entrance to applause that seemed a little bit too enthusiastic for someone like me, who wasn't a film star or singer or anyone of any real note.

The studio set was very familiar – I'd seen it lots of times on TV at my mother's house back in New Zealand, where the show's very popular. We settled into our seats, and in his customary light-hearted manner, Leighton got things moving with a nutshell description of what the whole *Willing* idea was about. He'd done his homework, and obviously had a good handle on the concept.

But the comfort I drew from that was short-lived, because

Leighton hadn't been joking when he warned me he'd be brutal. He turned to me and asked, 'So tell me, Reagan... Are the Willing a bunch of *shirkers*, who are too lazy to work, and just want to bludge off the rest of us?'

I coughed and must have balked a bit, because the audience laughed. 'Well no, of course not,' I began. 'It's not a lazy man's option to be Willing. It takes a lot of hard work just to live that way every day.'

'So how do you put food on the table, if you don't mind me asking?'

Actually, I did mind. I always felt crap when people asked me this, because whatever answer I came up with, it never seemed to dispel the outrage people felt at somebody choosing not to make the same sacrifices as everyone else.

I took a deep breath and gave it my best shot. 'I don't work in the traditional sense. But I do work quite hard at defining my own particular perspective on the world, and then sharing it.'

Leighton shrugged. 'You don't, erm... *eat and sleep* like the rest of us, then?' That got a laugh.

'I do, I do. Yes, of course. I just mean, I don't *earn* a living. I don't do work in exchange for food and shelter. Those things are secondary for me. The work is primary.'

'But surely you need at least *some* money to live. Do you get the dole...? Some kind of benefit?'

I squirmed in my seat. A quick mental probe came up zero on the Brynner front. I was on my own.

'No. To sign on you need to agree that you'll do whatever work is on offer. I can't do that. And to get any other kind of benefit, I'd have to lie.' I raised my hands. 'But yes, I do get help from people from time to time. I'd be a fool to refuse.'

'Financial help?'

'Financial help.'

'Enough to live on?'

'To a point. But it's like being freelance. You have to give up the need to be certain of your future. It's like, whatever you've got in your pocket will run out at some point, and what will you do then? It has to be a day-to-day thing. People have a bit of trouble with that, I find.'

'So what do you say to people who are concerned about your contribution to society? There's a whole raft of municipal facilities provided by society for its members. Parks, libraries, roads, clean water, sewerage systems. You walk on footpaths that are paid for out of their taxes.'

'I say, *hey, thanks very much for putting that footpath there*. But I'd be walking there anyway, footpath or no footpath. It's my planet as much as it's anybody else's.'

The other guests did their spots, and I stayed on to watch them on the monitor in the green room. One of Leighton's customary practices is to put all, or most, of his guests together on the couch and encourage a bit of playful banter between them, but he didn't include me in the mêlée – which I was actually pretty grateful for – I wouldn't have made a very entertaining part of the fun they seemed to have, throwing insults at each other and being hilarious.

But I did appreciate that I got a very valuable chance to talk about the *Willing*, and it was no small thing that Leighton chose to devote such a chunk of airtime to it. True to his word, he was fairly brutal. But his questions were designed to extract answers that might address the doubts people generally had. I admired his professionalism in deliberately playing dumb when he was actually in tune with what I was saying.

I'm also pretty sure this appearance on *Leighton Farmer* was the kick that got the *Willing* stuff moving, first in English-speaking countries, and ultimately the rest of the western world.

Recording for the show finished at about five, and one of the other guests, well-known Hollywood producer-actor Anthony Coleman, pulled me aside as we were leaving.

He asked me to call him Tony. We went to grab some dinner at his hotel room, where we ordered in, because it's hard for Tony to go anywhere in larger cities like London without being recognized and hassled.

Coleman had nearly twenty years on me, but you wouldn't know it. I guess he worked out daily and had some kind of amazing skin regimen going – if he'd had any kind of surgery it didn't show. Like a lot of big-name actors, he was a fairly small guy. He moved about with a restless, fizzing energy and talked *straight* to you with an intensity that reminded me vaguely of my Brynner, as I'd seen it on video. Talking with the guy was a bit overwhelming sometimes, but I felt like we had an unspoken understanding. Then again, maybe that's what everyone feels when they talk to Tony.

Tony ordered our dinner by phone, then said he'd like to talk business before the food came. He wanted to talk about the movie possibilities for the *Willing*.

I wasn't too keen on that idea, mostly because Tony had made a movie a year or two back, based on a favorite book of mine, and his movie version was mostly about how good the lead character was at kicking ass. I felt that the character's principles in the book version, and the way he lived, made him much more powerful than any amount of physical violence could, and I told Tony straight out how I felt.

He laughed. Then he pointed a finger at me. 'It's *you* I wanna make a movie about,' he said. 'A character based on *you*. A man who always does what he thinks is right, even when the choices are unimaginably hard. Yeah. I can see a movie in that.'

'Um, hasn't that been done before...?' I asked, but Tony was moving around the room now, waving his hands and glancing back at me with a passionate gleam in his eye.

'I'm not talking *Sophie's Choice* here. Nothing depressing like having to choose which of your kids dies. Fuck no. We want something *uplifting*. A real feelgood flick. We want the audience to go home feeling *they* can make the tough choices too. They can come out on top too...!'

Dinner arrived: two trolleys laden with incredibly good Chinese food, and a choice of desserts. We sat talking and eating until about nine, then Tony's phone suddenly erupted with a BAH-BAH-BAH-BAH – the *Mission Impossible* theme – and he jumped out of his chair and said he had to leave for another meeting. We swapped details and he was gone.

*   *   *

I had an early night because I was pretty hammered. Just as I was drifting off, my cellphone rang. It was Jo Bourne to say she'd seen the show, and to give her congratulations. It was nice to hear from her, and it helped ease a vaguely guilty conscience about having lived for the last year on her money, but not really having acknowledged the fact. She was in Bristol, which was a bit too far away for me to commit to meeting up before I left.

I considered asking Jo about getting some more money for maybe a nanosecond, but it really didn't feel right so I left it.

There were a few more things on my to-do list while I was in London. Akemi still wasn't answering texts or calls, so I put that one aside for the time being – figuring I'd go in person and knock on her door if I had the time. Which would be a squeeze, really. In the one day I had left, I'd scheduled two meetings with potential money people in London. One in the morning, one in the afternoon.

I say *potential*, but I wasn't really very hopeful. In fact it was touch and go whether I should bother at all.

Earlier in the year, I'd started getting email and Facebook messages from people all over the world. Some positive, some not. Some interested in being part of a new wave of consciousness like the *Willing*. Some wanting to help that wave along in some way. Some even offering to give me money. Most of this last bunch were obvious time-wasters, but there were also a few that could potentially – at a stretch – be on the level.

I was pretty cynical about offers of financial help by now, because apart from a very few exceptions, there's some kind of expectation that comes attached to money someone gives you. They want to somehow control things. Have a stake in the game. Maybe that works in the financial investment world, but not when it comes to helping an individual on a quest like mine. Principles are not for sale unless they're bullshit principles. People with money to throw around rarely understand this concept. Jo Bourne was maybe the closest thing to the exception, but for the most part it's like they say: there's no such thing as free money.

I had a weeding-out response that I sent to any potential contributors who'd passed the once-over stage. I said thanks for their interest; I'd like to meet and talk about it if they were clear of one thing: any money given would be a gift and not an investment. Some of the meetings would end very quickly, because they'd be miffed that I would dare presume that *I* was the one giving *them* the once over. They usually assumed it should be the other way around. Money does that to people, I find.

In the eight months before my trip up to London, I got a total of twenty-three messages offering money. The weeding-out process cut the twenty-three offers down to six possibles, four of whom I'd traveled to meet with in Spain, France and Italy.

Cost of travel to these meetings, plus accommodation: around eight hundred euros. Total resulting contributions: no cash, but two *air-promises.* These are heart-felt promises of money in the future that never seem to eventuate. So in real terms, a big fat zero.

But Jo Bourne had shown me there were people who really did want to contribute to change for the sake of it. Few though they were, I had to stay open to possibilities, and I was still ready to check out the last two on my list here in London.

The first, a guy called Eryn Glaister, had organized to meet me at the Paisley Club on the Strand at eleven in the morning. It was a members-and-their-guests-only club, and I was nervous about getting in. What if he was late? Would I have to stamp around outside in the cold until he arrived...?

But I guess he'd left my name at the door, because when I arrived ten minutes early, I was quickly ushered in and sat down and given a large pot of hot, spicy mulled wine. The atmosphere was wonderful. Nothing like the staid, conservative image I had of lofty establishments like this. There was a cultured, friendly air about the place. Sure, I didn't see any women there, but the men smiled and winked at each other – even at me. A complete stranger. Very un-London-like.

By the time Glaister arrived – I think he was pretty much on time – I was feeling the combined effects of the mulled wine and the cheerful atmosphere, and I was in a good mood. Glaister was about forty, I guessed. He was a bouncy, effeminate kind of a guy, whose expressive eyes seemed to be constantly shifting between extremes of emotion: surprised, angry, overjoyed, supremely relaxed. He greeted several of the other members with warm enthusiastic handshakes then made a little show of being surprised to see me.

We shook hands and Glaister started on his own pot of mulled wine. He leaned in towards me. 'I heard about your stoush with Lizard Lochlan,' he said with a conspiratorial smile, but in a voice loud enough to carry. 'Any enemy of Liz is a friend of mine.'

Some of the conversations around us stopped, and ears turned in our direction. I felt suddenly very uncomfortable. Glaister must have noticed, because he immediately looked appalled and asked, 'Oh! What did I say...?' He grimaced and bit into his lip. 'Did I hear wrong...?'

'Well... I'm not sure what you heard, but there was no stoush. We couldn't agree on something, that's all. Liz and I aren't exactly friends but... We aren't enemies. As far as I know, anyway.'

Glaister looked stricken. 'Oh. Okay... Hmmm. Well.'

'Would that have some bearing on whether or not you give me money?'

He gave a possum-caught-in-headlights grin. 'Oooh. We *are* a cards-on-table type of person, aren't we.'

I left the meeting ten minutes later with a generous *air-promise* from Eryn Glaister.

The next meeting was with a Joseph Noakes, who was meeting me at a café in East London at one o'clock. Noakes was twenty minutes late, which started things off badly. While I ate the cake I'd bought and taken to my table, I listened in on a conversation around a cluster of tables by the window. A group of nicely-dressed middle-aged men spoke earnestly in cockney accents about street fights and various acts of violence they'd witnessed recently.

When Noakes finally made his appearance, he had a big bloke in tow, who was carrying a small briefcase. I guessed it was Noakes, because he was dressed in an expensive suit and walked with an air of bulletproof self-assurance. His head was shaved bald, skin smooth, features brutal. He had the small, dark eyes of a shark and a wide down-turned mouth.

I stood up. 'Mister Noakes?'

The men at the tables by the window stopped talking and turned to look. They whispered and nodded to each other, obviously aware of who Noakes was. Noakes nodded and shook my hand. Then I offered my hand to the minder, who waited for a nod from his boss before accepting it. The minder's name was Mickey. Mickey pulled out his boss's chair and Noakes sat down with a grunt.

The café had gone dead quiet since Noakes's entrance, and as we ordered coffees, I was very conscious of the many pairs of ears in the room. Mickey sat a few feet back from the table, silently nursing the briefcase.

The coffees arrived double quick – as if the staff were on their best behavior. Noakes sipped his coffee and dabbed his mouth with a napkin. 'Show went well last night,' he said. It was a cockney accent with the edges rubbed off.

'Did it go over okay...?' I asked. 'I wasn't sure.'

His face folded into a smile, and he nodded. 'It went over just fine.' The guys by the window were whispering now. I heard the name *Leighton Farmer*, and several pair of eyes turned to look at me.

'I like what you're about, son,' said Noakes. 'And I'm interested in being a part of it. It's an ambition of mine...' He clasped his hands together on the table. '...To be a driving force behind change in the world. It's gonna happen anyway, so we might just as well do it properly, eh?'

Noakes was a real eye-opener. I'd been almost ready to get up and walk out when he first arrived. My prejudice was that strong. To be fair though, it was really hard to understand Joey Noakes's motivations. To reconcile his outward lifestyle with his inner values. His world seemed so brutal, but he spoke with a gentleness that wasn't forced. He was smart. He valued honesty. And he gave me a large whack of cash with no strings attached. I left the café with the briefcase Mickey'd been nursing so conscientiously. In it was a hundred thousand pounds. The ground was shifting under my feet again.

2

I stopped in Trafalgar square and looked up at the statue of Nelson. A pigeon did a long, dribbly shit down one massive shoulder.

It was just gone three in the afternoon, on the day before I was due to fly out of London Heathrow to Korea and then down to New Zealand. I had a briefcase in my hand with a hundred thousand pounds in it. That converted to one hundred-twenty thousand euros, or somewhere near two hundred thousand NZ dollars. Enough to last years if I carried on living simply.

Till today, it'd seemed my options in Europe had dried up. I'd come up to London with my last few thousand euros to do the *Leighton Farmer* spot, fully aware that I wouldn't be allowed back down into continental Europe – the Schengen area – for three months. This is one of the provisos on the relaxed visa requirements for New Zealand passport holders.

Because my mum's English, I had the option of registering as a British citizen and getting a British passport – which prior to Brexit, gave free access to continental Europe (still does at the time of writing) – but which would cost nearly a thousand pounds all up: too much.

Or, should I say, too much for Reagan of *yesterday*...

Speaking of my old mum, I'd told her I was on my way back down to see her, and she was expecting me home in time to watch *Leighton Farmer* together, with me on it – it screens three or four days later in NZ. I was due home in Whanganui two and a half hours before the show and would be trashed, but mum was excited about it, to say the least.

Then also there was the question of Grace. I'd organized to stay a night with her in her hometown of Incheon, near Seoul. I was really looking forward to seeing her, and she was even coming to meet me at the airport.

But up against all that was the case for staying on. I'd just got the *Willing* stuff up and running, and I don't mean to beat up on sweet little old New Zealand, but you can't get further away from where things are happening unless you head out into space.

And that wasn't the only thing. If you go to NZ from Europe, you have to go for a month at least, because the thirty-six hour journey each way really takes it out of you. It's possibly the most jet-lagged you can get. Because of the total day/ night switch-around (it's a twelve-hour time difference), you spend a whole week feeling out of sorts going one way, then a whole other week coming back. Of course, compared to our colonial ancestors, who suffered through a death-defying journey of around a hundred days by ship, we have it sweet.

In any case, I had some serious decision-making to do.

First up, I decided to deposit my briefcase at the hotel, and make all my other decisions overnight. I could afford a taxi, but chose to walk back across town to the hotel, because I meant to carry on living frugally. And apart from costing nothing but shoe-leather, walking's also healthy. And fun.

It was the middle of the day, with lots of people around, so the last thing I thought about was my personal safety. I mean, muggers work at night on deserted streets, don't they? I was so busy thinking over my options that I didn't notice the street I'd turned onto was very quiet, until a voice said in a cockney accent, 'Money, mista... *now.*'

I looked up. He was a dirty youth. Nice-looking clothes, but with stains all over them and filth in his hair, like he'd woken up in a skip somewhere. In his hand he held a stun gun – a high-voltage zapper. To add a bit of emphasis to his demand, he hit the button and a blue arc crackled at the weapon's tip.

I looked from the stun gun up to the guy's face. His pupils were dilated. He was chewing something so hard his cheek muscles were spasming. He meant business. But I was surprised to find that I felt nothing. Just a cold determination that I wasn't gonna give this fucker my hundred grand. No way.

That was the only thought in my mind as I swung the heavy briefcase. A corner of the case hit the guy smack in the temple, and he went straight down. The stun gun clattered to the road beside him.

I stood there for a moment. The street was like a sound trap. We weren't far from the main drag, but the city noises sounded distant.

The guy was lying perfectly still on the cobble-stone road. My next thought was *what if he's dead?* I slowly turned and looked up and own the street – up at street lamp level, where cameras would be if there were any. But I saw none: a rarity in modern-day London. Probably the very reason the guy chose this particular spot for his business.

I bent down and picked up the zapper, pocketed it, and walked away.

I'm not really sure why I took the guy's stun gun. Spoils of war? Didn't want him to use it again on someone else? Maybe I just thought it might come in handy. But as I walked the rest of the distance to the hotel, I started to shake. And to worry about carrying such a whopper chunk of cash on the streets of a big city like London. I got some small comfort from having that damn zapper in my pocket.

At the hotel I had to show my passport before they allowed the deposit of the briefcase, but I left again a few kilos lighter, and feeling very relieved.

So far, today had been the strangest day. I was very distracted. Moving around in auto-mode like a zombie. My next stop was to be Akemi's apartment – or at least the place she'd been living when I saw her last. Over a year ago.

I was sitting on the train before I reflected on how pointless the journey would very probably be. Why was I risking valuable time on a vague possibility? Was I factoring Akemi into my decisions? Putting them off in the hope that their was still something between us?

I guessed that Akemi represented some unfinished business for me. Our connection wasn't as deep as the one I had with Grace, but it was seriously passionate. I thought about Grace maybe once a week, apart from our Skype sessions.

But I thought about Akemi almost every day.

I knocked on the door to the apartment that'd belonged to Akemi eighteen months before. No sound from inside. I felt pretty silly.

I turned to go, then stopped as I saw a shape on the landing. 'Howdy...?'

The cat shied away, running back into shadows, but then ventured hesitantly back out. Cats are not always unique, but as I moved closer, I saw the mangled right ear that was as good as a fingerprint ID. It was Howdy, and he looked fed and healthy, so

Akemi was still here... Or maybe Howdy had adopted someone else in her place...? I took out my phone and bypassed the customary text – went straight to a call.

There was still a ringing tone, at least... Then a click as someone picked up.

'Hello...?' Akemi's voice. 'Reagan...?'

'Yeah, it's me.'

'Yes, your name is on my screen.'

'You didn't answer my texts.'

A long pause. 'I thought it's no point.'

'I was worried,' I said. 'I'm back in London.'

When I met her at the station, I could hardly recognize her. She was dressed very nicely, in some kind of smart suit, and her hair was now long – down past her shoulders. We hugged in a stiff sort of way, and looked for a long moment into each other's eyes. She smiled, and sang softly, *'Too true... Too blue...'* I felt a shiver run through my body. I'd heard that phrase many, many times in my head over the previous year and a half.

She opened the door to her apartment and let me inside. It was a completely different room to the one I remembered. As old and as threadbare as everything had been before, the furniture and wallpaper that'd replaced it all was new. Colorful. A bit gaudy for my tastes, but a massive improvement. The red plastic chair was still there – actually fitting quite well into the new overall scheme – and so was the tatty old guitar, but nothing else was the same.

We had dinner at Maharajah's. She told me she'd avoided the place while I was away because it made her sad. When it came time to pay, she wouldn't let me pay her share. She insisted she had no problem paying for herself.

We went back to her apartment and talked for a while, skirting around the reasons for the dramatic improvement in her lifestyle. I wasn't sure it was something I'd want to hear about, so I didn't ask. When I told her about the *SIR* business in France, and the *Willing* manifesto, and Matt's animation and the subsequent internet sensation, and the *Leighton Farmer* show, and the money from Joey Noakes, she smiled happily, but didn't seem to think any of it was a big deal. None of it had reached into her world, and it wouldn't in the future, either. I felt a little let down, but decided not to take it to heart.

She went to the bathroom, and before she closed the door, I saw that the whole setup in there had been upgraded to quality fittings as well. I used the time alone to think about where we were at, Akemi and I.

There was still a spark between us, but the underlying tension had gone. Was this a good thing? I thought maybe so. After my various experiences on the continent, I was a lot less frightened of her sexuality.

Her new bed was very comfortable and the sex was very nice. Different from before, but nice. This time she got me to wear a condom. I guessed her supply of birth-control pills hadn't been replenished.

In the morning, everything seemed to come clear. I was going to stay on in Britain for as long as it took to get my British passport. I kissed Akemi goodbye and went to make my calls. First to Grace in Korea: she was disappointed but supportive. Then to Mum in NZ: apart from a sad comment about Christmas, she was basically supportive too. I was off the hook.

I booked another night at the hotel, but found a cheaper B&B to stay at from the following day – it took a while to find one with a safe big enough to lock up my case of cash. Next, I started things rolling with the British registry entry and passport application. I was told it could take up to six weeks. Still. I'd heard stories about the many thousands of people who were desperate for British citizenship. It seemed odd that it should be so easy for me.

The B&B was an old Victorian house in Forest Hill that'd been decorated throughout to maximize its old-world charm. That's what it said in the advert, and the reality lived up to the hype. At fifty-five pounds a night, it was half the cost of my hotel room, and the weekly rate took the cost down further. It was a perfect spot to be for a number of reasons: the comfort of the place; its views out across the city – it was perched on the side of a hill; lots of cheap eateries nearby; not too far from London's CBD, and not too far from Akemi's apartment either. On the minus side it was a bit cold, despite their best efforts to heat the place. And you didn't have to look too far to spot signs of seediness on the street outside.

I wanted to warn Akemi about what Inspecteur Brouté of the DGSI had told me – that she was being monitored by international police – but I didn't feel good about broaching the subject because of the connection to her job as a sex worker. I was hesitant to mention something that could potentially spoil the fragile thing we had going. And to be honest, I preferred to be ignorant.

But where was her money coming from if she *wasn't* back on the game? I couldn't work out what Akemi did with her day. She didn't seem to have any work. I was still wary about broaching the subject, but sometime into the second week I was in London, she sat me down and played a music track she had on her iPod, through a set of docking speakers. She cranked it up

197

loud, but thankfully not loud enough to start her neighbors knocking on the walls again.

When it started, I thought I recognized the jangling guitar riff, but couldn't work out where from. Then the vocal started, and I realized it was Akemi. I looked at her, and she grinned – a big, proud, happy smile – and a tear in her eye. As we sat listening together, I could see it meant an awful lot to have me listen to the music she'd made.

She told me she'd been recording with a Canadian music student called Jeremie at his flat in Brixton. Jeremie had a little room set up as a studio and charged a cheap rate. For a young guy, she said, he seemed to know what he was about. She had nine songs she'd been working on, and three nearly done, which she played to me. All the vocals were in Japanese, but the songs had a melodic, haunting quality to them that I thought might transcend language and engage people anywhere. They jammed and they jangled, but often moved unexpectedly into a minor key, or a whole other timing, and kept the listener emotionally on their toes.

The two of us shared a blissful couple weeks, seeing just enough of each other to want more. But I was about to discover our time was up.

I dropped by Akemi's apartment building one afternoon. She'd said she'd be over at Jeremie's recording her music, but I meant to push a small gift through her mail slot: a box of condoms with reservoirs the shape of a guitar at the tip. Just for a bit of fun.

As I reached the top of the stairs and stepped onto the landing, I noticed someone strolling towards me and looked up. He had a goatee beard and a silly haircut, but I was pretty certain it was Simon Duchesne – the spy at SIR who did a runner when he knew he'd been found out.

The guy saw me and did the slightest of double-takes before nodding a nonchalant greeting and starting down the stairs. I called after him, 'Simon...?'

He threw a glance back over his shoulder. 'Sorry mate. Fink you got me mixed up with sa'an else.' It was a cockney accent, and his manner was very convincing, but I remembered how good Duchesne was at bullshitting. I watched him jog down the stairs out of sight, then continued down the landing to Akemi's door, where I stopped and listened.

I thought I could hear the sound of water running through pipes, but wasn't sure where it came from. I knocked on the door and waited.

Footsteps from inside, and the door opened on the chain. Akemi had a plush rose-colored towel wrapped around her waist, and another around her head. She peered through the gap at me, startled. 'Oh... Reagan...'

'I have to ask you something,' I said, taking a seat on Akemi's comfortable new couch. 'Did you ever have a client who would visit you from another country?'

She looked me in the eye. Bit her lip, then turned away. It was a while before she answered. 'Yes.'

'I didn't want to bring this stuff up. I'm just...'

'I see him once in every month,' she said, interrupting me. 'He's my only client now. He pays me ten thousand pounds each time, so I don't have to see any other clients. And I don't have to do the waitress job any more.'

'*Ten thousand pounds?* Jesus. That's uh... that's a lot of money.'

'It's enough.' Her back still turned, she adjusted the towel around her waist. I started to get a bad feeling about where this was all heading.

'Enough for what?'

'Enough for the sex... without a condom.'

I stopped breathing. There was a high-pitched buzzing in my head.

'He shows me a test report every time,' she continued. 'It shows negative HIV. It's our deal. And he plomised he will not hit me again, ever.'

'Hit you? It's *that* guy...?'

She rocked her head from side to side like she was trying to make up her mind. 'It's him. Yes.'

I took a deep breath. 'Look, an AIDS test doesn't mean anything if he's had unprotected sex recently. It might not show positive for...'

'I know.'

'You... you *know,* but you do it anyway?'

Her mouth compressed into an ugly grimace. 'Evelybody evelywhere do the things they don't like for money.'

'Not... *Jesus!* Not if their *life* is at risk!'

'*Yes*, if their life is risk! They do the job evely day for money. They are doing the job they don't like, or they are eating or they are are sleeping. It is the same as death! Can't you understand...? It's just one hour for me in the month. Then evely day I am free to be completely alive!'

I stared at Akemi. She suddenly seemed far, far away. I felt my investment in whatever relationship we had seeping away, and a blackness rushing in to fill the gap left behind.

With a real effort, I pulled myself together. Took a long, deep breath, and said, 'There's something I have to tell you. When I was in France, a guy from French internal security told me you were being monitored. I think he said your surname was uh, *Yoda*, like the Star Wars character...?' She spun around and stared at me, eyes huge.

'*Why didn't you tell me before?*' she spat, suddenly furious.

'I, uh...'

She covered her head with her arms and made a high-pitched howling sound that made the hairs on the back of my neck bristle. I stood up and took a few steps towards her. 'Hey, hey... it's okay. They've known about you for ages, but look... they haven't done a thing about it, have they... Why would they kick you out *now*?'

Her arms dropped, revealing her face. Her eyes were hard black stones. 'You don't understand. I have to start *again*. You think it's easy for the illegal person to find a place to live? A way to earn the money? It fucking is *not!*

'Evelything is recorded. Evelywhere you go, *they ask to see a passport!*' She dropped down into a squat, and coughed as if she was going to be sick. The towel unraveled and dropped away from her body, leaving her naked.

I didn't know what to say, so I sat and watched as she stumbled to her feet, pulled on some clothes, opened her wardrobe and pushed a bunch of shoes aside to reveal a small safe. She spun the dial on the safe and pulled out something that looked like a flotation belt, only it was heavy. Cash, maybe. Wrapping the bulky belt around her middle, she yanked a down jacket from a hanger, and put it on. She stood for a moment, looking around the room, then she slowly approached me, her eyes cast downwards.

'I know it's not your fault,' she said, and kissed me quickly on the cheek. She started to back slowly towards the door. 'Don't call me, okay...? Just... *Don't.*' She stopped and pulled her phone from her pocket. Stepped on a dustbin's peddle to open its lid, and dropped the phone inside.

Wiping a tear, she said, 'Bye.' and walked out.

3

SAN ANTONIO, SPAIN
Spring, Eighteen Months Later

I pulled off the road in my Toyota Estima van, and looked again at google maps. Yup. The narrow dirt track that snaked up among the dry, scrubby hills was indeed the one I needed to turn onto.

A dusty ten minutes later I parked at the entrance to the San Antonio settlement: around two thousand men, women and children who'd occupied a deserted town and made it their own. A proper road led up to the settlement from the south end of the cape, but I'd traveled down from Valencia in the North, so I used the track that the San Antonians had blazed themselves.

There was no fence, but surrounding the entrance from the end of the dirt road was a wooden archway that'd been crafted carefully out of wood, with the name *San Antonio* carved across its head. The dwellings started about fifty meters away, on the other side of a field that looked like it might've been a garden at one point, but had been left to go to seed.

San Antonio was a *Willing* community – one of many that'd sprung up around the world over the past few years. In continental Europe, they were mostly left alone to do their thing, because there was plenty of room – deserted towns like San Antonio, or scrub land that no one was interested in – and there'd already been a kind of established culture of individuals and small groups of people living this way, from centuries back.

Some other countries where a different story. In my birth

country of New Zealand, for example, there were strict laws about using public land, and the *Willing* communities were getting demands from local authorities to pay residential rates on the land they were occupying: money they didn't have, or weren't willing to part with. In the States, it was a similar thing – *Willing* communities were being threatened with arrest for vagrancy if they didn't move on.

But the *Willing* had begun something basically unprecedented, in terms of sheer numbers. People were swarming in to these communities from all over. The largest community I'd heard of at the time was eight-thousand strong, in Bologna, Northern Italy. *Eight thousand*. That's like a small town.

And instrumental to all this was Karl Donovan. My old friend Donno. Back then, just after the *Leighton Farmer* show aired, there was a sharp spike in interest in the *Willing* ideas, and I went on to appear on several more talk shows in Europe and the US. I felt sort of guilty I guess, and started mentioning the name Karl Donovan during some of my TV spots, crediting him with the foundational Willing concept.

From the start, I was against the idea of secluded communities calling themselves 'Willing' – after all, one of the core Willing principles was to remain open and connected to other people. I never believed it was healthy to go apart. But who was I to dictate what should and shouldn't be done, or to set my personal definition of *Willingness* in stone? By now, the Willing were gathering together in small, isolated groups all around the world, and they weren't satisfied with my deliberately hands-off approach. They clearly wanted some kind of central directorship. Which seemed ridiculous to me – wasn't this the very thing they were trying to *escape* from?

But this is where Donno stepped in. It was Donno himself

who started up the first settlement at San Antonio, which became a model example for other communities around the world to follow. He then started up an online commentary on practical ways to change one's life in a *Willing* way, which he updated every day, and which got an enormous number of followers. Donno's *WILLING WORLD* website soon became the central hub of the worldwide Willing community. A digital meeting-place where they could chat about issues, exchange stuff, organize events and generally be Willing.

The basic Willingness concepts were there, albeit communicated in a haphazard, syrupy fashion. Donno was obviously still keen to sugar the pill. But there were also one or two new aspects that he'd taken it on himself to add. For example, fluffy little esoteric tidbits here and there, like

> *THERE IS NO ACCIDENT; MERELY*
> *CONSEQUENCES OF YOUR OWN UNCONSCIOUS*
> *CHOICES*

and

> *YOU CHOOSE TO BE ALIVE, SO WHY NOT ALSO*
> *CHOOSE TO MAKE LIFE WORK FOR YOU?*

This stuff was not typical of the deeply-discerning Donovan I knew.

Top and center on the site's homepage was a picture of Donno that I recognized from our days in Valencia together. Or perhaps more accurately, a picture of some guy with a cream panama hat tilted down to conceal his face: *I* knew it was Donno because I was standing next to him when that particular picture was taken. But he was faceless. As far as the rest of the world was concerned, it could've been anybody under that hat.

Unlike the esoteric stuff, this was classic, *under-the-radar* Karl Donovan. It was also a stylishly mysterious online entity that seemed to have exactly the effect Donno was aiming at: it was drawing people in.

I'd recently taken to visiting *WILLING WORLD* and reading Donno's posts more often, because I was really starting to worry about the direction things were heading in. A few weeks earlier, a *Willing* community in Greece had taken in refugees from Syria, without any suggestion that they might need to have an interest in Willing principles, and Donno supported the move.

I didn't. Generously providing shelter for a person was one thing; whether that person was going to actually have an interest in *Willing* principles, was another. I thought it added a whole other layer of bullshit to the *Willing* community idea.

All this had been weighing heavily on my mind, but what finally prompted my visit to San Antonio was the arrival of eighteen different requests for media interviews within the space of a week, including the *Leighton Farmer Show* in London. Leighton himself emailed me, suggesting I might like to tell my side of the story.

I was nervous about fronting up, especially on *Leighton Farmer*, where my public profile had been launched, and I wanted to go prepared.

I needed some answers from Donno.

The last time I'd met face to face with Donno was in Valencia, over two years before, when I saw him off at the Estació del

Nord. I left my van parked to one side of San Antonio's front entrance, alongside a collection of decaying vehicles, and strained my eyes to catch sight of a San Antonian. There was no one around so I let myself in – in a manner of speaking – walking through the archway and past the ex-garden to where I could see some kids playing. When they saw me coming, the kids laughed and ran away to hide.

The dwellings at the outer edge of San Antonio were cobbled together mostly with stones from the ruins of the old town, and anything else lying around. Bits of rusty tin. Moldy boards and planks. Blankets. Towels. Pieces of furniture lay out in the open, smelling of damp. I have to say, I wasn't impressed.

I peered into several of the empty dwellings before I heard some laughter in one of the larger shanties nearby. It was a low-to-the-ground lean-to that looked set to collapse in on itself. I called out, *'Hello...?'*

A head poked out from a hole in the wall: a young woman with blonde dreadlocks. The head disappeared again, then three women stepped out into the weak sunlight, where they stood blinking at me.

'Hi, I said. 'Is Karl Donovan around?'

The women looked at each other. The one with the dreadlocks said, 'He's not here.' A northern British accent.

'Okay... Well, where will I find him?'

Dreadlocks folded her arms and squinted at me. 'What do you want him for?'

Clearly, they had no idea who I was. I guessed they weren't regular watchers of the evening news. Not that I held that against them. 'He's a friend of mine,' I said.

One of the other women, a squat thing with a pretty face and a patterned scarf on her head, seemed a bit embarrassed by her friend's surly manner. She explained kindly in an East-London accent, 'It's just that we get a lot of folks just like, dropping in, an' asking to see Karl Donovan. Like he's got nothing better to do with his time.'

The scarf's name was Maisy. Maisy and her two mates said they'd take me to see a bloke called Micmac, and I got to see a bit more of the settlement on the way. There were more substantial structures further in towards the center, where a kind of courtyard had been cleared with sheltered areas around it. A group of kids were being taught to write in one corner, and two older guys were playing their guitars quietly in another.

Micmac was a muscular, square-faced scowler of maybe forty-five. He shook my hand with a strong grip, and seemed momentarily appalled by my weaker response. But he let it go. 'Donno's not here, man' he confirmed in a strong South African twang. 'He doesn't like to be disturbed.'

'Yeah, so I hear, but he's expecting me. I notice there's no cell coverage out here. Do you have a way of getting in touch with him?' Micmac took a breath, like he was suppressing an urge to clobber me, and fixed me with a hard stare.

'He didn't say anything about it to me.' he grumbled.

'Tell him it's *Brynner*.'

Finally he nodded and said, 'Wait here,' then went inside his hut.

Maisy and her friends sat with me while we waited. There was a row of tables nearby where several people were busy preparing food. Smoke from an earth oven hung in the air and stung the eyes just a bit. Naked children played on the dusty ground.

'You know Karl Donovan?' asked Maisy. By the look on her

face, I could see she thought that was a big deal.

I confirmed that yes, I was privileged to know Karl Donovan. Maisy exchanged a look with her friends, and said. 'It's just we've never actually met him.'

Micmac stepped out of his hut and announced that Donno was on his way – he'd be here in an hour or so.

I heard Donno before I saw him. Rather than parking out at the entrance, he rode in to the settlement's center on his motorbike and stopped a few meters from where we were sitting, his shiny blue helmet obscuring most of his face.

Maisy and her friends took a hesitant step forward, but Donno ignored them. He nodded towards the rear of the bike. 'Jump on.' He was never big on niceties.

'Oh, nah,' I said. 'I'll just follow you in the van.'

I could just make out the familiar squinty grin through his visor. 'Don't think so, mate. Not where we're going.'

It was a scary journey. I was a terrible pillion passenger, and Donno stopped every few Ks to tell me off.

'Lean!' he shouted through his helmet. 'You're gonna spill us onto the fuckin' road!' Once we got back on the main road, Donno really let rip, but leaning with the bike on the curves and corners somehow went counter to my intuition. I heard muffled grunting and swearing from Donno the whole way.

About an hour in, we went off-road again. Donno just stopped and turned onto a narrow track that went into a forest. It was slower going from that point because we had to negotiate a muddy, twisting and turning path through trees and bushes. Multiple knobbly tire tracks showed that the path was fairly well-used.

At last we came to a stop outside a collection of buildings that couldn't have been less like San Antonio if it tried. It looked very civilized.

The central structure was a large A-frame house, surrounded by wooden decking. Two small huts sat at the periphery of the clearing, and a long ladder at the rear of the house led up to a box-like tree-house, nestled high in the branches of a tree. Well covered by the forest's canopy, the structures were painted in earthy camo greens and browns so that they blended in with their surroundings.

Donno parked his bike next to two others under a shelter and took off his helmet, muttering all the while about my lack of skills as a passenger. Then he joined me where I was standing admiring the scene. I glanced at him and saw he'd done another fairly radical transformation. His hair was long now. Tied back in a ponytail, which seemed to change the whole shape of his face.

'Flew it all in by helicopter, he explained, his mood improving. 'Took a bit of putting together.'

The occupants of the two huts came out to say hi. One was a young blond guy with a deep tan and what I took to be a Californian accent. He had a slow smile and a pronounced slouch, and kept his hands in his shorts pockets the whole time. The other guest was a woman of maybe thirty-five with short dark hair and soft brown eyes that I was taken with right away. From her accent, I guessed she was from Germany, but we never did exchange names or personal details.

Donno enthusiastically showed me around, calling the forest dwelling *the Nines;* explaining the name was an allusion to the expression *to the nines,* meaning *to the highest order.* The best of the best.

'Plus,' he added, 'It's a kind of tribute to *you*.'

'To *me*?'

'Yeah. It's your numerology. You're a *Nine*.'

'My numerology.'

'Well, your birthday, right...? *Ninth of the ninth, eighty-one.* The eight and the one make nine, and the whole lot adds up to twenty-seven, which in turn adds up to nine. You're a *Nine*, through and through.'

'Right.'

He leaned against the thick trunk of a tree. 'It's supposed to tie up with the kind of energies that determine who you are, and how you reincarnate,' he said, nodding. 'Apparently a *Nine* is coming to the end of his incarnation cycle.'

I blinked. 'Numerology and reincarnation.'

'That's right. Numerology and reincarnation.'

'I'm er, just surprised you would believe in stuff like that.'

He snorted. 'Me? Shit no. But it's interesting, ain't it.'

The Nines was nicely furnished and had electricity throughout, as well as computers, large-screen televisions, ovens, and fridges. It was kind of weird to find such a comfortable set-up in a forest in the middle of nowhere. Internet was provided by a Chinese satellite signal bounced off a decoy station on the other side of the forest, to prevent the location being tracked – or to at least give advance warning if someone came looking.

Donno told me he'd found his own "tooth-fairy" who funded the Nines and kept him in food, beer and petrol for his bike. He was cagey about the tooth-fairy's identity though, and when I tried to push it, he said, 'If I told you who he was, I'd have to kill ya.'

I laughed.

'I'm not joking, mate. It's in the contract I signed.'

I saw he wasn't pulling my leg, but I wasn't impressed. 'Right. Well, that's some contract. You think it'll be legally binding if it requires you to do *illegal* stuff like kill people?'

'There's no actual mention of killing. Just nasty consequences if you let the cat out of the bag.' He shrugged. 'But I doubt they had any laws in mind when they wrote it.'

I sighed and shook my head. 'Why all the secrecy? Seems like silly games to me.'

'Well, come on. Think about it. If you're a thorn in some bloke's side, and the bugger knows who you are and where to find you, your life ain't worth shit.' He spread his hands. 'If you're gonna do something, you gotta at least give yourself a decent shot at success. I ain't doing this stuff to be a martyr.'

I saw it was a serious matter as far as Donno was concerned, and decided to let it lie. We sat with a beer each on the decking, early evening sun shining through the trees onto our upturned faces. I waved a hand, indicating the cluster of buildings that made up the Nines, and said, 'Silly games or not, that tooth-fairy of yours has got some seriously deep pockets.'

Donno was fetching a fresh can from a box nestled between us. He gave a reluctant grin. 'He's a good bloke, but he's a bit mad.' Donno popped his can and took a swallow. 'I told him I wanted to set up a kind of HQ for the Willing. He says to me, *tell me what you need and it's yours.*

'So. I really went to town on it. Well, you would, wouldn't ya. I slap my plan on his desk. Six hundred grand's worth. And he just shrugs and goes, *yeah, fine.*'

I was stunned. 'Six hundred thousand euros...?'

'Yeah. Bugger didn't even blink.'

'That's some serious money.'

Donno settled back in his chair. 'Pretty fuckin' serious.'

'And you're happy with the arrangement?'

'You mean, *does he have his claws in me...?*' he asked' 'Nope. He doesn't.'

'Okay, good.'

We sat for a bit, quietly drinking our beers and enjoying the evening, then Donno finally said, 'I know why you're here, mate. Greek settlement, right? Syrian refugees.'

I nodded. 'It's good to catch up, but, yeah. That's basically why I came. I've got media coming outta my ears, calling me up and emailing me, looking for answers.'

Donno sat up and turned towards me. 'Muslims, right? *Why would we invite them into a Willing settlement...? They'll never embrace Willing concepts. They'll be Willing in name only...* Yeah. We've had this one out before, haven't we, you an' me.' He pointed at my can. 'How's your beer?'

'Fine.'

'Okay, well. There's a big-picture thing here. Fast-forward a few years... The *Willing* is expanding outwards, becoming a more mainstream concept. How are we gonna blend with the rest of the population if we isolate ourselves? We have to integrate. And we have to start integrating now. It'll encourage tolerance and understanding.' He spread his hands. 'How does that sound?'

I took a moment to consider what Donno had said. For sure, Donno's own, hermit-like anonymity made a joke of what he was telling me, but it seemed to make sense in the wider scheme of things. I nodded. 'Yeah... it works, I guess.'

'Yeah?'

'... Yeah.'

'Okay, good. That's the media-friendly version.' He held up a hand to halt my protest before I got out a word. 'And it's also *true*. You won't be bullshitting them, so don't worry yourself... But there's a deeper thing happening. We've got to give everyone an opportunity to see the truth, to understand it, and to start living it. That's the best we can do...'

He turned his face toward the sun. 'If they *see* the truth, but choose *not to live by it*, then that's their look-out. "Cause, mate... at the end of the day, *they're* gonna be the ones out in the cold.'

I spent an uncomfortable night in the Nines' tree house, about ten meters up above the ground. Didn't sleep particularly well, wondering about Donno and his secret dealings with his tooth-fairy and his mysterious *nasty consequences*.

But I didn't feel I had the right to take issue with it all. While I might have been the one to introduce the Willing concept to the world, Donno *did* have a real stake in its genesis. He was, after all, doing his own thing, and doing it his way. It was unfortunate that it was *my* face people associated with the Willing, but there you go. I had thrown my hat in the ring with Karl Donovan, and I had to deal with that.

One thing that Donno had got very good at was selling his ideas. What was a bit fishy about that, as far as I was concerned, was his own accusation a few years back in Valencia, that I was manipulative. He'd likened my own desire to speak to truth in people's hearts, to a politician's clever rhetoric. It seemed to me Donno had become very skillful at nailing down what it was people *wanted to hear,* and speaking to that.

To my mind, if anything was clever rhetoric, *that* was.

The next morning when Donno dropped me off at my van at San Antonio, he revved his bike a few times then lifted his visor and said, 'Don't forget about the contract, mate.'

'Um. Contract...? I don't remember signing anything.'

'You didn't. But don't forget what I said about *consequences*.'

'Meaning what?'

'Have to spell it out for ya, do I?'

'Yeah.' I folded my arms. 'Guess so.'

He rubbed his brow through the helmet's front aperture. 'You're a good bloke, Reags. One of the very few really decent buggers in the world. But the stakes are high now, an' well... I wouldn't wanna see anything happen to ya. So better to just keep everything you've seen these last few days under your hat, yeah? If you don't, there might just be consequences neither of us likes.'

*   *   *

I went back to Valencia and did my interviews. Some by phone, some in person. My schedule was full of media stuff for about a month. They seemed to buy it. It sounded pretty good that the Willing wanted to integrate and share and be tolerant. It made them less threatening and a little bit less weird.

Clever rhetoric or not, Donovan's explanation had made sense, so I was fairly happy to trot it out verbatim. And I did. I repeated the same *integration-tolerance-understanding* phrases over and over for cameras and microphones until they seemed to lose their meaning.

By the time I flew up to London and appeared on the Leighton Farmer show, I'd had so much practice that we covered the whole thing in about two minutes. There was plenty of time left, so Leighton picked up where he'd left off eighteen months or so before. With his awkward questions that I appreciated gave the audience a deeper insight, but which had me squirming on the studio set's couch.

He started out gently enough, asking me, 'What advice to do have for people who would *like* to live by Willing principles, but who are put off by how difficult it all seems?'

'I'd say, give it a shot. In the end it might not actually be for you, you know? But it's a very meaningful thing to do. It beats the hell out of the treadmill – working to stay alive, and staying alive to work.'

'So what would happen if say, tomorrow morning, everyone across the whole wide world decided to just up-sticks and become *Willing*? What if they all packed their jobs in?' He shrugged. 'How would we all eat?'

I sighed deeply. There were little titters of embarrassment among the audience. They clearly didn't know what to make of my frank discomfort.

I guess Leighton saw that too, He added, 'Well, because that's what some people might be thinking out there, right?'

I took a deep breath. 'Sure, yes. I imagine so. Well, it seems to me a fresh start would be a good thing. I think the current social systems have way outlived their usefulness. We'd be forced into finding better systems that recognize the uniqueness of every individual, and if – like you say – the entire population were suddenly *Willing*, there'd be no problem with doing that...

'But, to be frank, I really don't think this is gonna happen,' I continued. 'Willingness is a voluntary attitude, and the world is clearly *not* going to embrace it overnight. People won't suddenly ditch everything they know and value, for something they can't fully appreciate. It takes quite a big shift in focus and probably a massive overhaul of a person's fundamental values.'

Leighton smiled. 'I think you're probably right there.' The audience gave a relieved laugh and I felt some of the tension lift. 'So let's say – for the sake of argument – that people around the world *do* adopt Willingness. You're advocating a complete dissolution of the structures that we base our lives on. Isn't that a giant step *backwards...?* Surely we're going to see a big downturn in the progress of the human race.

'I mean, we won't be sending many more billion-dollar probes to Mars, will we. Important research will be halted in its tracks. We might never find the cure for cancer. What do we live for, if not to move forward?'

I nodded. 'Well, firstly, you can't *adopt* Willingness like it's a religion or some other pre-existing format. It has to start and end in *here*.' I thumped my chest. 'You're either truthfully Willing, or you're *not...*'

Just at that point, I gratefully felt the first faint fuzz of warm confidence that characterized the Brynner. It was like meeting a trusted old friend and it felt good.

Clasping my hands together, I sat forward in my seat. 'But mostly it comes down to our definition of *moving forward*. What is *progress*, really...? How do we measure it in our day-to-day lives? By our level of comfort and convenience? How *safe* we feel? By how much money we have, or how much stuff we own...?'

I caught sight of a studio monitor nearby – on the screen I was framed in medium close-up, looking very Brynner-like and intense and brimming with confidence. 'See, I think we're really confused about this. When comfort and convenience are our goal, our ideas shrink and our appreciation of uniqueness is one of the first things to go.

'Because, hey. Uniqueness is *not* a convenient thing. We absolutely have to stop acting like it is, or like it *can* be. We can't measure all our kids against the same ruler just because it's convenient to do it that way, and expect them to grow up recognizing and treasuring their own uniqueness. Or that of others around them. They *won't.* They'll grow up believing some form of mimicry is their own. And their concept of progress – of a meaningful life – will be an adopted idea too. *Someone else's* picture of happiness. *Someone else's* idea of success. And they'll wonder why it doesn't feel so good.'

'What about you, Reagan?' Leighton interjected. 'What's *your* idea of success?'

'My idea of success? My personal idea of success is doing exactly what I want to do. Every minute, every hour, of every single day.'

He raised an eyebrow. 'And how does that work out for you?' The audience laughed. '... I mean, can you actually *achieve* that?'

I nodded. 'I can achieve that, and I do. All the time. Whether I have money in my pocket or not.'

'You're a lucky man.'

This time I shook my head in the negative. 'Truly, Leighton, it has nothing to do with luck. It's all about *choice*. About having the flexibility, the integrity and the strength, firstly to identify your best choices. Then to act on them.'

4

The autumn of that year brought trouble.

It was getting colder, and the situation in some of the settlements – in the European continent and in some states of the US – was getting serious. The Willing had shown their Willingness by opening their doors to all comers, and their numbers had swelled way beyond capacity. Way beyond any capability they might have had of feeding, clothing or even sheltering their members.

I'd hoped that people who called themselves *Willing* would be smarter, but they'd mindlessly followed Donno's direction, and taken in a huge raft of people who'd never even considered the possibility of being the driving force in their own lives. A news item on TV showed a woman in a *hijab* – a garment some Muslim women wear that completely covers the body, head and in this case the face – waiting in line for food at a settlement in Italy. I guessed the TV reporter meant to rark up distrust of fundamentalist Islam, but to me it just epitomized the general hopelessness of the situation. The Willing settlements now had swarms of people sitting waiting to be fed like so many sheep. As the weather gradually grew colder, we had a crisis on our hands.

But sitting in his little forest castle in the middle of nowhere, Donno was still happily preaching the righteousness of accepting all comers into the settlements. I sent him message after message, asking *was he watching the news? Did he realize he was setting up a disaster?* But I only ever got one reply:

219

No, mate. Everything is going just fine.

Still, Donno continued to take a totally hands-off approach. Almost none of the Willing had ever seen him in person, let alone the general population.

He was the man with the hat. A digital presence only. A faceless guy at a computer somewhere who tapped out advice on his *WILLING WORLD* site, but didn't get involved beyond that. And despite his distant stance, he was becoming a bit of a celebrity out in the world.

In Donno's absence, I felt a tug of responsibility – emotionally, if not intellectually – and started visiting the settlements to see what could be done.

The first visits went fairly well, I guess. I talked to them about Willing principles. I asked them to shoulder responsibility for their own lives and their own existence. After all, this was the foundational idea behind Willingness. I suggested practical strategies that they could use, on an individual basis, to feed and clothe themselves: personal visits to businesses, shops, companies, looking for sponsorship for the *noble challenge* they were engaged in.

As I said it, I knew the words sounded hollow. Their eyes had a blank look when I talked about these ideas. Like, *what the hell was I talking about...* ? I soon quit that strategy because I could see it was just annoying people. They just wanted to know when the food and the shelter was coming.

The climax to these visits was a trip up to a place called Mount Katahdin, in the US state of Maine. I have no idea why they chose to start up a settlement somewhere so damned cold. It was pretty cold when I was there, anyway.

The visit started badly and ended worse. I was introduced to a heavy-set guy with a mustache called Jim Hutchens, who was the designated leader of the settlement of "twelve to fifteen thousand." He couldn't give me anything like an accurate headcount. When I asked Jim how he thought his position as leader fit with Willing principles, and produced a copy of the original manifesto, he did his nut at me.

'Who the fuck d'you think you are, in your warm clothes, with a warm bed and a hot dinner to go home to tonight? Look around you, buddy... This is a fuckin' disaster. Someone's gotta step in...' he looked at me pointedly *'... In the absence of anyone else who'll take any fuckin' responsibility.'*

Like the people in all the other settlements, Jim just wanted to know when the food and clothing and stuff was coming. And he wasn't happy when I had no answers. I was getting pretty pissed off with his attitude, too. I asked, 'How can *I* be responsible for all the cold, starving people out there? If they'd actually paid attention to the principles I set out, everything would've...'

I didn't get to finish, because Jim belted me in the face, and I woke up on the floor after he'd left.

Last stop on my US trip was in Los Angeles, for a spot on the Ed Rymes show. I still had a bruise on my face from Jim Hutchens's punch, and was regretting having accepted the invitation.

Rymes was a big, bald white guy with cold dark eyes, whose thing was to lead in to video clips and interviews with some rhyming rap. He was massively popular in California, but he had an annoying way of making snide comments out of the corner of his mouth to get a laugh. Leighton Farmer in the UK did a similar side-of-the-mouth thing, but in a totally friendly, inclusive manner. Personality-wise, the two talk show hosts couldn't have been more different.

My *Ed Rymes* spot started so-so and ended badly. Rymes's silly rap lead-in was shouted to a loud, pumping beat from a drum machine, and featured the words *willin'*, *chillin'* and *fillin'*. Something about filling the stomachs of the cold, hungry Willing, I supposed.

Rymes then sat down and kicked the interview off with a suggestion that Willingness was a form of communism. I denied that and launched into a bit of a speel about choice.

'We're making very clumsy decisions in our everyday lives,' I said, 'because we have a very narrow idea of our choices. Are we a *communist,* or a *capitalist?* Are we a *leader* or are we a *follower?* A *Republican* or a *Democrat?* As if it's the *one*, or it's the *other*.' I spread my hands. 'But what if we say, *none of the above...?* I personally think *none* of those choices are good choices. They're all somebody else's ideas. We have to look further and wider and come up with ideas of our own. It's a good example right now, how you have to choose whether you vote for someone you dislike *intensely*, or for someone you just *dislike*. This is what...'

I stopped while the studio audience shouted and clapped to show their appreciation.

Rymes wasn't impressed. He gave an exaggerated shrug. 'And, what... *Willingness* is the alternative? How does Willingness help us make better choices?'

'I'm not saying Willingness *itself* is the alternative. Willingness is a way to get a *handle* on what a wide range of choices we actually have. A way to expand our horizons. I'll give you an example...' Recently I'd started wondering if short, illustrative stories might help get ideas across, and I'd prepped the following gem on the plane to LA.

'... Back in the days of steam locomotives, the train drivers used to come across the occasional sheep or cow standing in the train tracks. They'd give a good solid blow on the train's whistle, and the animal would start running, but often it'd just run straight ahead, along the tracks in front of the train...'

This got an appreciative laugh.

'I mean, the animal could just step *this* way, or *that* way, and let the train pass, right? But it doesn't realize it *has* that choice.'

'I get the point,' Rymes said. 'But is a choice we *don't understand*, really a choice?'

I nodded and wondered if maybe the guy wasn't so dumb. 'True. That's why in our learning we need to focus more on what choices we have. We have to learn to define our *own* choices, instead of choosing from an existing menu someone else thought up. Instead of making the default choice to like, go to college, get a job, get married, have kids, buy a house, etcetera etcetera, just because that's what people *do*.

'It's so easy to live in auto-mode. To mess up our lives by making unconscious choices, like having two, three, four kids because tradition or hormones or testosterone tell us to. Then we buy the *house* and the *car*, and suddenly find ourselves with a big fat monthly bill that we have to subjugate ourselves to pay. This is how we give away our freedom.'

'You think there's something *wrong* with getting married and having kids?' Rymes asked, his dark eyes boring into mine. 'A lot of people would say it's the most natural thing in the world.' I was moving onto very shaky ground, but hadn't yet realized it.

'Sure, it's a very natural thing to get married and have kids. I'm saying we have to *understand the choice to do so...* What the ramifications are, and whether that tallies with what we want out of life.' I spread my hands. 'I mean, a few hundred years ago we thought beating our children and our wives was a natural part of life. We thought having *slaves* was a natural part of life. We're more careful about those things now because we understand how damaging they are.'

'Let me get this right...' Rymes said, his jaw set. 'You're saying marriage and kids and owning a house cause us *damage...?* Wow.' He did one of his side of mouth comments. *'Is this guy for real?'*

Not really dumb. Just opinionated and cold-hearted. And the audience were so besotted with his smoothly twisted logic that they stuck right by him. I could hear by their grumblings that the tide of opinion had turned against me, and believe me, things just went downhill from there.

It was a bad, bad interview. By the time it was over, I was feeling hopelessly flustered and misunderstood. I pulled off my mic and hoofed it out of the studio without saying goodbye.

I was getting pretty tired by now, and found myself very quick to judge people like Rymes in LA, and the Willing guy Hutchens over in Maine. Having been on the receiving end of judgment all my life, I knew it wasn't a good thing, and yet here I was, doling it out. I needed a rest very badly.

I took the long way back to Europe from the west coast of the US, and went across the Pacific – stopping first in Korea to see Grace. We'd stayed in touch over the previous couple years with weekly conversations over Skype, and she'd come to stay with me in Valencia once, but couldn't take more than two weeks off her job, so the time together was short. I'd planned, again and again, to visit her there in Korea, but *Willing* stuff kept coming up, and this visit was the first time I'd set foot on Korean soil. Grace met me at the airport in Seoul, and we bussed down to her mum's house in Incheon.

The two of us had grown less and less satisfied with a relationship at a distance, and had recently been talking about some kind of radical change in status. This had become a more urgent issue for Grace a few months before, when she'd finally got up the courage to quit her job. She'd gone to live with her mother, and was going crazy from the batty things her mother demanded of her. It was the usual stuff of course: *get married, give me grandchildren, be useful*. It'd got to the point where everything the old lady said was about one of those things.

My marriage proposal over Skype was probably the least romantic proposal in the history of human relationships. I said something like, *hey, it'd be way more convenient just to get married. A whole bunch of our legal problems and social obligations would go away.* She agreed straight off, and we started talking about the price of food in Spain again.

So yeah, it was all decided in a minute or two. Don't be fooled into thinking that I didn't put any thought into my proposal. It was a purely practical decision, to allow the both of us to live the way we wanted.

Grace's Mum was all smiley and made a big deal of being welcoming, but Grace kept destroying the illusion by telling me what else was going on in the old lady's mind, so my time at their house was not comfortable, or much fun.

Mother and daughter had a big bust-up on the third day of my stay. Apparently Grace had tentatively broached the subject of marriage, and her mum had responded by saying, *yes, whatever. Go. But I can't guarantee my health will last more than ten more years.* Meaning she expected her daughter to be back in Korea from that point on, to look after her. Grace made it very clear this was not gonna happen, and the old lady bust a boiler. She wanted me out of the house. I didn't see much of her after that. That was pretty much the note I left on.

Next stop was New Zealand to rest up and catch a bit of southern-hemisphere summer.

The warmth of an NZ summer is a dry, very comfortable kind of warmth. The sky is an intense blue, and bright sunlight combines with fresh air to make everything seem wholesome and clean.

In Whanganui, I was very glad to find my old mum in good spirits. Dad had died some years back from a heart-attack, but she was doing pretty well on her own. She was in her late sixties at this point but wasn't interested in the concept of retirement – she kept herself busy working as a pottery teacher, making her pots and selling them, or visiting friends.

Mum'd made me a favorite cake of mine when I arrived, and it felt great to be home. We sat out on the deck most days – mum under the sun umbrella, and me catching as much NZ sun as I could – and we talked about any old thing that came into our heads. I'd forgotten how nice it was to do that.

My old mum had always been puzzled about the way I looked at the world, and I think she'd suffered more than once when I walked away from stable situations in favor of freedom, self knowledge or just plain adventure. But she never tried to manipulate or influence my decisions, which I've always been thankful for.

The most delicious thing about my stay down in the South Pacific was the very reason I'd previously avoided the place: it was so far away from where things were happening in the rest of the world. Though there were three or four Willing settlements in New Zealand, they weren't a newsworthy issue because they were small in numbers, and they'd managed to come to a peaceful arrangement with the crown about paying taxes for the land they were using: a small yearly fee that equated to roughly a week's rent for a single dwelling in town. Everyone was fairly happy with the arrangement.

Though I was pretty much a household name by now, people didn't really seem to recognize me when I was out and about in Europe or the US, and even less so in NZ. I noticed people checking me out at the airport in Whanganui, but thankfully they let me be. Kiwis are not overly impressed by celebrity.

While Willingness was well known in the western world, I never heard of any Willing settlements in East Asia. The Willing concept seemed to be completely alien to cultures like Korea, China and Japan. It occurred to me around this time that the major difference between east and west, was that western cultures clung to an ideal of individual expression that was seldom-realized, but at least thought to be a good idea. Eastern cultures were *deliberately* group-driven. Though I disagreed with the eastern way, I respected the straight-forward honesty of their approach.

*   *   *

I flew in to London Heathrow on December 12th, where I planned to set the legal stuff for my marriage to Grace in motion. There was a long list of documents that Grace needed to collect and have translated into English before she could get a visa to stay in England, and in turn be allowed to live in Spain. Our marriage itself would be a registry affair.

At Heathrow, I was drinking coffee at a counter when a woman stepped in next to me and ordered a coffee. The voice was familiar. When I looked up I did a double take – she was the spitting image of Karl Donovan's girlfriend Di. The same wide features and piercing blue eyes. The husky voice was the same, except for the accent, which was British, rather than Australian. Of course, the Di I knew had died some time ago in a car accident, so it couldn't have been her.

She turned and saw me staring, but apart from a little smile, gave no indication that she recognized me. Which is hardly surprising, I guess. I decided there was no point in pushing the issue, and watched out of the corner of my eye as she took a seat at a table nearby and read a magazine while she drank her coffee.

I hooked up with Tony Coleman while I was in London. He was there doing a big action movie, but wasn't pleased about it. Everything had been in place to do his shoot at an Australian studio on the Gold Coast, but a stiff budget shakeup at the last minute meant Tony was forced to use a cheaper studio in London, with a British crew. He didn't mind working with the Brits, but hated the fact that half the Australian film industry would now doubt his word. Literally thousands of people had been told at the last minute that the job was off. I figured things in Hollywood must be pretty bleak if big stars like Anthony Coleman were getting budget-crunched.

But Tony was smiling as he handed me a glass of champagne. We were celebrating, because he had some good news: he'd signed a really good screenwriter to write the script for our *Willing* movie. I'd okayed an outline a few months earlier by email, and the project was gathering some momentum. The only thing that bothered me was that Tony was paying for the project's development out of his own pocket.

'Could you get a studio on board to fund it?' I asked.

He made a face. 'Reagan,' he said, 'I could get a studio on board with this tomorrow. Right *now*, if I made a call. But trust me, that is *not* what we want.'

I figured he was going to tell me why, so I waited.

'You ever wonder why most Hollywood pictures are *shit* nowadays?' he continued at last. '... Why they have a great cast, great director, great effects, but they absolutely *suck ass?*'

'Well, yeah, actually.'

'It's because all you need to get a Hollywood movie up and running now is a great pitch, and a couple big names attached. A big star or two. A big director.

'Sure, it seems like a major fuckin' victory when they say, *yeah*, they wanna develop your movie. Sure, it's very tempting to say, *wow! Great!* And pick up that ball and run like mad...'

He shook his head. 'But, it's *not* great. Once you're signed to a studio, your project *belongs to them*. Every minute the project is in development is costing the studio money, and they don't wanna fuck around. They want it to go into production yesterday. Worse than that, they have a lot to say about what you're doing, and they wanna see all of it on the pages of your script. That would be fine if what they said actually made sense, but buddy, let me tell ya... what these guys know about storytelling, you could tattoo on the inside of my foreskin...' He grinned. '... And I'm *circumcised*.' Tony was getting a rhythm going now. He took a sip of his champagne and waved his glass in my direction.

'I'm not exaggerating. Doesn't matter how good your writer is, they need the time and the space to get a good script happening. Sure, they can pump out some kind of a script, but with the time pressures, and with all the infuriating studio input, it always turns out like a sad cut-'n'-paste pastiche of shit we've seen an' heard dozens of times before, no matter how good the story pitch was.' He nodded. 'Fresh material can't be forced. It needs to be gently coaxed.'

5

As winter took hold in the northern hemisphere, the next wave of trouble came. Some Islamic State members had been found living in a Willing settlement in Belgium.

This was the beginning of a big turn in the tide of public opinion regarding the Willing. Indifference turned into distrust and suspicion. Some of the smaller settlements were forcefully disbanded by police and army. A politician on a TV news program I saw said the authorities would like to disband the whole lot of them, but the logistics of relocating so many people during the winter made this impossible. Instead, they were going to bring in an ID-card system to keep tabs on each and every member of the Willing – The ones in the settlements, anyway.

On his *WILLING WORLD* site, Karl Donovan responded to all this with a kind of team spirit: *stick together; tough it out.* He didn't use any deliberately provocative language at this point, but he was clearly drawing up 'them and us' lines.

Someone posted an emblem on *WILLING WORLD* that they thought might symbolize the Willing: a looping capital *W* with its ends joining up underneath, like a person with their arms above their head.

The symbol started appearing on walls, bridges, footpaths and buildings around continental Europe – perhaps elsewhere too, but I couldn't say for sure – I didn't make any more international trips after my disastrous visit to the US.

The very-visible *W* symbol seemed to strengthen the Willing's team spirit: their posts became more and more gung-ho anti-establishment. A post that openly suggested collecting weapons was jumped on by Donno – which I was relieved to see. He even went a step further and banned any and all fighting talk on the site.

I wondered if that would be enough.

*   *   *

If the European authorities were hoping the cold weather over Christmas would cull the numbers in the Willing settlements, they were disappointed. News of increased populations, and groups of keen refugees striking out across the continent in search of what'd come to be known as a *Willing Welcome*, spurred along the drive to get a registration system in place.

They announced in January that the registrations would be done on-site at each settlement, and photo ID cards issued on March 1st, in all the Schengen countries. I heard the UK, Hungary and some other non-Schengen states had coordinated similar plans. The settlements were to be be patrolled regularly by police, and anyone who couldn't show an official registration ID could be arrested and detained.

There was a huge amount of angry stuff on the net about how the Willing would be tagged and monitored like animals. Rumors even started that micro-chipping was on the agenda too, but I think this was just overenthusiastic paranoia – there certainly was plenty of that to go around.

On *WILLING WORLD*, Karl Donovan's reaction to all this was:

> Throw away your ID cards, everyone! I mean it. They can't arrest everyone in a camp of ten thousand.

– Which was true, of course, but it seemed to me this attitude just represented one more nail in the coffin for the Willing.

*   *   *

My apartment in Valencia was near the beach – near– but separated from the sea by a wall of dun-colored buildings. I chose a two-minute walk from the sand over shelling out an extra hundred euros per week for partial sea views, or an extra two-to-three-hundred for being right on the waterfront.

The state of the place was several notches up from the dump

Emiléne had been living in back when we were hanging out, but I discovered during my search that unless you had a lot of money to spend, you had two distinct choices: either

1) *crappy exterior/ okay interior*, or

2) *okay exterior/ crappy interior*.

It was either the one or the other. I went with a drab-looking five-floor concrete box, whose rooms were spacious, light and actually pretty comfortable.

A British news crew tracked me down in Valencia. I said yes, I'd do an interview, because I wanted to air my opinions – which, by now, had grown quite impassioned.

But the night before they came to interview me, I had a panic attack: whatever I said to them, I was in trouble. From the Willing's perspective, I'd be a traitor turning his back on the team. And from the mainstream viewer's perspective, I'd be a chump whose stupid pet project had spun out of control, and who refused to take responsibility for his mistakes.

But that period between 3 and 5am always brings me clarity. I saw that my reluctance sprang only from a need for approval. The truth was the truth, and I would tell it.

The crew wanted to film all sorts of fancy rubbish of me in a lovely Spanish setting, but I didn't appreciate their keenness to show me living it up when the Willing folks were starving and cold. Nor did I really want to tell the world they could find me there in Valencia. The crew grudgingly set up the shot against a neutral stone wall.

'I always saw *Willing*ness as an individual thing, but something that needs to be practiced *alongside* mainstream society. Not separate from it,' I told them when the camera was

234

finally rolling.

'The settlements are *Willing* in name only. They don't hold by the principles set out in the original manifesto. Yes, they're refugees from a system that failed them, but they won't solve anything by just running away. Their problems are still with them, in their own hearts. Willingness is about facing up to those problems and owning them. Mastering them. I don't see that happening.'

I visited the WILLING WORLD site the day after the interview aired, and it was just as I'd feared. They hated me.

As I'd often found throughout my life, the truth was not welcome. The Willing decided I was not *with* them, so I was *against* them. A particularly moronic brand of logic that just further convinced me that the Willing were nothing even *close* to being Willing. Some clever person had 'shopped up a wild-west style *WANTED* poster with my face on it and posted it on the site.

When they interviewed me, the Brit news crew had been very interested in Karl Donovan. I didn't offer any answers to their questions about him – not that I really had any to give – but I knew it was time for me to go pay him another visit.

It wasn't easy to get hold of Donno. The email addresses and numbers I had turned up nothing. The Nines were hidden somewhere in a hundred-K radius, inland from the San-Antonio settlement, and though I'd visited once I didn't have a hope of locating them. I was equally doubtful about relying on any of the San Antonians to help me find it.

So I ended up posting a coded message on *WILLING WORLD:*

Brynner would like a chat

He replied the next day – I guessed it was him, anyway:

Brynner See MM

By *MM* he surely meant Micmac, the angry South African at San Antonio. But if I'd guessed wrong, the picturesque two-hour drive from Valencia wouldn't be such a big waste of time, so I went. I wasn't exactly spoiled for options, anyway.

It turned out Micmac was expecting me this time, but he was just as prickly as before, in fact more so. I got the cold shoulder from Maisy and the other San Antonians, too – evidently I was very much on the San-Antonian radar now. Hardly surprising, I guess.

Donno turned up on his bike and eyed me for a long moment through his helmet visor. Then he said, 'Aw, shit. I wish there was some other way to cart you up to the Nines.'

I was just as bad on the back of his bike as the last time. He rode slowly, constantly complaining what a pain-in-the-ass I was, and we arrived at the forest hideout late in the afternoon. It was already pretty dark inside the forest, and the lights of the Nines lit up the surrounding bush.

I'd noticed some extra body fat on Donno when he was on the bike, but when he took off his helmet I was appalled at how unhealthy Donno now looked. His hair, still in a ponytail, was long and greasy. His skin was pasty white, and his neck was a wobbly roll of flab.

We dumped my bag in one of the huts where I'd be sleeping this time. Donno said he was billeted up in the tree-hut – he'd been kicked out of the main house, because his tooth-fairy had come visiting, and it seemed only right to give him the best digs. There were no Willing guests there at the moment, so the three of us had the Nines to ourselves.

We approached the A-frame house that Donno had vacated so the tooth-fairy could have adequate space to sleep and breathe in comfort. Donno even knocked on the door. Very polite, I thought. For Karl Donovan, anyway. A voice called out for us to come in.

We found the guy cooking in the kitchen. He turned to face us.

It was Simon Duchesne. Alias whatever he was calling himself now. Haircut different from London, but goatee still in place.

Whether he knew I was coming or not, I had to hand it to the guy: he was the coolest cucumber you could ever meet. Donno introduced him by some other name, but I didn't catch it. I was too razzed up.

We sat around the kitchen table, while Duchesne twittered away in his East London-style English. At last the buzzing in my ears eased off a bit.

'I think you'll find we're all on the same page here,' Duchesne was saying. 'We can get the job done quicker and more effectively if we...'

'We are absolutely *not* on the same page!' I said in a louder voice than I'd intended. '... and I abso-fucking-lutely do *not* want to join in your twisted game.'

Duchesne shared a look with Donno, who clicked his fingers in front of my face a few times like I was a lunatic. 'Reags. Reags... Hold your horses there, mate. You're with friends.' But I wasn't done yet.

'I know what you did to Akemi, and to Marianne,' I told Duchesne. 'You're a bully, and you're a liar...'

Donno grabbed my shoulder and twisted me to face him. *'Reags!* What the fuck...? What are you on about, you idiot?'

Duchesne was smiling and shaking his head. He stood from the table, and walked over to an iron wood stove. Opened it, and dug around inside with a brass poker.

Donno had a dangerous light in his eye. 'What's the problem, Reags?' he asked.

I pointed at Donno's tooth-fairy. 'Ask *him*.'

'Okay Reagan.' Duchesne spoke without turning around. 'We get the picture. I take it you won't be joining us for dinner, then?'

Five minutes later, Donno and I stood in the hut that was my shelter for the night.

'No way, man,' said Donno. His jowls wobbled as he shook his head. 'Russell's a bit wonky, but he's legit. I'd stake my life on it.'

'He's an expert liar,' I threw back at him. 'I can usually pick them right off, but he had me fooled.'

'Well, yeah. Perhaps that's because he's not fuckin' *lying*...? Trust me. He's not that sort of guy. Russell and me go way back. I've known the guy longer'n I've known *you*. Now if you'll excuse me, I'm gonna go get some dinner.'

'Yeah, wouldn't want to keep Russell waiting.'

He stopped in the doorway, and turned back around to face me, eyes glinting with fury. 'What is your fuckin' problem, man...?' He titled his head. 'You *jealous?*'

'Jealous...? I'm not jealous of *you*. You're being played by a con-man. And you're buying the whole package. What's there to be jealous of?'

I thought Donno was going to belt me one, but he checked himself and glanced nervously in the direction of the A-frame. He eased the door closed. When he turned back around, his body was rigid with anger. 'Mate. You're really pushing it.'

I was embarrassed to realize that I'd been steadily losing my rag, and that Donno, easily the more volatile in nature, was showing more restraint.

I took a breath and said, 'Did you ever see Di's body after her so-called accident?'

'Did I what...? *No*. Fuck no. Why the hell would you ask that?'

'I... well...'

It was on the tip of my tongue to tell Donovan about my possible sighting of Di at Heathrow airport. About my growing theory of a deeper, darker conspiracy. But suddenly it hit me: had Donno himself lied to me about Di's death? How did I know *he'd* been straight with me all this time?

I backpedalled a bit. 'Look, this whole thing stinks. You think you know this guy. But how much do you *not* know about him? Like, who does he work for? Because – mate – his masters are *your* masters...'

'Of course I've fuckin' thought about it! You think I'm an idiot?'

'And?'

'And nothing. Not a whisper of interference.'

'Okay, so how much of this strategy of yours – with the Willing settlements and stuff – how much of that comes from your mate Russell?'

'Aren't you listening to me? It's all *mine!* I'm the man here.'

'Even the rationale behind it all? All that fuzzy, vague stuff?

Choice and *accident?* The *big-picture..?* The consequences of *not stepping up to the plate?* Is that *you* talking...? Or is it your tooth-fairy?'

As I spoke, I saw it in Donno's eyes for just a fraction of a second. I'd hit home. But the moment of clarity didn't stick around for long. Donno drew himself up.

'You think I've sold out, don't ya.'

I took a deep breath, then nodded. 'Yeah, Donno. I do.'

'Fuck you,' he spat, and started for the door. Then he stopped and turned back.

'If it wasn't dark out, you'd be out on your arse right now,' he said, and pointed a finger. 'I want you gone first thing in the morning. An' I'm not takin' you on the bike again. You can *walk*, fella. Find your own fuckin' way home.'

Plonking myself down on the bed, I was surprised to find I felt nothing about the fight with Donno. My conscience was clear. But when I tried to read an ebook on my iPad, I found I was too jittery to make sense of it. After-effects of the adrenaline rush, I guessed.

I'd undressed for bed and turned out my light when there was a soft knocking at the door. I figured it was Donno, wanting to talk some more. But I opened the door to Russell/ Simon Duchesne. He was apologetic.

'Sorry to barge in when you're in bed, mate,' he said when I'd let him in and closed the door. His accent was a bit more cultured than I remembered it from the sighting in London, but it seemed authentic. Everything about the guy seemed authentic – that's what gave me the heebie-jeebies.

'Mind of I sit down?' he asked, but he'd taken a seat before I had the chance to respond. He sat looking at me, hands clasped

240

between his knees, the picture of relaxed camaraderie. 'Got off to a bit of a bad start, didn't we.'

'What do you want?' I asked, my tone a bit harsher than I'd meant it to be. He flinched, as if I'd slapped him.

'All right, well... I'd like to make this right.' He spread his hands. 'Whatever you think there is between us.'

'How...? Money?'

'Well.' He coughed. 'That's not beyond the realms of possibility, but...'

'I'm not for sale.'

He looked puzzled. Hurt. Despite myself I felt pangs of remorse. Like I was giving the guy a hard time. Being unreasonable. But then the energy in the room shifted. He sat up straight and nodded.

'Donno told me you don't like contracts.'

'That's right, I don't.'

Duchesne chewed at his cheek then turned to look at me. 'Well, that makes things a bit awkward, you see...'

'You mean there'll be nasty consequences if I let on about you and your shady dealings.'

He smirked. 'Very perceptive of you.'

'Well I don't care. I have nothing to lose.'

'You sure about that?'

'My only possession that I really care about is the truth, and you can't take that away.' I cringed inwardly at how sanctimonious that must've sounded.

Duchesne said, 'I have a very long reach, you know.'

'I'm glad for you.'

'No, I don't think you follow...' He folded his arms and fixed me with a steady gaze.

'I know where Akemi is. She thinks she's off-grid, but she isn't. Not as far as I'm concerned, anyway. And your girlfriend, er, *Min-Ji?* No, you know her as *Grace*, don't you... I know where she lives in Incheon, too.' He stopped and licked his lips, like he was enjoying a good meal. 'I also know where your old mum lives down in little old New Zealand. *Durie Hill,* right? I checked it out on Google maps. Nice view.'

I stopped breathing.

'So.' He clasped his hands together again. Put them in his lap. 'Ball's in your court.'

'You're... threatening my *mother?*' It came out like a strangled croak.

He shrugged. 'I'm doing whatever it'll take, for you and me to put our problems behind us and move ahead.'

My head pounded. I was furious, but I couldn't move or speak.

Duchesne finally stood up. 'Your choice, mate,' he said, and let himself out.

I stood there on the wooden floor of the hut for an hour, maybe more, until I could feel the chill start to bite through my socks. I struggled to get a grip. Did some alliterative gymnastics in my head and forced myself to breathe slowly and deeply. I started to feel the cool edge of clarity take shape.

Duchesne thought he was giving me just two choices: blow the whistle and take the nasty consequences, or play the game and keep everyone safe.

But there was a third choice.

Kill Simon Duchesne.

The idea of it nauseated me, but the alternatives were worse. There was just no way I could live with either choice he offered. The first choice *dragged me down into Duchesne's dark dungeon of deceit*, and the second *dumped my dearest into dreadful danger*.

So he would have to die. The only question left was *how*. I turned out the light and sat down on the edge of the bed to think.

I had my stun gun from the mugging in London in the side pocket of my bag. Since that experience, I'd never quite taken my safety for granted again, and I'd kept the weapon charged up with a charger I bought in Valencia.

I was wearing a dark-navy down jacket. Sliding the stun gun into the right-hand pocket of the jacket, I pushed the two metal contact prongs through the lining and the outer material, so the business-end of the weapon was exposed, but barely visible.

I found a plastic shopping bag in a drawer in the hut. Took the belt off my jeans and put it in my other jacket pocket.

I was ready for business. But not looking forward to it.

I peered through the window of the big A-frame house. In the dimly-lit lounge, the coals in the iron wood stove glowed an angry orange. At the other end of the room, Duchesne's face was lit up blue by the computer screen he was working at.

I tapped on the window and Duchesne looked up.

He opened the door and nodded me inside, then sat back down behind the computer. 'Something on your mind?' he asked.

'I was uh, thinking about what you said,' I replied, and moved around to stand behind him, hands deep in my jacket pockets. I saw a flash of a refresh on the computer screen: he'd switched apps to a game of *Patience*. Both our reflections were clearly visible in the window, and I saw Duchesne warily check my position.

'Anyone ever tell you you look like that actor, Yul Brynner?' he asked, and started to say something else, but then jerked back in his chair as I pushed the stun gun contacts into his shoulder and gave him a clicking, flashing burst of ten-thousand volts. He slid like a bag of potatoes off his chair and onto the carpeted floor, where he lay softly grunting and groaning.

There was a smell of burnt flesh and nylon, and of ionized air. I was mortified at what I'd done, and stood there, paralyzed, gawping down at Duchesne for way too long. At last I found the presence of mind to pull the plastic bag and belt from my pocket. Slid the bag over Duchesne's head, and wrapped the belt around his neck – sealing the bag, and cutting off his oxygen. I fastened the belt behind his neck, medium-tight – didn't trust myself to manage the violence of strangulation – deciding he'd have to make do with slow suffocation inside the bag.

Duchesne was moaning softly and his limbs began to move, so I gave him another zap, which put him down for maybe thirty seconds. But then he started moving again – this time with more purpose. I started to panic. Pulled the stun gun out of my pocket and zapped him – one long, searing burst – until it was obvious that the stun gun's charge was weakening.

It only gave me a few measly seconds' grace. Duchesne jerked back into motion, and as I stood by, wondering what the fuck to do, he started a slow, spasmodic crawl across the floor. He was obviously getting enough oxygen to keep him going –

the plastic bag ballooned out and sucked in with each breath. None of his limbs was working right, but he knew his life was on the line, and he was putting everything he had into making them move.

This wasn't working out the way I'd planned. I'd reckoned on a certain level of violence that, at a push, I might just be able to handle. But things were moving way beyond the limits of my savagery. I briefly considered whipping the bag off his head and calling the whole murder thing off, but I knew this was not a realistic option.

If I didn't act quickly, Duchesne was going to take control of the situation. Which would be a really bad thing. Unacceptable. The overriding emotion I was feeling was pity for a fellow human being: not in the least bit helpful right at that moment. I badly needed something to motivate me to finish him off.

I vigorously shook my head. Mentally fought for some kind of hate, anger, vengefulness, that would help me get the job done, and remembered Duchesne's shabby treatment of Akemi. He'd hit her, at least once. So hard she'd puked. He'd put her life at risk with his bullshit HIV tests. And he'd degraded her by paying her the price of her integrity. The fact that she'd set that price herself didn't help me with my motivation problem, so I thrust it aside, and at last found myself quite pissed off with Simon Duchesne.

Reaching down, I grabbed the belt and ratcheted it a notch tighter around his neck, finding the buckle's pin wouldn't go into the next hole on the strap without some serious tension. He swatted furiously at me with hands like fleshy clubs, but he was too uncoordinated. I planted my foot between his shoulder blades and pulled hard on the strap. At last the pin slid home, and I stood back, expecting to watch him die.

But Duchesne wasn't done yet. Scissoring his body in a

desperate inch-worm *push-drag; push-drag* motion, he moved across the lounge floor. Which was dark, but I could make out the silhouette of the brass fire pokers on a stand by the wood stove, back-lit with orange firelight.

I launched myself toward the pokers, planning to beat him to it, but Duchesne's leg shot out and tripped me. I went down, bashing my head on the edge of a coffee table.

I guess I was only down for a moment, but when I scrambled back to my feet, Duchesne was already next to the stove, reaching for the poker stand. Which I managed to snatch away just in time. I jumped back, holding a poker like I meant to use it. But Duchesne was weakening now. He batted at his head, trying with his useless fingers to rip open the bag, but it wasn't happening.

I had to look away when the bag started drawing into his desperately sucking mouth.

No matter what sense you might get from movies about the timely death of a "bad" guy, there was absolutely no satisfaction in watching Simon Duchesne die. It was appalling. Every nerve and muscle in my body screamed at me to *help*. It was in my power to do so. *How could I just be standing by and watching someone die?*

But die he did, eventually. And the moment of his death was announced by a squelching noise and a horrible smell. His bowels had relaxed and he'd shit himself.

It was difficult to get myself moving, but I had to figure out what to do next. Replacing the poker on the stand, I removed the bag and belt from Duchesne's body and lay him back down on the floor. There was no obvious sign of foul play – I hoped it might look like an accident, or maybe a heart attack.

Thankfully the whole thing had gone off with very little noise, so I could leave without any fuss if I had to, and I thought I might.

It was a shame that my absence would dump a load of suspicion on me, but there was no point in me sticking around because I wasn't capable of the level of bullshitting that'd be required to fake my ignorance: *Oh what? Russell died? Gee, how sad...*

Nope. Couldn't see it happening. Nor did I feel I could trust Donno to give a damn about my own interests. He wasn't going to be pleased that his tooth-fairy had been zapped to death and was lying on the floor in his own shit; no doubt he'd see it as a poisonous act of jealousy.

So I left without saying goodbye. Donno had pretty much indicated that was what he wanted anyway. There was a torch in the cupboard in my hut, and some spare warm clothing I figured I'd need, so I loaded my bag and headed out on the track.

After about half an hour of jogging through the forest, I was starting to wonder if I'd taken the wrong track and had gone off in a completely different direction, but at last I came to the tar-sealed road. It was a relief to see the stark white center lines, painted there by human hand. I was jogging along the shoulder in the dark, breathing hard, when I heard a motorbike engine in the distance and stopped to listen.

The sound was getting closer. I ducked into the some bushes near the road and waited there for several minutes, trying to control my breathing and worrying whether its steam would be visible in headlights. My clothes were soaked with sweat from my running, and crouching motionless I was getting pretty cold, but was too nervous to open my bag and take out extra clothing.

The road suddenly lit up, and a bike growled slowly past. The engine sound faded, but I waited and listened. Donno was out looking for me.

Time to make some decisions. Too cold to sleep in the open, and nowhere handy to get under cover. I couldn't go back to San Antonio for my van because I wouldn't get back there until light, and the San Antonians would certainly shop me to Donno when they saw me. Too risky to keep moving along the road. I'd have to somehow navigate my way across open country.

I took out my phone, then an extra jacket from the bag, and made a tent over my head to keep light from the screen from being seen off in the distance. There was no cell coverage, but I still had a saved map of the greater area in Google maps, and an in-app compass.

I decided to head for the town of Cansalades – about a two-hour journey on foot, over hills and through scrub. I quickly established my north-west heading, which required me to cross the road and strike out across open scrub land on the other side. I'd be visible from the road for a while, so I had to get moving.

*   *   *

The next day, I took a bus from Cansalades up to Valencia, and on the way cleared a voice message on my phone. It was my old pal Inspecteur Brouté from the DGSI wanting me to call him back.

I was feeling pretty rotten about having killed Duchesne, or Russell, or whatever the hell his name was. Given my inability to lie, I thought a call to police right at that point was a bad idea, and I put off answering Brouté for the time being.

Back at my apartment in Valencia, I switched on the TV in time to catch a news story about a big bush fire. I didn't pay it much attention until they said the fire was near Cansalades. They showed aerial footage, but it was all just bush and smoke. No sign or mention of a cluster of buildings.

Was it the Nines going up in flames? If not, it was a hell of a coincidence. Donno was so secretive and careful about the place. I thought he might've decided I was gonna let the cat out of the bag, and torched the place before the cops came. Or it might've just been an accident... but I doubted it.

Just then my phone – the land line at my apartment – rang. I moved towards it, then stopped. The message counter said 14. I'd forgotten to check when I got back – people were obviously keen to get hold of me. I let the phone ring till it clicked over to answerphone, but the caller rang off.

I didn't want to worry Grace, so I sent her a text message saying I was busy with Willing stuff. That was another conversation I couldn't stomach right now. *Hey, Grace. I just killed someone and left him on the floor lying in his own shit.* There was only one person in the world I could imagine spilling the beans to without fear of judgment or consequences: Herbert Drus. I took a bus up to Montpellier.

Drus was his grumpy old self, but he didn't give me the brush-off, like so many people seemed to be doing recently – except people I didn't particularly want to talk to, that is.

I was a mess. Feeling lost and confused. I'm ashamed to admit it, but I asked Drus's advice about shadowy ways to get around my troubles, like buying a fake passport. He said *No, you absolutely do not want to go down that path.* And then he gave me advice that I didn't really want to hear, but which I knew was quite correct:

Go to Brouté. Tell him everything. It didn't sound like something Drus would normally suggest, but I knew he was right.

PART FIVE

1

Paris was raining and cold. We met at Brouté's office in the Parisian CBD. He was as laid-back as ever, but had a bad cold and was keen to get down to business. It turned out the Spanish cops had found my van outside the San Antonio settlement, and had wasted no time tracing it to me.

We sat with a coffee each, in a room that seemed too furnished to be an interview room, but not furnished enough to be an office. Brouté's nose was red from constantly wiping and blowing it. He fussed with his handkerchief as I told him first about the Nines, and about my meeting with Donno, then when I moved on to tell him about Russell/ Simon Duchesne, I noticed I suddenly had his undivided attention.

I told him about Duchesne spying on SIR then disappearing when he was discovered. About the sighting in London. About Donno intro'ing me to a guy called Russell, who financed Donno's *Willing* operations, and about my certainty that 'Russell' and 'Duchesne' were one and the same person. About the threat to Akemi, Grace and my mother. And finally about my killing Duchesne/ Russell. I felt acid in my throat as I described the unintentionally dramatic death, but gradually managed to get the whole story out.

When I'd finished, Brouté nodded very slowly. We sat in silence for a full minute as he mulled over what I'd said, then turned his eyes back to me, his gaze suddenly sharp. 'This conversation must remain between us only,' he said in a low voice. 'We can agree on that...?'

I felt a faint twinge of hope. 'I guess so.'

'No, I must have your solemn promise you will not share anything we say here.'

'Okay, sure. I promise.'

He nodded. '... Simon Duchesne... alias Russell Weill... alias one other name we know of, is – *was* – known to us. We were watching him for a long time. But we couldn't touch him.

'He was a key member of a group that's almost as insubstantial as smoke. They never have official meetings. They don't even have a name. We've traced some of its membership to people in very influential positions, who are very, *very* clever at covering their tracks. On the rare occasion we *can* trace them, they shut down our investigations by political means. Little threats and promises in the right ear. I think you understand what I'm saying.'

He took out his handkerchief and blew his nose. 'In any case, Duchesne's story is not one that can be told without embarrassing some powerful people. His murder will not be tried in a court of law.'

I blinked. 'You mean... I'm off the hook?'

Brouté pursed his lips. 'Taking a person's life is a very serious matter. And not one I can close my eyes to as a policeman...'

I nodded slowly.

'But I am open to making a deal. First, you will promise me never to take such extreme measures again, unless your life is under *immediate* threat, of course.'

'Um... yes, I promise.' I was humoring him. *I* knew that *he* knew these promises were worth nothing. And I sensed this was just a preamble to bigger things. I was right.

'Second, you will tell us every detail you can remember about Duchesne. Everything you saw him do and say. Everything you heard about him. Every minor scrap of information, no matter how insubstantial it may seem.'

'Agreed.'

'And third, you will give us Karl Donovan.'

I blinked. 'What...? I... I'm not sure I can do that. For a start, I don't know where he is. But he's also my *friend*...'

Brouté shrugged. 'If he really is your friend, I think you have a strange idea of friendship. But in any case, such little niceties are not important now.' He pulled a sheet of paper from his briefcase and handed it to me. The *Willing World* logo headed the page.

'This was posted yesterday,' he said.

> *THE BRIDGES*
> *Posted 4:32am, Tuesday March 3, 2015*
>
> *Authorities around the world have so far disbanded 12 of the smaller Willing settlements, and they have made their intention clear to disband the remaining 37, including large settlements like Posafe in Oregon, where 32,000 people now live. They say they will do this in April when the weather is warmer. How kind of them.*
> *This is not acceptable to the Willing. Therefore we make the following promise: For each Willing settlement disbanded, we will destroy one major bridge, in a major city center. We will not announce which bridge, or where.*
> *It will be destroyed early in the morning when there is no traffic, without threat to human life.*
> *Our aim is not to cause harm, but to disrupt the lifestyle society in general takes for granted, just as*

they cause disruption to ours.

Brouté told me the message was posted by someone with administrator rights, via the Chinese satellite that provided the Nines with its internet. The time shown on the document – four thirty-two in the morning – was after Duchesne's death.

Donno's work? Probably. Brouté said the post hadn't yet been picked up by the media, but it would be very soon. His office would be making a statement later in the day, to encourage the general public to keep an eye on bridges across the continent. Police resources alone wouldn't stretch to such a mammoth surveillance job.

'Obviously, we cannot allow the Willing to dictate security policy,' Brouté said, snorting into his hankie again and quickly checking its contents. 'But even at ground level, it's a very grave safety issue. I'm sure you can appreciate there's more at stake than a sentimental memory of a friendship.'

Brouté was right. Donno's friendship was nothing more than a memory.

I told Brouté about Micmac and the people at San Antonio who could possibly ID Donno, and might know where he could be found. Then I teamed up with a DGSI artist – a pretty, but aloof young French woman – to render identikit pictures of Donno, of Micmac from the San Antonio settlement, and of the two Willing guests I'd met at the Nines during my first visit there.

With all of the shape-shifting he'd done over the years I'd known him, it was a tough job to nail down a specific likeness of Donno – presumably, that'd been a deliberate move on his part. What we ended up with was a cross between the Donno I'd known in London, and the Donno I'd spent time with in Valencia. I managed to pinpoint two identifying aspects of his face that had remained unchanged: his almost-permanent squint, and the surly curl of his lower lip.

Then I spilled everything I knew about Karl Donovan. Every tiny little detail I could remember, from our first meeting at the pub in London till the moment I did a runner from the Nines a few days before. From time to time we segued into questions about Duchesne, but finding Donno was clearly our number-one priority.

The Spanish police moved quickly, swooping on the settlement at San Antonio and rounding people up for questioning. But they drew a blank.

They'd found Micmac easily enough, but Micmac said he didn't know where Karl Donovan could be found. He said the identikit I'd helped draw up in Paris looked nothing like the Donovan *he* knew, and then – very helpfully – he worked with the cops in Spain to draw up a new one.

When Brouté showed me a faxed copy of Micmac's identikit picture of Karl Donovan, I noticed he was watching me very carefully. I thought it didn't look like Donno at all, and I told him so.

Brouté nodded slowly and said, 'All right. But tell me... Who do you think it *does* look like?'

I looked again at the picture, and saw what he was driving at.

'Me.' I snorted and shook my head. 'It looks like *me*. Micmac's trying to protect Donovan. And to set me up. They're in it together.'

Brouté nodded again. 'Yes, the thought had crossed my mind. The Spanish police are keeping an eye on him.'

I did my best to help in any way I could, but Brouté grew impatient. He seemed to think I must either be holding back, or I'd failed to notice some important detail that would lead straight to Karl Donovan.

Using my phone, I posted another *Brynner* message on the *Willing World* site, hoping that Donno might answer like he did last time, but I knew it was fairly unlikely now.

We finished at about nine in the evening on the third day of our Paris stay. Brouté seemed hesitant about letting me go, and he warned me to expect more calls and more meetings.

I ate a seafood dinner by myself at a small restaurant near the hotel I was booked into. Prawns without their shells. When I ordered, I asked the waitress about the shell situation, and was told they could do them without shells. But evidently this wasn't correct, because after she'd talked with the cook, I saw her tug her apron off and run out the door. She came bag with a plastic bag two minutes later and delivered it quickly to the kitchen, then slipped the apron back on and gave me a little smile. *Merci*, I called across the room, grateful that she'd gone to the extra trouble. It was a nice meal and a nice ambiance.

I knew Brouté was cutting me some slack and was grateful, but it felt horrible to be on a kind of leash, knowing I'd have to answer to Brouté and the DGSI until Donno was found. And he *had* to be found. Karl Donovan was the axle that the current Willing culture revolved around. He was in the wind, but he could still write posts and influence the Willing communities around the world from any computer in any country.

The bridges thing spelled the end of any credibility the

Willing may have had, but more importantly, it was a potential catastrophe. Like Brouté said, the risk to people's lives was very real.

Over in Korea, Grace was having mother-trouble again. Mum was refusing to give permission for her daughter to marry me. A quick check of the UK marriage rules told me the mother's permission wasn't needed, which took the teeth out of the threat, but Grace was still wary of her single status in Korea. I was surprised that this would bother her, but it clearly did.

The next weapon her mother used was the big guns. Or so she thought. She said, *right – I'll cut you off and you'll not get a penny from me in my will, and the house will go to some random distant relative.*

Grace said *fine with me*.

The following week, during our next Skype session, we laid all this cultural stuff out. She'd been thinking about it a lot, and she knew the cultural pull was much stronger when she was in-country. It was a prime reason why she wanted to get out ASAP.

I'd told Grace I'd book and pay for her ticket to the UK, but I'd been worrying so much about the Willing stuff that I'd kept putting it off. I promised to book her flight right away.

The next few weeks were a relative calm before the storm. Everyday life at my apartment in Valencia. Two-euro movies at the Rialto. Coffees and napolitanas with an American neighbor called Lorenzo – an ex-army sergeant with a kind nature and a great sense of humor. Good company in difficult times.

Brouté called one Monday night with a question for me. 'What can you tell me about the word *Brynner?*' he asked.

I told him about my similarity to the actor Yul Brynner when I was nervous.

'So Brynner is you?'

'Well, it would be a reference to me. Donno used to have me on sometimes.'

'Do you mind if I ask, when were you born?'

'Me...? September 9, 1981.' A detail Brouté would have ready access to, surely. One of his little tests?

I heard him breathing at the other end of the line. 'Yes. That's very interesting,' he said at last. 'You see, we cracked the administrator password for Karl Donovan's website. It was *BryNneR9981* with capitals *B,* first *N* and *R.*'

After that Brouté called me every couple days, to check in and see if I had any new info about Donno, but I had nothing to tell him. Each time we talked, Brouté's voice was more strained. I guessed he was under a lot of pressure.

The Brynner password with my birth-date tagged on the end was another niggling little thing that pointed in my direction. Though I was unhappy about Donno and Micmac's efforts to set me up, I wasn't particularly worried. I was confident that the truth would prevail and I'd be in the clear.

I got an email from Joey Noakes up in London. He'd heard about the bridges thing, of course, and was worried about where the Willing were headed. I started on a reply about three times, but really had no idea what to say, so in the end I just left it. I felt a bit rotten about that because it was thanks to Joey that I could eat and pay my rent, but I already had a lot of pressure from other sources to deal with.

My financial situation was still fairly buoyant – I had seventy-nine thousand euros left. Spain was great for cheap living. I'd developed a habit of steering clear of banks, preferring to keep my money in cash in a safe bolted to the floor of my wardrobe.

From one point of view, at least, I was doing okay.

2

I met Grace at London Heathrow on March 26th. I watched her from a distance as she stepped out of the arrivals exit and scanned the nearby faces. She had a bulky down jacket wrapped around her waist and was trailing a battered leather bag on a trolley. She looked sleepy but lovely.

We had a hotel room booked because I'd made the mistake of telling Herbert Drus I was getting married in London, and he'd insisted on coming up to witness the registry wedding. I hadn't wanted it to be any kind of event – meaning to just drop in to the registry office on the way somewhere – but having an out-of-town guest in attendance kind of locked things down. It's mean and ungrateful of me, I know, but I was in a hurry to get Grace back down to Valencia, and was irritated at having to factor Herbert into the equation. The fact that our last minute re-bookings cost three times the price of the original tickets certainly contributed to my feelings about it. I guess I'd become quite a cheapskate by this point.

We waited at the airport for two more hours for Drus's flight to arrive. When he came out through the exit, he kissed Grace on both cheeks and gave her a crinkled, kindly grin of welcome. The two of them seemed to take a shine to each other straight away.

I managed to get a room for Drus at our hotel and we decided to do our registration business the next day and just relax. While Grace was looking at some clothes in a shop we were passing by, I warned Drus that she didn't know the juicy details about the previous couple months, in case he brought it up. He was fine with keeping mum for the time being.

It was nice to see Grace and Drus talking happily over dinner. He had that same expressive facial mobility I remembered from my stay with him in Montpellier a few years before, when he was with the younger woman from SIR. It seemed to me he liked a bit of harmless flirting as much as the next man, but he didn't bring that face out for just anybody.

Drus had brought along a suit to wear to our marriage at the registry office. Which shocked me, because I'd thought he'd be the last person to go for any form of ceremony. *It's just a couple people signing a piece of paper,* I'd said, but he insisted, saying it was important to observe a happy event like a marriage, even in the most minor way. He said it with so much feeling that I really wondered if I'd short-changed things.

The young office clerk who did our registration was a bit on the surly side – which, combined with Drus's determinedly festive mood, and Grace's puzzlement – made the whole thing a bit bizarre.

The next step was an interview at the Immigration Office, conducted separately, to check that our stories tallied. We sailed through. Grace had brought a bundle of paperwork from Korea – all translated into English – that proved she was who we said she was, and that she wasn't bringing any nasty illnesses with her. Added to my own bundle of papers, it was going to be a massive mission for some poor immigration official to wade through.

We waved goodbye to Drus the following day, and left the UK with a six-month marriage-visitor's visa in Grace's passport, so we could come back again when her full-blown resident's visa was ready.

When we got back down to Valencia, and were safely home in the apartment, I felt it was time to tell Grace about the nasty stuff that had happened recently. She knew about most of it from press reports, and she shrugged and said we could cope with it together. But when I told her about killing Duchesne, she was suddenly quiet.

'This is very bad,' she said. 'You should have told me this before.'

'Why...? Would it have made a difference?'

'Yes. Maybe it would. How can we know we are safe, Reagan? Who will come for you next?'

That night she closed her bedroom door in my face, saying she wanted to be alone. We had our own rooms and our own separate beds, but I'd been looking forward to some of our *scientific research*, and it really shocked me that she would react this way. Obviously, I didn't know her as well as I'd thought.

I was hardly a stranger to sleepless nights, but that night was harder than usual. Usually, I at least know that the pieces of the puzzle are somewhere in my mind, waiting to be identified and slotted into place, but this time someone else was holding some of those pieces. I'd plunged myself into a level of commitment and shared responsibility that I was unprepared for.

Grace joined me in my bed first thing in the morning and said we'd find a way through the difficulties together. But she said it with a firmness I didn't think she felt.

The day of the first planned Willing settlement closure came. I was very nervous. I got up early and took some breakfast to eat in front of the TV.

The settlement was a two-thousand-strong camp near Spa, in Belgium, the one where four IS members had been discovered the year before. It was one of the few settlements whose numbers had actually decreased – mostly, it seemed, because of the IS issue.

Grace came to join me in front of the box, and we watched together. It looked like Belgium was still pretty cold. The folk from the settlement plodded away from their dwellings, their breath misting about their heads. Woolly-hatted kids looking puzzled, and their parents glaring angrily at the camera. It was a sad, sad event. I felt an anger stirring inside me, but I wasn't sure who, or what, to direct it at.

*   *   *

Grace and I still had some good talks, but I noticed she was always on tenterhooks, and it was very easy to trigger suspicion with a single word. It didn't help when I tried to talk about it. On the rare occasion that she laid everything out and opened her soul to me, she admitted that she felt like she was gambling everything on our relationship working out, and the stakes were terrifyingly high. Her head and her heart were badly out of sync, and she didn't know how to deal with it.

Right after the Spa disbanding, I opened the wardrobe in my room to find my stuff had been disturbed. One of my little weirdnesses is lining up my shoes in a single neat line, but today the line was a scattered mess. Relatively speaking, that is.

I asked Grace if she'd been in my wardrobe, and she was insulted that I'd even ask. Again, I'd triggered the kind of frosty afternoon that was becoming way too familiar.

PART SIX

1

Now that the first disbanding was a done deal, everyone was waiting to see if the Willing were actually serious about their *Bridges* threat.

They were. The bridge they targeted was a major motorway connection near Marseilles, in France. Several bombs had been set among the supports, and the structure was badly weakened, but only a small section of the actual bridge came down. One person was injured, mostly because he was stupid. There's no excusing the bombing, but the idiot did get out of his car and climb over rubble to have a look, then fall and fracture his skull. Still, the media interviewed him in hospital later that day as a victim of the Willing's "terrorist action".

The Marseilles bridge bombing was the first time I heard the Willing – as a group – referred to as *Terrorists*. Until this point, they'd been a quirky bunch of misfits who rubbed shoulders with bad types, and who idly threatened, but they didn't represent any significant danger. Now the public in general were dead set against them.

I got a call the next day from Brouté. He didn't mess about with pleasantries.

'What time can you come to Paris?' he asked.

'What time...? You mean *today?*'

'Yes. Today.'

I hemmed and hawed.

'You have no legal obligation to deal with me. If you prefer you can deal with the Spanish authorities.'

It wasn't a choice I cared to make, but I certainly preferred Brouté. 'I'll come. When do you want me there?'

'Name a time. I have the booking site on my screen.'

He hesitated for a second or two about paying for Grace to go along too, but I told him how she was my newly-arrived wife, and he agreed. I managed to sell the whole thing to Grace without worrying her too much: I was *doing my best to help the police catch the people behind the bridges threat*.

I felt a sneaking relief that English wasn't her native language. She wasn't familiar with the vernacular connected to legal trouble – that slippery slope that starts with *assisting police with their inquiries*, then escalates to *person of interest*, then to *suspect*, to *defendant* and finally to *convicted felon*. My aim was, of course, to keep Grace happy, and as far away from freaking out as possible. As far as I knew, I had nothing to worry about anyway.

Brouté had found a French police psychologist who was planning to use hypnosis to extract more info about Karl Donovan from my head.

The psychologist's name was Mouton: French for *sheep*. Which I found funny and ironic. Doctor Mouton – or Doctor *Sheep*, as I thought of him from the first meeting – was about my age, smoothly handsome. Curly, sandy-colored hair plastered to his head. He spoke and moved in a clipped, efficient sort of way, but was friendly enough.

I told him, 'I think you'll find I'm not much good as a hypnosis subject. I'm too conscious. Not very suggestible.'

'Oh, we will see about that,' Mouton replied with a smile.

Two and a half hours later, Mouton was a bit less smiley. None of the methods he'd learned seemed to be working. Brouté was popping his head in from time to time, and Mouton seemed embarrassed that he wasn't getting any results. And I got the feeling he blamed me. He turned and clapped his hands.

'Right,' he announced. 'We will take an *associative* approach.'

He worked from notes, firing bits of info at me in different combinations to try and trigger something. I was starting to feel really frustrated, and resented having to play a part in something so stupid. I mean, it was a *joke*. No way was I hypnotized. My eyes were closed, but my state of mind was anything but trance-state.

Then he tried asking questions after each combination, firing them quickly at me. Barely giving me time to answer. *The hostel in Valencia... Girls... The building is where...? Which room are you in...? The color of the walls is what...?*

I did my best to keep up. At least it staved off the boredom. But somewhere in among the questions he asked, *who are you?* and I rapped out an answer:

'Karl Donovan.'

I really don't know why I said that.

Confusion...? An ill-considered, sarcastic joke, maybe. But it had slipped out, and the room was suddenly quiet. I opened my eyes.

Mouton and Brouté were staring at me. There was surprise in their eyes, but something else too. Something that worried me.

The satisfaction of a suspicion confirmed.

I stood outside our hotel room for a brief moment before going in to confront Grace with the news. We were staying in Paris. For the time being, anyway. What I wouldn't tell her – *yet* – was that I'd graduated in status from *assisting the police,* to *person of interest*. Not something I'd be celebrating. Brouté didn't have to tell me my movements could be easily monitored. I wasn't going anywhere without them knowing about it. I suppose I was under a sort of open arrest.

The only way I would, or *could* be cheerful enough to reassure Grace, was to dump any desire I had to be dramatic about the situation. In a way it helped to have that extra motivation to stay calm and collected and un-flustered. We went out for dinner at the little seafood restaurant I'd visited the last time I was in Paris, and the same waitress was on. I'm not sure if she remembered me, but she was very friendly. I didn't feel like complications today, so I skipped ordering the prawns.

Grace chatted away about stuff she'd seen in the town while I was with Brouté – the Louvre; the Luxembourg gardens; the Notre Dame Cathedral – not *completely* oblivious to the trouble I was in, but still in tourist mode. Fairly happy to have some free time to get a look at Paris in the Spring. Personally, Paris was the last place I felt like being, but one small consolation was the sudden sexual energy that the new environment triggered in Grace. She was all over me.

It was the strangest mixture of feelings. Little hollows of fear would open up in the pit of my belly, then Grace would fill those hollows with a heightened sexual desire. Once she attacked me behind a stone wall, with the sounds of voices and shoes on cobblestones coming from nearby. She pulled me out of my trousers and took me in her mouth. The tension and the immediacy of the whole situation was so full-on that I came in seconds.

The next day Brouté called me in at one in the afternoon. The Spanish police had searched our apartment overnight in Valencia, and had sent up a box of our things. I'd given my permission for them to do this, but it felt pretty horrible. The psych guy Doctor Mouton and I watched as Brouté opened the box and pulled out a cream-colored panama hat.

'What can you tell me about this?' he asked. I shrugged.

'Nothing. Why?'

Brouté shared a look with Doctor Sheep, then turned back to me. 'Because it happens to be the same type of hat worn by Karl Donovan in the picture on the *Willing World* website. And because the hat was found in your safe.'

'*My safe*...? You mean the safe in my apartment?'

'The safe in your apartment.'

I sat with my mouth gaping open for several long seconds. 'I... uh, I have no idea how it got there. It wasn't in there last time I looked.'

'You're certain?'

'*Yes,* I'm certain!' I said with sudden ferocity. I licked my dry lips.

Brouté put the hat down. 'Okay. So, now explain to me why you were logged in to the *Willing World* site, with administrator rights.'

'I was *what*...?'

'We looked at your computer this morning. Your browser was set up to remember the administrator password for Karl

Donovan's site. The *new* password.'

Then it suddenly hit me. 'Oh, God. The shoes...'

'Pardon?'

'The... shoes in my wardrobe last week. I thought someone had been in my wardrobe because my stuff had been disturbed.'

'Ah,' said Brouté. 'You think the person who was in your wardrobe logged in to your computer? And put the hat in the safe?'

'Yes. *Yes...!*' It was all beginning to make sense. 'He'll have guessed the combination because it was my birth-date. It's Karl Donovan, I'm sure of it!'

Brouté and Mouton couldn't have looked less convinced if they'd tried.

Things were really starting to unravel now. That evening when I left, Brouté asked me not to leave the immediate area. I knew I'd graduated in status again.

Grace was getting worried now. I started thinking seriously about sending her back down to Valencia, or even back to Korea, but that would be an extreme move that just confirmed her concerns.

But as things turned out, it didn't matter. The next day, Brouté forced my hand and arrested me. I had thirty minutes of supervised talk-time with Grace before they shut me away in a cell.

2

The cell they put me in was nicer than some apartments I'd lived in. Sparse, but clean and practical. All the amenities in one ergonomically designed room, like a bedsit or a compact-sized hotel. There was a TV that I could watch until 9pm, when the thing shut off – part-way through a movie, or not. I had a phone I could use to call out as often as I liked, free national calls; three cents per minute international. I wasn't allowed access to the internet.

I'd laid it out for Grace that I couldn't say when I'd be released, but she chose to believe that I'd be out sooner rather than later, and headed back down to Valencia. Her eyes were hard when she left.

Brouté came to see me on the evening of my first day in the cell. He was polite, asking if he could sit down. I sat facing him on the bed.

'I've been doing a lot of talking with Doctor Mouton these last few days,' he said after a moment's brooding. 'He has some theories... which are are troubling, but also quite convincing. You see, he thinks you are either a brilliant liar, or you have something known in English as *DID*: Dissociative Identity Disorder. He's leaning quite strongly towards the second one.' He looked me in the eye. 'When it comes to lying, I am quite a

275

good judge. I believe you *think* what you tell us is the truth.'

'Of course it is!' I buried my head in my hands. 'Jesus. I can't believe this is happening.'

Brouté took a deep breath and waited. When I looked up a him again, his eyes were gentle. 'If it is *DID*, and you are ill,' he said, 'it's unlikely you have a firm grasp of the truth.'

I watched an English-language news program that night on the TV in my cell:

> *WILLING'S REAGAN JAMES ARRESTED ON*
> *SUSPICION OF CONSPIRACY TO COMMIT*
> *TERRORIST ACTS*

Footage of the guy who'd cracked his daft skull at the bridge-bombing in Marseilles was inter-cut with clips from *Leighton Farmer*, and the black-and-white *WANTED* poster off the net. It was sickening to see, but I couldn't turn it off or look away.

The news of my arrest coincided with the announcement of an imminent disbanding of another Willing settlement in Portugal. I could see politically why they'd want someone to point the finger at at this point. I just wished the hell it wasn't me.

3

The decision was made to keep me in France, because the Marseilles bridge bombing was local, and was thought to be my work. Or at least directed by my words, if not my own hand.

The reality of my situation didn't kick in right away. My door was locked, but my environment was quite pleasant, and everyone treated me politely. I lounged through the first days in my cell, sleeping soundly and catching up on lots of movies I'd missed, certain it was just a matter of time before my innocence was proven.

My lawyer – a soft-spoken black Parisian called Elia – was a court-appointed job. I rashly chose this option because it seemed to me there was no way they could make this thing stick. It shouldn't take a genius to chase down some of the umpteen witnesses who could swear to the existence of a guy called Karl Donovan. I mean, *surely*.

But I was wrong.

Avocat Elia Katon had small round glasses and a thick afro tied back in a bun. He was tall and skinny and did everything in a slow, measured kind of way. His huge bony hands hovered over pages of text and rocked this way and that as he pondered. When I first met Elia I took him to be in his twenties. But the first time he took his glasses off to clean them, and looked up to meet my eye, I saw the weary lines of someone much older. Mid, or even late forties. He didn't smile much, but cracked the occasional dry joke in his excellent English.

Elia was fairly onto-it in his plodding, methodical kind of

way. He tracked down most of the people on the long list of names I gave him – people Donno and I had related to in some way or other together, but in our obviously separate contexts.

He sent out copies of both versions of identikit picture – the one I'd dictated to look like Donno, and the one Micmac had dictated to look like me. Lots of people recognized *my* likeness right off, but Donno's? No such luck.

It seemed the Willing had closed ranks, and the few people who'd actually met Donno were protecting him. At this point, that was hardly any kind of surprise. But the thousands of *other* people in the world who'd presumably met Karl Donovan during his thirty-something years of existence? Now *that* was totally nuts. I had several fights with Elia about drawing up alternative identikits for Donno, showing him in his various guises, but Elia said nope, this couldn't be done. Two was enough already.

Bill Sykes from WARF had no record of a Karl Donovan having talked at WARF 2012; or 2010, when he supposedly met Simon Duchesne/ Russel Weill. Nor did the hospital in Newcastle have any record of having treated Karl Donovan's elbow.

Most of the Valencia crowd were tracked down to their four corners of the globe via Facebook and email addresses I had for them. Emiléne, Matt and staff at the Valencian Hostels were keen to help, but had nothing we could use. Karl Donovan was not listed as a hostel guest. Some thought they recognized Donno's identikit likeness, but couldn't remember a name or a context.

And to make matters worse, the few people who could most likely help were nowhere to be found. Either Simon Duchesne had been bullshitting when he said he knew where Akemi was, or he knew more than the combined internal security services of the entire EU, because she was certainly beyond the legitimately long reach of the DGSI. Elia managed to contact the owner of the St. Pancras flat where Donno's ex-girlfriend Di had lived, but the trail stopped there. I still had my suspicions, but as far as everyone knew, she'd died in the car crash as reported.

Three acquaintances from Valencia including Christian Sam were still in the wind. Sam's family told us via Facebook that he was somewhere in the Middle East and not in regular contact. I'd been hoping that the edgy existential conversation Sam shared with Donno might've somehow stuck in his memory.

A dozen or so "Karl Donovan" sightings came in from around the globe. There was a painter-and-decorator guy in Sydney who the DGSI got briefly excited about, but who could prove he'd never set foot outside Australia. He looked a bit like Donno, but wasn't.

None of the other sightings led anywhere either.

The prosecution sent Elia CCTV footage they got from a supermarket in Valencia, that showed me buying a load of cleaning chemicals. They'd decided that the chemicals, mixed the right way, could be used to make a bomb. Which was really stupid, but it got me thinking. I got excited about street cameras in London and Spain: maybe there was footage of Donno and me walking around together. I made a list of dates and places, but Elia checked and found all the storage drives that held the footage had been recycled after a mandatory thirty-one day period.

Of course, the video from the supermarket in Valencia was Matt and me gearing up to help clean up Emiléne's new apartment. Elia and I found it odd that the footage still existed after all this time, despite the thirty-one day cycle, but we couldn't get info from the prosecution about where they got it.

As each thread of my defense frayed and petered out to nothing, Elia gradually became less and less communicative. I thought it might be frustration, but there was something else in his manner I couldn't put a finger on. It'd actually only been a few weeks since I was put away, but it was a depressing kind of existence in my cell, waiting for the smallest of developments in my case, as if my life depended on it – and in some ways, I guess it did. Anyway, I was starved of human contact by this point, and was pretty sad about Elia's coldness.

So all in all, things were not going well. I briefly considered taking a different tack and shelling out some cash for another lawyer, who perhaps had more incentive to give it his or her best shot, and was a bit more amicable. But as it turned out, I didn't have much choice but to stick with Elia. I'll tell you why.

A few days after I was arrested, Grace was lonely and depressed down in Valencia, and decided to head back to Korea. On the phone, I told her to take the seventy-odd thousand euros from the safe, and put it on the visa card so she had some money to keep her going when she got to Incheon. I told her about the ten-thousand-euro limit on taking cash out of the EU territory, and about the way they automatically confiscate the whole lot if you try to take more.

So I was pretty shocked when I heard she'd ignored my warning.

My phone call to Grace in Korea nearly didn't get to happen at all. Her mum picked up, and despite my repeated requests for Grace... Grace, *just get me Grace*, she yabbered on at me in Korean, and grew more and more angry.

At last, she banged the phone down. I thought she'd cut me

off, but then I could hear her in the background, shouting at her daughter. Grace picked up the phone. 'Sorry about that,' she said in a breathless voice.

I told her about the problems with my case, and how I was thinking about paying for some extra legal clout. 'You'll see a sudden drop in the Visa balance when I pay the retainer,' I said. There was a longer silence than the usual time-lag on an international call. 'Grace...? You still there?'

'Yes. Ah, Reagan...? There's something I have to tell you. I um... The money was taken.'

'What? *Gone*...? You mean it was stolen...?'

'No, it... It was taken at the airport. The customs in Barcelona.'

'But... *What*...? I told you to put it on the Visa.'

'Yes, I know. I was scared. I didn't think they would look in my bag, so I just took the money in cash. It's terrible. I'm very sorry.'

I was stunned. I wished I'd mentioned that thick bricks of paper money are one of the things the customs people are on the lookout for when they scan carry-on luggage. '*All* of it...?' I asked. 'It's all gone?' I heard a hesitation.

'There was... There was forty thousand in the suitcase and thirty thousand in my pockets. They didn't find the thirty.'

Well that was something at least. But my mind started clicking and whirring: Grace had been ready to let the info about the remaining money slip by. She wasn't planning on telling me about it. Which meant she had her own plans for the money, and I very likely wasn't part of that plan.

I told her to keep the money and said goodbye.

*   *   *

Twenty-two days after my arrest, the Portuguese Willing settlement was disbanded as per schedule. The following day saw an interesting development. The low-brow French newspaper *Média Large* reported (Translated into English):

> WILLING TO DESTROY:
> REAGAN JAMES IS KARL DONOVAN – ONE AND
> THE SAME

Brouté had promised he'd keep the multiple-personality aspect of my case under wraps as long as possible, and so far he'd kept his word. But the timing seemed to suggest there was a strategy in place. I reasoned that if the Willing made good on their threat, and hit another bridge in retribution for the closure of the Portuguese settlement, I'd be a convenient focus for people's wrath.

But then I had a visit from Brouté himself. We sat down in the cramped space of my cell, and in spite of the media leak, I found myself pathetically pleased to see a familiar face.

Brouté had some strange news. He folded his arms and asked, 'I suppose you heard about the details of your case being made public?'

I said I had.

'Well, we know who leaked the information. It was your lawyer, Elia Katon.'

'What? *Elia...?* You're joking.' I was stunned.

Brouté shook his head. 'He went to two other newspapers before *Média Large*, and they called us to confirm the information.' He raised his eyebrows. 'Yes, it's a very underhand thing for a lawyer to do. You can certainly ask for another lawyer, and if you make a complaint against Elia Katon, he will probably be disemb... er...'

'Disbarred.'

'Yes, disbarred. The damage is done, but we may be able to benefit from it...' He licked his thin lips. 'Whether or not you believe yourself to be Karl Donovan, I think you can help us.'

The following day, an official from the prosecution announced to the media that, while I was yet to have my day in court, it was true that the evidence suggested I was Karl Donovan.

In my cell at Sainte Celeste, I was given full access to a computer and to the internet, and administrator access to the Willing website.

Brouté explained his theory. As unpopular as I'd been with the Willing till now, I'd suddenly be flavor of the month if they bought the idea. If they believed that I was Karl Donovan, and I'd been their single driving force all along. I seriously doubted they'd be so gullible. How could anyone be so foolish as to accept, out of hand, some random, unproven theory?

But they did. There were literally hundreds of messages of apology and many more pledges of allegiance. Even some offers to fight to the death. I was sickened by it all. And at the same time I felt a pathetic pleasure that at least *somebody* was rooting for me – misguidedly or not.

As far as Brouté was concerned, this was where my usefulness came in. My first active role as "Karl Donovan" was to post a message to the Willing, urging restraint. Telling them to lay off the bridges thing, at least for now. Brouté assured me that, if and when it was proved I was actually *not* Karl Donovan, everything would be fine. It seemed to me he wasn't seeing such an outcome as being very likely.

283

My next sit-down with Elia was not a comfortable one.

Without meeting my gaze, he made a show of pulling a stack of papers from his leather case and setting them deliberately on the table between us.

But I jumped straight in, and asked, 'Why did you tell *Média Large* about the case?'

His head jerked subtly. He finally met my eye with a defiant stare. 'You can ask for a new lawyer. I'd have no objections.'

'You could've just quit.'

He snorted quietly. 'No I couldn't. I'd lose my job.'

'From the advice I got, if I fire you and then tell people *why*, you'll lose your job anyway.'

His mouth compressed into a tight line.

I repeated my question. 'So, why?'

Elia leaned back in his seat. The relaxed line of his body didn't match the sour expression on his face. 'I've defended murderers, thieves, mobsters and child molesters,' he said slowly. 'And it never bothered me if they were guilty or not. I just did my job like a lawyer should. But your case makes me sick.' He adjusted his suit jacket and looked up at me. 'I don't think you're sick. I think you're a liar. And I think you're the worst kind of terrorist: you don't even do it for a cause you believe in enough to come clean about it.'

I think it was a combination of loneliness, and the overwhelming evidence against me that started me sliding down the slippery slope of self-doubt. For the first time I contemplated, what if I really *did* have DID? What if I *was* a total whack-job?

Looking back over all the time I'd spent with Karl Donovan, I had to admit that it looked bad that there were no witnesses to his existence. But the most damning evidence – to my own tired and confused mind, at least – was how Donno reflected a deep, unexpressed side of myself. It was just proud of conceivable that he was a projection of my mind that represented the Brynner in me. My Mister Hyde. My Tyler Durden.

So it was *possible*. And the more I allowed myself to recognize the possibility, the greater was my sense of coming adrift.

Early in my life, I'd started off on a path to truthful thinking and action, and even when everything in the world around me seemed to reject my idea of truth, I'd taken comfort from that strong central pillar of rightness I felt inside. And now that pillar was crumbling. I couldn't sleep at night, which further weakened my resolve and made things even worse. I was on a massive downward slope.

Until one Monday morning, Elia Katon walked into my cell looking very contrite.

4

Elia had been in touch with Christian Sam at last.

His hand was trembling as he took out his phone and pulled up a picture on the screen. It was a wide-shot across the rooftops of central Valencia, taken from the rooftop at my old hostel. The light was good, and the image resolution high. Elia enlarged the image on his screen and panned to one corner.

Standing to one side of the picture, obviously unaware the picture was being taken, was Karl Donovan. He was squinting against an evening sun, in serious conversation with someone just on the edge of the frame. It was a clear three-quarter shot, easily identifiable, and the most welcome sight I'd seen in my whole goddamn life.

With a building rush of excitement and relief, I shouted a loud *woohooo!* and threw my arms around Elia – crushing him in a big bear-hug, and in that moment forgiving his betrayal.

Elia apologized. He admitted he'd behaved like a complete prick, but he made it clear that we weren't out of the woods yet. The burden of proof was still very much on our shoulders, because the prosecution had a strong case against me.

At long last we'd established there *was* actually someone answering the description I'd given, and that his name was Karl – Christian Sam recalled the name – but we still had to track 'Karl' down and prove he wasn't just some guy I'd met somewhere and built a whole delusional story around – which was what the prosecution would undoubtedly say.

So Elia was being cautiously optimistic, but hell, I wasn't

holding back. I figured it was just a matter of time. My sense of equilibrium had righted itself as soon as I saw the squinting Donno pic. Deep down, I'd really known it all along, but was very glad to have confirmation that I wasn't the whack-job Mouton said I was.

Days after the Karl Donovan photo came to light, a bridge in Madrid was badly damaged by an explosion at four o'clock in the morning. Brouté's little ruse with the Willing website didn't appear to have worked, but now my case was looking healthier, I found myself hoping I wouldn't be accused of knowingly having bullshitted the Willing after my innocence was finally proved.

There were no calls to claim responsibility for Madrid, but it was pretty much taken as a given that the Willing did it. Though the bombing lit a fire under our tails, it also led to our second major break. This break came in the form of a German woman called Claudia Haffner.

As it turned out, Claudia was the woman I'd met during my first trip to the Nines with Donno, and whose name was unknown to me until now. She'd been a founding member of the settlement at San Antonio, so she'd had a fairly long association with Karl Donovan. She was a keen *Willing* practitioner, but had never been impressed with secrecy contracts, or threats of 'nasty consequences'. She'd packed up and left after the Marseilles bridge bombing. Since then she'd been drifting around the European continent, waitressing here and there, avoiding the Willing settlements, and not really keeping up with current world events. She decided to come forward when she overheard a conversation in a café about the bridge at Madrid.

Claudia started the dominoes toppling when she told police that my old San Antonian mate Micmac (full name Michael McDonald) was an engineer and probably Donno's explosive expert. She'd seen things at San Antonio that had her worried.

Micmac was arrested the next day. With the help of street cameras, he was placed in Madrid around the time of the bridge bombing there, and quickly tied to the actual incident. When they sweated him, he gave up some very useful info about Karl Donovan: Donno was not an Australian national after all – he was a South African who'd done some of his high-schooling in Australia. At last the police had the info that helped them track down the details of Donno's true identity. His real name was Terence Peat and he was from Johannesburg.

They picked him up three days later in the Portuguese town of Oporto.

Brouté himself delivered the news that all charges were to be dropped and I was to be released. He held out his hand and said, 'I hope you won't hold it against me.'

I felt nothing but relief and I willingly shook his hand.

*   *   *

The day of my release, Herbert Drus came to pick me up at the Sainte Celeste forensic psych hospital. His manner was understandably very stiff, given the level of courage it must have taken for him to voluntarily enter a police facility. I knew how much effort he usually put into avoiding such places. We climbed into his old car and didn't speak until we'd been on the road for almost an hour. It was Herbert who finally broke the silence.

'I have invited some friends for dinner tonight,' he said. '*Une petite célébration.* Jo Bourne will be there.'

'Sounds good,' I said, stretching my back and yawning. 'What are you celebrating?'

'What are we celebrating? *Merde! Tu rigoles...* Are you joking?'

'Uh... No.... Why?'

'Well, of course, we are celebrating everything you've achieved!' He banged the steering wheel and threw me an outraged glare.

'Oh God,' I said, suddenly feeling very tired. 'What is there to celebrate? The whole fucking thing was... ' I almost said *big fucking disaster*, but it seemed too sad to quote Akemi. I didn't even know if she was alive.

'I'm just happy to be free,' I continued. 'I don't wanna like, *kid* myself I achieved anything worthwhile.'

Drus took a deep breath and spoke between gritted teeth. 'Reagan, Reagan, *Reagan*... All right, tell me. What was it you hoped to achieve when you started out?'

I opened my mouth to speak, then stopped. Nodded slowly.

'Yeah... Yeah, I see.' I leaned back in the seat. 'Okay.'

Still looking sour, Herbert muttered and shook his head. Then at length, he shot me a rare smile.

*   *   *

The following month found me back in summertime New Zealand. Brouté had done some digging around and found some funds to help me buy a ticket home. And this time it really did feel like I was home. Mum was over the moon to have me back in one piece.

I took a call on mum's phone from Tony Coleman, who was very keen to get our movie happening. He told me its working title was now *Inner Brynner*.

I was getting some sun in the garden a few days later, when I heard my mum's voice calling, 'Mail for you... From Japan!'

I wasn't in any big hurry to disturb my sunbathing. I'd met very few Japanese people on my travels and I'd traded details with virtually none of them. Akemi was pretty much the only one – but as you'll probably recall, she was always dead set against going back to Japan.

Anyway, my curiosity got the better of me and I found the postcard on the kitchen table where mum had left it.

It was covered in small, garishly-colored pictures and most of the writing was Japanese hieroglyphics I couldn't read, except for a hand-written section in one corner, which said *HAPPY NEW YEAR*. This was followed by an address in Kyoto.

And under that was scrawled the name *Yoda*.

Like the Star Wars character.

Photograph by Liya Pearson

RAPHAEL FOREST was born in New Zealand, where he suffered through his schooling, then went on to work in television, film and music.

Currently he's based in Japan, where he writes his books and produces his own music. His debut album *Cleverno Deepyeah*, also a Roof Media project, is scheduled for release in early 2018.

Forest has begun work on a follow-up to *Inner Brynner*, titled *Outer Edges,* in which Reagan James is confronted by colleagues of the late Simon Duchesne, and must re-evaluate everything he knows.

A date for release of *Outer Edges* has not yet been set.

Made in the USA
San Bernardino, CA
16 August 2017